Texas-
Land of the
Big Hair

*(Big Money Divorce
Texas Style!)*

by Sonya Bernhardt

Penelope
Books

The characters and locations depicted in this work of fiction are the fabrication of the author's imagination and are not meant to portray actual persons, places or events. Any errors are the product of the author's faulty understanding.

ISBN 978-1-4243-4400-0

Published by Penelope Books
www.penelopebooks.com

Cover art and book design by Good & Wright

First printing June 2007.

Dedicated to Patrick Dennis,
author of Auntie Mame.

Table of Contents

Texas - Land of the Big Hair
Big Money Divorce Texas Style!

1

The Genie is out of the Bottle Now

The big excitement this week was meeting billionaire Ray Calhoun. Texas is littered with millionaires, multimillionaires and even mega-millionaires but being told that a billionaire wants to meet you can still get a girl's attention.

My money manager, Ted Drapas, called and told me that he'd been on a pheasant hunt with a bunch of guys at someone's ranch. He said if he was a woman he'd join a gun club. There was one woman on the hunt with a bunch of wealthy men.

"You should seriously think of joining a gun club and coming with us on some hunts."

I told him, "Oh yeah, that's real attractive to a man. Men go into the woods not to hunt, but to be men, to drink and spit and curse and scratch themselves without some woman there to make them feel uncomfortable. Bringing a woman along ruins the whole purpose of the trip."

"Oh no. This woman was drinking and cursing right along with the rest of us."

"Exactly my point. Women are supposed to be all soft and pink and sweet smelling to come home to when you men are ready to hear someone's voice with a higher pitch than your own. Cursing and spitting? *Real* attractive."

"Well, I don't think she actually spit, but I get your point. Anyway, the reason that I'm calling is that Lynn and I would like to invite you to attend the 'after the hunt' dinner party. It's going to be held in the home of one of the hunters. He's got a furniture company and years ago needed a warehouse to store furniture, and now he's converted the building into residential loft space. It is really cool. He's left it warehouse looking with exposed beams and the original oak wood plank floors, very New York." Ted's voice became quite animated. As he spoke, his voice rose and fell like a roller coaster. He sounded like an eight-year old child describing his secret clubhouse. "He just drives his motorcycle into the freight elevator and parks his bike right there in his living room. The building used to be a wagon wheel factory, so the freight elevator can handle the weight."

"Where is this located?"

"Down near the baseball stadium."

"I think you and Lynn had better drive me then. I don't want to leave an eighty thousand dollar sports car exposed in that area of town. If the car was still there at all, it would at least be missing all the wheels or something."

"Good point. The parking area is gated off. I'll have to ask him how to get in to park." Ted paused for a moment aware that I was still debating whether or not I'd go, "So, we'll pick you up?"

"What is Lynn wearing?"

"I'll tell her to call you."

My sort of live in, French-Algerian boyfriend was going to be out of town. The children were with my ex that weekend.

Wednesday, two days before the Friday party, I went out to Hank's restaurant with my friend from the Vermillion Art Gallery, Taylor, and his new friend, Corey. Corey was an assistant director he'd met through his makeup artist cousin on the movie set of the Antonio Banderas movie, *Pancho Villa*, in San Miguel, Mexico.

Taylor called me as I was dropping the kids off with Richard, my ex-husband, after our Wednesday visit together. Taylor advised me that his friend was traveling and was used to dressing very laid back grunge like the other workers in the film industry. He suggested that I might not want to dress as elaborately as he knew I sometimes do, since his friend might be uncomfortable and feel underdressed. I told Taylor that if someone felt uncomfortable around me it was a deeply rooted problem within themselves best dealt with on a psychiatrist's couch and not at dinner with me. I reminded him that it was very difficult for someone to feel uncomfortable around me; they had to really try.

"We are going to Hank's restaurant and Hank is a biker, a Harley guy, and all of his Harley friends come in dressed in their leathers and sit right next to the hoity toity, ooh laa laa people. He'll fit right in."

"You are right, sweetie. You never make anyone feel uncomfortable. What was I thinking?"

"Tonight I am wearing suede pants, Donald Pliner pony skin boots and Yves Saint Laurent bag - the one you like with the bone handle. The pants match the brown stretch velvet top I found in Crested Butte when I was there on my last ski trip. You know the one, Taylor. Remember? It has a fake mink collar and a gold zipper that unzips to a modest point. That is *very* dressed down. I am not in full Penelope costume, so don't worry. I'm sure it won't make him feel uncomfortable."

The day of the 'after the hunt' dinner party arrived. I took a nap, so I didn't look tired and stressed. Lynn called me. She was drinking with her friends at a sushi bar after a day of shopping at Neiman Marcus. She said she had dressed really cute for lunch in a whip-stitched leather jacket and miniskirt and had decided to just wear that and not change for the party. She told me Ted was going to pick me up. She was going to go home, get the baby from the sitter and bring her to the party and would meet us there.

I was relieved she no longer thought of me as a potential threat to her marriage and was comfortable enough to have Ted pick me up. When she was pregnant, Ted told me she asked if he was having an affair with me.

I had said, "Oh, no! Poor Lynn! She must really think that it is true or she wouldn't have actually come out and said it. She would have just worried awhile and let it go. Poor Lynn! Does she really think I would have an affair with a married man? Do I seem like that kind of woman? Do I give off that impression to people?"

"Oh no, no. It is nothing like that, definitely not. It is my fault. I have not been paying her enough attention. It has nothing to do with you, Penelope. I assure you. It is near the end of her pregnancy, and it has more to do with hormones than anything else."

"What gave her the idea that you were having an affair with *me*?"

"Well, you see what happened is that the other day when I stopped by on my way to the office to get you to sign some papers, Mr. Guillory came to give you a massage. Then, the next time he massaged Lynn, he said to her, 'Oh, I saw your husband the other day leaving Penelope's house at eight in the morning.'"

"Oh, no! Poor Lynn! You are lucky you didn't drive home to a lump of burning cinders! I would have burned the house down! I would have been so upset!"

"She's over it now. I'm sorry I even mentioned it to you."

"Should I talk to her? Do you want me to reassure her?"

"No, no. Everything is okay now. Like I said, it was me. I wasn't paying her enough attention."

After Ted picked me up, we drove to pick up another party guest. She was from Dallas and staying at a friend's home just down the street from me on Chevy Chase. Ted was drinking a Coors with a squeezed lime slipped down the bottleneck. We have open container laws in Texas, not allowed. When he went to the door to get her, I told him I wanted to stay in the car and finish off his beer if he didn't mind.

"Oh, no, go right ahead. I've got plenty more in the trunk. We're bringing beer, ice, charcoal and other stuff to the party."

I drank the beer and hid the bottle away. I don't need any incident to ever cause me problems in a child custody battle. I was in the process of putting the bottle under the front passenger seat when

Ted opened the car door on his side to introduce me to the Dallasite, Ellen. She was wearing a fingertip length conservatively cut brown mink coat of near best, but not top grade quality fur. I hoped she hadn't paid too much for it. Ellen had on chandelier style gold earrings that dangled like two miniature grape clusters on either side of her face.

Women in Texas are very much not afraid to wear big, big jewelry. I was, in fact, wearing what I lovingly refer to as my 'doorknob ring.' It is so named because when I stopped by my divorce attorney's office immediately after purchasing the ring to apologize to him for saying the f-word, his secretary, a beautiful blonde from Beaumont, Texas, noted that my ring was as big as the doorknob on her office door. With the secretary's encouragement, I held the ring up to the doorknob for comparison and indeed it was nearly as big. Of course, it was a rather *smallish* brass knob, but it is a rather *largish* ring. The center stone is a massive purple amethyst surrounded by pink citrine daisies with yellow citrine centers set in white gold.

Fariq, my favorite jeweler, had just returned from a jewelry show in New York and had purchased the ring on the chance that I would love it. He never purchases on speculation. He just goes to the shows for inspiration and designs custom things for his clients, but this time was an exception. Fariq said he couldn't control himself. He had to get this for me and another very modern ring for a different client. I asked him who the client was and it turned out to be Andrea, the princess from Romania who was married to Prince Raim from Saudi Arabia. I knew her. She was a friend of my realtor, Becky Bugle. We had been to lunch together with Becky and I had been Andrea's guest at her Opera gala table. The jeweler thought it was great that we knew each other. He said we were his two best customers.

Anyway, back to meeting the billionaire.

The first words out of this Dallas woman's mouth were, "Oh, you've got beer in those beer condom things! Give me one."

Ted must have thought that she'd already had enough to drink because he suddenly forgot that the trunk was full of beer. To slow her down he announced that there was beer at the party.

"Okay, let's get the show on the road then," she said as she climbed into the backseat of Ted's car.

Ellen spoke in a raspy-edged voice that can only be earned by a lifetime of hard liquor and smoking. Her hair was dark brown and fell to her waist, not unusual on a Texas woman, even a widow in her fifties.

Once settled in the back seat, she told me she loved my coat and asked me what kind it was. I told her it was lynx. I didn't tell her that it was the finest lynx that my furrier had ever seen in his entire career, and he had started out as a furcutter at the age of sixteen working for his uncle. It was full length, the purest white and the spotting? *Perfect*, in different shades of brown. The coat had been cut very dramatically to take advantage of the lines of spotting across the back of the garment. My furrier loves to use the word 'garment.'

I had dressed up my outfit worn to Hank's restaurant earlier in the week by adding the coat, twenty carat diamond earrings (twenty total- I haven't lost my mind, a simple pair of five carat round stones with five carat pear shaped drops), and of course, the doorknob ring.

Ted had forgotten to call ahead to find out how to get in the security gate so we parked across the street in a nearly empty parking lot. That part of downtown is deserted at night. The two Rays came out to the car to meet us. They must have been watching for us from the upstairs window. When I say 'the two Rays,' I am referring to the Ray who owned the building and his close friend, the third generation billionaire, Ray Calhoun. Calhoun had the previous week had too much to drink out in the woods with the guys and cried about how lonely he was. He asked Ted Drapas if he knew a nice woman with her own money who would not be a gold digger.

Of course, some debate followed if a woman like that even existed. Ted mentioned he knew someone with her own money who had broken off an engagement with an oilman because he didn't call her for a week, so she definitely had not been in it for the money. The men arranged that I would come to the party for a look see.

The first thing I said to Calhoun was, "You look strong. Here. Carry this." I handed him a case of beer to carry and crossed the street ahead of the group turning my back on him, so he could admire my coat.

Ted even said, "Great coat, Penelope."

"Thank you, Ted. I *love* fur." I looked back at Calhoun over my shoulder and smiled flirtatiously. I knew my blonde ponytail flipped in a cute way when I did that.

Once inside, I admired the beautiful wood floors and told the owner he had a fortune just in the antique wood. To get wood like that for my kitchen floor, salvaged from torn down buildings in the Northeast, my contractor had to give the supplier at least six months lead time and pay a mint.

Ray Malloy, our host, gave me a tour. I hung up my coat on a coat rack in the long closet that ran the length of his entire condo. Now, *this* was closet space! I noted there were no women's clothes. Hmmm. No women in this man's life, at least not the kind allowed to leave behind a few things.

Inspecting this bachelor's closet made me think of the early days of my relationship with my Greek boyfriend. Ulysses told me he loved me, which shocked his friends. He never said this sort of thing to his lovers. He had only said, "I love you," to his ex-wife, Monica, to whom he had been married for eight years, and from whom he had been divorced almost as many.

After the first night with Ulysses, he immediately cleared space for my clothes in a closet, gave me two drawers for my personal things and offered to take my dry cleaning with his to the cleaners. He was so sweet. He kept my photo next to his bed in a pink crystal and antique brass frame along with another framed picture of my three children. Our photos were placed on the dresser next to a picture of his nieces, a prayer candle and a vase of purple orchids.

Every time I see purple orchids I think of him rushing to the store because I had asked him if I could stay the night with him. He said he had nothing in the refrigerator, nothing at all, so he went out and bought eight bottles of German water and orchids.

It was a sweet confession. He said at the time of the call he knew I wasn't calling to spend the night as in 'going to bed with him' but in the sense of 'help me I have nowhere else to turn.' But he was in love with me. He was in love with me, I was running away from home and he had nothing in the refrigerator.

Orchids and German water and a heart full of hope.

Everything makes me think of him.

Back to the party. So, the entire back wall of the closet was used to hang art. Ray said he didn't want to clutter the clean lines of the space in the front rooms, so he kept all of his art on this one wall.

We returned to the main room where I was introduced around to the other party guests. I got a beer and became involved in conversation with another of Calhoun's friends. I told him my legs were shaking from walking too many miles around Memorial Park that day, and that my knees were about to go out from under me if I didn't sit down immediately.

"Would you mind if we sat on that couch over there?"

About a mile away, there were two separate living areas, conversation spaces created by chairs and couches arranged to form rooms without walls. 'Pods of space' is the official decorating term. We sat together far away from everyone else on a big comfortable down couch covered in off white cotton duck cloth. There was a modern square chrome and glass coffee table that had Fisher-Price toys on it for the kiddos at the party. If Ray Calhoun wanted to meet me he would have to cross the large expanse of antique wood floor. In cattlemen talk this is called 'cutting a cow from the herd.' Sitting so far away also gave Calhoun a chance to observe me from a safe distance.

Ray Calhoun's friend, a dreamy blue eyed hunk named Gunnison, and I talked about forty-five minutes. I could see Calhoun in the kitchen watching me, sipping a beer and talking to Ted Drapas. Ted was not so discreet in his body language. He kept tossing his head in my direction encouraging Calhoun to 'go on over there and meet her.'

Calhoun was dressed in billionaire disguise. All the billionaires I know all dress the same, in baggy, shabby, worn out high quality cotton. It feels good to be caressed by old, good cotton, and you derive a secondary benefit from interacting with people who respond to you and not to your wealth because, until they hear your name, they don't know who you are. Sometimes, you even luck out and people don't know that your name means money. Billionaire camouflage.

Ray could clearly witness from the safety of the kitchen that Gunnison was having a grand old time with me. We were laughing and talking and laughing, having the kind of fun you are supposed to have at a party. I observed one woman after another throw themselves at Calhoun, even the married ones. As the night wore on and the women were emboldened by booze, they became more and more blatantly sexually aggressive. Believe it or not, men get tired of that.

My Greek boyfriend grew up in the nightclub business. His family started the first strip clubs in Houston. They had twenty-four clubs. When he was eight, he was captain of the busboys at his uncle's nightclub. He collected all of the tips and doled the money out at the end of the week according to how hard he thought the workers had worked. He gave this one elderly man double tips and fewer tables to work because he thought that was fair. He didn't give out the tips nightly because he said the Cuban immigrant workers had wives and children to feed and if he gave them the money on a nightly basis the men would buy beer and gamble it all away and not have grocery and rent money at the end of the week. That is a lot to know about life at age eight.

He'd been in his uncle's care in the evening since age six. That is when my confidant and closest friend, Mr. Guillory, first met Ulysses, age six, running back and forth across the dance floor zip, zip, zip cutting through all the couples.

Mr. Guillory loves my Greek boyfriend. Ulysses is like a son to him. I once asked Mr. G. to tell me something about Ulysses that I didn't already know.

He asked, "Which Ulysses? I've known so many. He has been through so many changes. There was the Ulysses when he was six years old, then Ulysses as a teenager working in his father's restaurant, the nightclub owner, then Ulysses in the dark years that he pulled out of and now the new Ulysses. I call him the 'after Penelope Ulysses.' He is a changed man. Now, he has purpose. Someone to live for. Something real to work for."

Ulysses was there for me at a turning point in my life. I never spoke badly about my husband to anyone. I guess that would have made it too real for me to deal with. I expended much energy trying to pretend to others that everything was okay. I told Ulysses the truth about my life the night I spent with him. I told him I was afraid. I remember Mr. Guillory hugged me that night trying to give me his good energy like he knows how to do, telling me to breathe in deeply and saying, "There, there Cherie."

But, that evening he could not give me his good energy. He pulled back away from me. I was such a black hole of fear, doubt and confusion.

Mr. Guillory said, "You are afraid. What are you afraid of?"

I told him, "My husband is going to kill me. I know it, but I don't know why."

Anyway, as part and parcel of his position as a nightclub manager, Ulysses had many, many women throw themselves at him every night. He'd come over to my house in River Oaks, an exclusive section of Houston, after he had closed the club, and my body guard would let him in. We'd have decaf coffee in the kitchen and just sit together. We just liked to be near one another, drawing strength from one another. He said it made him feel normal again after dealing with the club people to just sit with me. Sometimes, I would wake up and he would be at my bedside watching me sleep, sitting in an old fashioned needlepointed desk chair from the master bedroom desk. I'd wake up and he'd say, "Hello, Princess." We jokingly had a body count of how many women had basically demanded sex from him each evening. Tuesday night was always the worst - tequila night, salsa dancing night. The fewest women ever to throw themselves at him on a Tuesday was fourteen, including my own sister!

Rejecting a woman who has thrown herself at you sexually is a very tricky business for a man, especially on tequila night. Once rejected, the woman is embarrassed, horny, angry, drunk and set on revenge. She may, for example, once rejected, sidle up to the biggest, stupidest drunken man at the bar and play the role of innocent woman inappropriately approached by 'that man over there' and ask the big guy to rescue her and bat her eyelashes promising a reward to the defender. Then, sit back and wait for the show to begin, as the big ox goes to take out the one who just rejected her amorous advances. It went on like that all night, every night.

I could just imagine how difficult it must have been for the billionaire. I hate to refer to him that way, but beyond a certain point of wealth it is difficult to have an identity that looms larger than the money. What a burden to be born into that. I truly believe that God does not give you more than you can handle. What kind of life lessons was Ray Calhoun sent here to learn? What struggles to endure? I once joked in my big Jacuzzi bathtub with my French-Algerian beau, after telling him about a horrific incident, that God knew I could only handle so much, and he knew I couldn't handle my most recent tragedy without Jacuzzi bathtubs and seven hundred thread count Egyptian cotton sheets.

I thought about all this as I sat with Gunnison and watched Calhoun from afar. He would briefly interact with people and then recoil in horror at something inappropriate they would say. Then, he would extract himself from the situation. Calhoun kept looking over at his friend on the couch with me. We were throwing our heads back and laughing our guts out. Calhoun began to look downright miserable. He wanted to be having *that* great time with *that* blonde over there.

Gunnison and I went into the kitchen at some point to get a cigar. I had brought some Monte Cristos and Romeo and Juliets for everyone to enjoy as my gift instead of the usual bottle of wine. After all, this was an 'after the hunt' party. As I was holding out the cigars for Gunnison to make his selection, Ray Calhoun appeared. He looked directly at his friend and not at me.

"You two look like you've been having a good time. What have you been talking about?" There was more than just a hint of an accusatory tone in Ray's voice.

Gunnision stepped back in an expansive gesture throwing his

arms open wide, a Monte Cristo firmly between the fingers of his right hand. His body language said, 'Hey, Brother. I'm not doing anything wrong here.'

Gunnison laughed and spoke joyously, "This woman has an amazing memory for the history of deregulation of the trucking industry. She wanted to know how that had impacted the propane business, so I was just telling her."

Ray had a somewhat shocked look on his face. The topic of deregulation does not normally elicit guffaws from people.

So, I was able to say the second thing I ever said to Mr. Calhoun. I turned to him and said, "And, of course, how that parallels the deregulation of the airline industry." To lighten the mood since Ray was in stunned silence I added, "Oh, I'm all for free enterprise, free markets and capitalism. Don't get me wrong. I'm just not for it when it impacts *my* industry. Then, I want a total worldwide monopoly, baby." I was speaking loudly, but then moved close to Ray and whispered in a conspiratorial hushed tone, "Which we achieved by acquiring nineteen companies in a single year." I turned at that point and gave a big high five to Gunnison who raised his hand high over our heads. My voice louder again, I said, "Yeah, baby! World-Wide. Monopoly. After all, that is what is best for MY consumer. Wouldn't want to muddy the waters with a lot of unnecessary decisions for the consumers to wade through, now would we?" I grinned at Calhoun, a twinkle in my eye.

We were all giggling now. Calhoun had caught our infectious laughter. "And what industry is that may I ask?" Eew, I thought. He's terribly polite. I would learn with several opportunities to observe him that Ray had impeccable manners and graciousness at all times.

"The computer software business. My husband, I mean my EX-husband, negotiated an ironclad contract with Microsoft. Then, we bought up all the competition. We'd lure these owners of small companies and their wives to Texas and show them the lifestyle they could have here compared to California or wherever they were from and tempt them into coming to work for us.

It was an easy sell. All I had to do was show them how much

I admired and respected my husband and thought he hung both the moon and the stars and talk up the wonderful life they could have in Texas. I helped him recruit many of his top employees. I am actually a very good salesman."

Ray locked eyes with me and said in a sort of isolated dead calm that made everyone else's conversation fall away from my ears, "I know you are."

I wasn't embarrassed for rambling on a bit, after all, I was full of enthusiasm for my topic. I knew he was referring to the fact that I was there selling myself to him and not in the manner of the other women. I had more to offer than my sexuality. I represented the total package. I was indeed a potential life partner, an entirely different category of woman.

Gunnison and I invited him out on the terrace to smoke a cigar, and he declined. I don't think he is used to women ending the conversation and walking away.

The whole evening I kept watching people circling Calhoun like vultures, each with their own agenda. Each lunging out with their sharpened birds of prey beaks and ripping the flesh. This must have been going on his whole life. Even at the age of three, social climbing mothers must have vied for their children's positions at his sandbox throwing their frilly skirted daughters in black patent Mary Janes at him. How exhausting. What kind of life view would one develop? How hideous to see the entire human population at its worst through the prism of money. This made me think of Ulysses again.

The first time I made love with Ulysses he cried. He said, "That is the way it is supposed to be."

I asked him what he was talking about. He said it was one of the only times in his life he had ever felt loved in a woman's arms. He said there was no other agenda, nothing I was trying to get out of him. It was just love and laughing together.

He asked me why I had laughed and I told him because I was so happy.

He said, "Because you've got to know for future reference that it throws a man off more than just a little bit when the woman starts laughing during sex."

Ulysses told me again that he loved me, and he wanted to share whatever small sliver of my life I was willing to give to him.

He asked me, "What do you want from me?"

I told him he should be ashamed of himself for being willing to settle for a small sliver of my life. He used that word, 'sliver.' I told him that I, on the other hand, wanted the whole enchilada. I wanted more from him than any other woman had ever asked. I wanted it all. I wanted for him to love me and to show my children what it looks like for a man to love, really love, a woman. I wanted him to show them what it was to be a man.

The next time I spoke to Calhoun at the party, I was alongside others at one of the stainless steel cooking islands in the kitchen area. The pheasant had been barbecued and served up with potato salad on paper plates with plasticware. I had a second beer and worked my way along the island from one plate to the next using my toothpick to spear and sample all the different venison sausages. Each hunter had his own venison recipe to offer. One was so awful I discreetly spit it into my napkin. At the end of the table was one plate with the absolute best sausage I'd ever had in my life. A huge portion of spicy mustard had been put off to one side of the plate. Ray Malloy encouraged everyone to dip the sausages in mustard.

I made groaning sounds and quickly put three bites into my mouth. I announced to everyone that this one was the absolute best. I told the people on the other side of the counter from me that I didn't care if they never invited me back. This venison was all mine, and I wasn't sharing. For emphasis, I drew the plate closer to me and began stabbing the sausages as quickly as I could and shoved them into my mouth, chewing. I wrinkled up my nose and made pig grunting noises and everyone laughed.

Someone then reached over my shoulder and squirted more mustard onto the plate just as I was nearly running out – very observant. I turned and looked over my shoulder to see who was taking care of me. It was Calhoun.

"This is the best venison sausage I ever had in my life," I said as

I stuffed even more into my mouth. Then, I grinned and said, "If you can't eat with meat falling out of your mouth in front of someone, then you don't need that person in your life anyway."

He laughed. Each interaction he had with me was positive and made him laugh. I got the impression he had not laughed often recently. I asked Ted Drapas, my money manager, for another beer and walked to the other side of the kitchen to follow him to the ice chest.

When I turned, Ray was near me again, and I had the chance to make a little small talk.

"Your friend races motorcycles. Do you race also?"

Of course, I already knew the answer was 'yes.' That is the reason I had asked him the question. Before I continue, let me explain to you, reader, a little theory I have about sex and men. If a man is capable of risking his life for the thrill of speed and possesses the skill and control to survive the experience, he has the correct attitude towards life to be a really great lover. My word of advice is avoid the timid.

I asked Calhoun a very important question, "What is the fastest you've ever gone?"

"On wheels, one hundred and forty miles per hour. But, that is not the fastest I've ever gone. I've gone one hundred and seventy miles per hour."

Now, this man really had my attention.

"Oh! So, you've got a little cigarette boat then. How fun! "

I think I stole from him the explanation he anticipated giving me as the next obvious tack for the conversation to follow.

He blinked a few times, "How did you guess?"

I shrugged, took a swig of beer and asked him when the last time was that he had fun.

"To tell you the truth, I don't remember the last time I had fun it has been so long."

"So, you are captain of a boat and you are not having any fun. What you need is a cruise director," I announced this with a bit of girlish laughter in my voice. Then, I stepped towards him and stood very near looking directly up at him. I thought, 'God, he's tall.'

With my voice lower in a stage whisper I added, "There is no shame in delegating. Put someone in charge of fun."

He looked down into my face. He was nervous, I suddenly realized.

"Oh, come on," I pressed, "Tell me. What was the last, best, most fun you've had?"

He looked up and to his right at an imaginary point about two feet above his head. "I guess it would have to be a couple of Saturdays ago when I took my five year old son to pick out his birthday gift. I was in luck because this year his birthday fell on my weekend. Last year, it fell on his mother's weekend, and I didn't get to see him at all."

Before I got to ask what toy his son had picked out, the Dallasite came into the kitchen and took him by the arm and pulled on him.

"Excuse me, for just a moment, honey. I'm going to borrow him."

Helpless, he was led away from me to the dining table. I spoke to someone in the kitchen awhile and followed, sitting next to Calhoun but turning my back so that I faced another guest. I introduced myself and shook hands. I don't know what the Dallasite said, but suddenly Ray jumped up from the table and fled. Recoiled.

"OH, Huuuuneee! Come baaack," she drawled, patting his chair and swinging her long dark brown hair in a flirtatious gesture over her shoulder. Her hair additions on one-inch wide black combs were beginning to come loose. They sagged in three or four different spots around her head. Ray had retreated to the safety of the kitchen again. Ted Drapas was icing down more beer and handed Calhoun a cold one. Ted called me over and asked if I wanted a beer. He and Calhoun were talking about hedge funds, so I went, fresh beer in hand, in search of more food.

In the dining room, I became involved in a horrible conversation with a family law attorney who insinuated, after she asked the name of my lawyer, that I had been charged too much. I told her I had gotten exactly what I had paid for, as the list of lawyers willing to take your case becomes extremely short when there is almost a one hundred per cent certainty that both the client and the lawyer will be shot during the course of the suit. She, for example, would not have made that list.

These people were vulgar. How dare she demand to know something as private as my divorce attorney's name. I fell into that one. These people had no idea how to make conversation.

I excused myself and returned to the kitchen to get away from her and was standing opposite Calhoun and Ted on the other side of the stainless steel kitchen island when the Dallasite joined us. She positioned herself between the two men and threw her arms around Calhoun's neck. Her fingers were interlaced making escape impossible. Her hair combs had now slid even farther and chunks of hair dangled here, there, and yon.

"Excuse me, Ted," she at least acknowledged the fact that she had interrupted their conversation, "Excuse me, but I've just got to say something to Calhoun here."

Now, she turned her gaze full on Calhoun. She was clearly inebriated, and I knew he was experiencing a spray of drunken spit on his face.

"Calhoun, all of my friends have been after me, telling me the two of us should get together. I just want to tell you straight out that I want to be first in line to marry you when your divorce is final." She turned to face me but did not let go of her death grip around his neck. The word 'albatross' popped into my head. "I've got dibs on him. All my friends say we'd be a great couple. He says he's separated now, but not ready to date yet."

She shared this confidence with me at full volume but lowered her voice an octave.

I spoke to her, but I looked at him.

"Oh, but he's married."

I sang out the word 'married.'

She released him and stepped back almost losing her balance on her Manalo spike heels. She'd clearly been shocked. She gaped at him open mouthed. He had endured her hanging onto him fairly good naturedly, I thought. Sadly, he appeared to be used to such behavior from women. Now, he looked panicked. He realized he'd been caught in his lie. Earlier, he clearly claimed he was divorced.

"No. I really am separated." He spoke directly to me.

There was a tinge of desperation in his voice. Now, he faced the English teacher on the day the term paper was due and the dog really did eat it, but he knows it will never be believed.

"I'm separated. I really am."

The Dallasite faced me, desiring the truth.

I explained, "Oh, no. He's married." I told her, "You see in Texas we don't have papers of separation like they do in New Jersey and other states. In order to be legally separated in the state of Texas, you must file for divorce." I looked him dead in the eye now. "Which he has not."

She drew a deep breath of indignation at having been led on so. "Well, we just don't act like that in Dallas!"

Calhoun's eyes fixed on mine, "But, I am separated. We haven't lived under the same roof in years."

I had him locked in my sights, my eyes never shifting away from his nor his from mine. His eyes seemed to be pleading now, mine accusing, "Words have meaning."

Completely exasperated, he looked up and to the right just as he did when he searched his memory earlier.

"Estranged," he strangled the word as he spit it out, "We're estranged then."

His eyes searched mine for forgiveness, as if saying, 'I am not a liar. I am not a liar.'

I answered simply and with emotion, "How sad."

The Dallasite seemed to have been visiting her friend in Houston for too long because after a moment of consideration she decided to relax her morals to local standards. Recovered now from the shock to her decency, she threw her arms around his neck again and brought hers lips precariously near his.

"Well, that is different then. Let me just make myself clear. I want to marry you, and I am first in line when you file for divorce."

I spoke to her but looked directly at him. I said each word slowly and with conviction.

"Oh. This. Is. A. Very. Attractive. Man."

His face softened. He was forgiven.

"I'm quite sure the line for him already wraps around the block three times by now."

Anxiety crashed down like a hurricane swell in Galveston impacting every molecule of his body. He stepped forward, forgetting the albatross, and caused her to tilt backwards from his sudden movement. He raised his hand as if swearing an oath.

"NO. Trust me. There is no line."

At that I smiled. The wave of anxiety retreated, and he stood there, smiling back.

Ellen, the Dallasite, released Calhoun and returned to her table of buddies but not without taking me by the arm. "There is someone I want to introduce you to," she said by way of explanation. "Be right back," she mouthed silently to Calhoun.

Soon Ellen announced that a friend had invited us all over to the St. Regis Hotel jazz bar. Ted was talking to Calhoun in the kitchen, and I approached them both.

"Okay, Ted. We're going to the St. Regis Hotel."

Ted laughed and turned to Calhoun, "What did I tell you about her? She's direct."

They laughed.

"You know what I mean. We are Ellen's ride, and she wants to join her friends at the St. Regis. You are welcome to come with us if you wish," I added for Calhoun.

"No, I think I'll stay here. Thank you, though."

Ted offered to get my coat, winked at Calhoun, and disappeared into the back of the condo. He returned and asked if he could try on my coat. Robert Newhouse, the recently divorced divorce attorney, put on Ellen's coat and they both mugged it up for pictures using Ted's digital camera. They posed with cigars and looked liked 1920's style mobsters.

I got out of camera range to give them both room to pose and found Calhoun standing right next to me doing the same. The entire length of his body was against mine. The sides of our arms touched. It was possible to speak in a low voice and be heard by him easily.

"I know that it is unsolicited advice, but I've just been through a separation and divorce and it is not easy. You don't have to do things according to anyone else's timetable but your own. I didn't even leave my house for a year, for goodness sakes. I didn't even begin to think about dating for two years. You are ready when you are ready and not a moment sooner."

His voice cracked a bit when he replied, "You are the only one who seems to understand."

I reached up and in a very nonsexual way scratched his back just above the shoulder blades. "Remember that you are a human being and humans require touch and lots of it each day. You can not ignore your basic needs. It helped me to get a massage every day. A massage therapist would come to my home. Now, I have a great massage gal. Her name is Madeline. I go to her. She works at Avalon Nails on Shepherd. I'm sure she would probably come to your house each day. I'll tell her you are going to call her. If she doesn't have a portable massage table, I'll buy her one."

His voice was shaking when he whispered, "I do need touch."

Just then, Ted appeared with his camera, "Anyone else want a picture taken before I go?"

Ray pressed his cheek next to mine, "Over here."

We smiled. I'd never taken a cheek to cheek photo with anyone before. It felt nice to have his cheek pressed next to mine. I decided to ask my French-Algerian lover to break up. I needed to be available in case someone came along who was a good match for me. Being in a relationship that I knew was going nowhere was just preventing me from really looking. I was missing opportunities and using up valuable time. Besides, I liked being alone.

Ted called a couple of days later and said the photo turned out great, and he was going to send a copy of it to Calhoun. I asked if I looked good in it.

"No, no. Not to worry. It looks great of both of you. You both look really happy. It doesn't look like the two of you just met. It looks like you've been together a thousand years."

After we posed for the photo, Calhoun said he thought he had met me before. I thought to myself, 'Certainly, you have a better line than that. I'm sure you are used to the girls all falling over themselves at that suggestion.'

I said, "Nope. Not possible."

Ted held my coat for me, and I eased my arms down into the sleeves and shrugged it on. Calhoun only had a few seconds to make small talk.

I said the word 'nope' in such a way that it made a sound similar to pulling your thumb out of a pop bottle. "Nope, not possible. I never leave my house. There is really no reason to. It is so wonderful there. I'm sort of a recluse. Whenever I feel like being around people I throw a party and invite them over."

Ted's wife overheard and stopped.

"She throws awesome parties. The best parties I've ever been to. She celebrated the anniversary of the sinking of the Titanic with a four course meal that was exactly like the historic records of the ship."

"We had six wines, including champagne with chocolate éclairs, and port with cigars on the smoking deck. The smoking deck was my outside patio," I explained.

"One thing that impresses me, Penelope," Ted added, " is how you never drink at your parties. Usually, when I go to a party the host is smashed by the end of the evening. I didn't even see you drink at your wine tasting."

"I have a responsibility to my guests to make the evening run smoothly. I do drink at the very end, usually two glasses of wine as the guests are beginning to leave."

"The band is always so wonderful," Lynn smiled broadly, hanging onto the word 'sooo' like only a true Southerner can. She swayed back and forth with her daughter on her hip. Clearly, we were on our way out the door. The host, Ray Malloy, was at Lynn's side. She continued, "She had jazz musicians for the Titanic party. I think they were the same ones for her wine tasting."

"I've been to your house before, to your party," fibbed Ray, the host.

"Oh, I'm so sorry. I apologize that I didn't recognize you from before. Sometimes, I'm not in charge of the guest list. I just have a party idea and ask people to invite other people. I try to meet everyone. I'm so sorry. Which party did you go to?"

"The wine tasting."

"Oh, really? Which one? I had more than one this year. Was it the one with the poets and the interpretive dancers out on the back patio? Or was it the one with the man who only had one wine, but he also imported coffee and his grandfather invented the elevator?"

Ray blinked a few times. Fibber.

"Maybe, it wasn't a wine tasting. It was a party in December."

"Oh, the toga party!" Ted cried out. "We really wanted to go to that, but the baby got sick. We had cancelled our vacation and everything to go."

"I only give one or two days notice for a party," I explained to Calhoun who once again stood very close to me as I spoke to Ray Malloy. "I found out on Wednesday night I could get the Gallant Knights, and we had the party Friday."

"The Gallant Knights?" asked Calhoun.

"You know them? They play at this dive bar that has been around for years that caters to college kids. It's a band just like the one in the movie *Animal House*. They play songs like 'She's a Brick da da da daaaa House.'" I sang a line for everyone raising my arms above my head and snapping my fingers. "A six piece funk band. I'm lucky my neighbors are old and deaf."

"Yeah. I had my toga all ironed and ready to go and ended up with a crying baby on my hands all night driving around trying to get her to go to sleep. I even drove all the way to Penelope's house and drove around the circle. I could hear the band and she had a lot of cars there, but I couldn't go inside." Ted sounded truly forlorn recounting his memory.

"I wish I had known. We could have paid one of the valet parking guys to drive her around."

I turned to Ray again and asked him what I was wearing at the party because that would help me identify what party it was.

He said he didn't pay much attention to women's clothes, normally. He couldn't possibly be asked to remember something like that.

"Oh, you would remember Penelope's clothes." Ted said, "They are memorable."

"They aren't really clothes. They are more like costumes designed for each party, very elaborate," I explained. I hoped that Ted would have the sense to not describe the outfits to Calhoun and his friend. After all, I had worn nothing but body paint, a bikini, and a gold net dress for the conservative judge's fundraiser in my home. It was a fish fry and people spending five hundred dollars each deserve a show.

I held my breath as Ted continued talking, "She dressed everyone at her toga party. She got all different colored sheets and grape leaves and stuff like that. Everyone had a custom made toga. God, I wish I could have gone."

"Next year, I promise. I'll do it again."

"I would like to get to know you better," said Ray, the fibber, who had apparently never been to one of my parties.

"I'd like to get to know you better, too, Ray. Thank you for inviting me to your 'after the hunt' party. I've had a wonderful time."

"May I call you?"

"Sure, and I'll make sure to put you on my party list. But I must warn you that I'm cutting back this year on the elaborate parties. I'm going to keep it simpler like the last party I had. I just got a bunch of theatre tickets and we all went to see 'Who's Afraid of Virginia Wolfe?' and then out to Katz's deli for sandwiches. Easy and simpler and a cheap way to entertain. Afterwards, we just went back to my house and had caviar and wine and cheese."

So, Calhoun got to see me get invited out by his friend. He also witnessed his best bud get rejected, but nicely.

2

You Simply Can't Make This Up

Suddenly, I remembered meeting Ray Calhoun once before. It was at Memorial Park on the jogging path just as he had said at the party.

I told him, "Nope, not possible. I never leave my house." But, I just remembered. Oh, my God.

The things I told him! You know, the sorts of things you tell a total stranger that you never expect to ever see again. Oh, my God. I racked my brains for days trying to remember all that I told him about myself. Did I tell him that my husband, Richard, tried to kill me? No, I don't think I did since I tried to seem attractive to him because he had such gorgeous legs. Then, all in a rush, I remembered everything. The whole conversation came back to me. Talk about coincidences! You can't make this up!

He asked me where I lived and initially I told him near the medical center or inside the loop, something vague like that. It sounds like bragging or it could get you followed home and mugged if you tell a stranger that you live in the most expensive neighborhood in the city. In fact, I later found out from my realtor that there are five different sections in the neighborhood, and I live in the best section. "Buy the little house on the street with all of the big houses," my dad has always said. That is what I did.

Then later in the conversation, when I asked him what he did for a living and he said he managed office buildings, and he had several buildings I realized he was doing the same thing, trying not to let me know he was rich. He owned the buildings, I was certain. He had only given me his first name, Ray. He had intentionally omitted his last name leading me to think he was either very wealthy, married or both. So mystery Ray, no last name, 'managed' office buildings.

I apologized to him and told him I lived on Chevy Chase. I told him that before I was rich I had probably only lied once or twice in my entire life, but now that I was rich I lied all the time. It was the only way to draw boundaries in a socially acceptable way when people asked you all kinds of inappropriate questions that were none of their business.

I admire my friend Michael Strauss's ability to handle such questions. He had something to do with the invention of Lasik eye surgery and is very wealthy. People will ask him things about his money and lifestyle that are none of their concern. People have no manners!

Michael just turns the question back on them by saying, "That is an interesting question for you to ask me. What would cause you to ask me something of that nature?"

Ha! There! Back in their lap, forcing them to justify their right to know something so personal.

I remember talking about boundaries to Calhoun emphasizing my point by rubbing the flat of my palm up and down my arm and saying, "My job is me. I end here with my skin. My job is not you or anyone else. It is my responsibility to be happy. God put me here on earth to enjoy this life and be fulfilled. The fact that I was placed in this body is a big clue. This is the body I am responsible for. This is my job. No one else can make me happy except for me. I am completely in charge of those decisions."

The day I met Calhoun in the park, I told him my philosophy of life. Each day was a gift and to be respected as such, a gift from God. In order to show gratitude for that gift I needed to make sure that the world was a better place due to my existence each day. I told him I played a little game with myself that had developed elaborate rules over the years in order to live my life in accordance with this philosophy. Using my effort and energy and creativity, I had to do something each day to honor the gift of life. The tricky part was to do my good deed anonymously.

I told him how the judge had blocked my gift to Rotary Club International that would have built a clinic in Chinandega, Nicaragua for Father Marcos and the mud slide victims. I told him how I also couldn't buy one of the art cows for the children's hospital fundraiser. The children's hospital would get its funds without my contribution, but the money to Nicaragua was going to be slower to come if at all. Those people had been living exposed in the city dump for years now, unclothed, with severely malnourished children that had distended bellies and shocks of bright white hair sticking up as a result of severe mineral deficiencies.

All they needed was a water pipeline that cost eighty-seven thousand five hundred dollars so they could begin farming again. These were small farm farmers that had been there for generations. The land was so rich from the volcanic soil that a very small plot of land had an enormous yield. This area of Nicaragua had once yielded most of the beans eaten in South America and Mexico. Now, the people starved for want of a single water pipeline. The judge blocked me from giving the money for the pipeline and for the clinic.

Later, I found out someone had contacted Rotary and given two hundred thousand dollars. I wonder if it was Ray after he met me that day in the park? I also told him that it was my belief that I must help someone in need if God placed them directly in my path. That is why I had stopped to help Ray when he seemed to be injured in the park. He was limping badly, and I offered to go get my car and drive him to his car. He rejected my offer and said he was going to try to walk. He had suffered the injury on another day and was taking it easy and walking instead of running to keep it loose and let it heal. He told me he was a marathon runner.

I told him that Byron McCoy was my company's sales manager. He was also a marathon runner. I asked if they were friends. He said the name sounded familiar. We walked together about two miles. I was a jabberbox. He was smiling and encouraging me though. I didn't pick up any signals that my talking was annoying to him.

I told him that a friend of mine had told me that the luckiest thing that ever happened to me in my life was that my family turned on me after about two seconds of becoming rich. I explained that during the divorce my mother had testified for my husband resulting in him getting the children. She had been led to believe that he would financially compensate her by paying off her house in Kingwood. My parents had purchased the house, knowing that it was too much for them to afford. I guess they thought of me as their backup plan. When they got in a hole my mother came to me to pay it off, and I couldn't just write her the check without asking Richard as she suggested.

When I had asked my husband, he had not just said no, but, "Hell no! She's been a terrible mother to you. She didn't even help you out when you were in college and has never helped with the kids."

I didn't know what to tell her when she asked me what Richard had said because I didn't want to create a family rift so I took the blame. I told her that dad was a real estate broker and that they knew full well what they were getting into when they purchased that house.

She was livid. Richard knew about this breach between Norma and I just prior to me running away from him, and he worked it to his advantage. He held out the promise of taking care of her without actually coming out and saying it just leaving it hanging there in the air between them unspoken but hoped for by Norma.

She knew she'd get little more from me. In China, I had picked out a huge room sized oriental rug for our fifteen thousand square foot home while my mother toured the jade factory upstairs with the tour group. I met with the family that had spent four years weaving the rug and had my photo taken with them. I paid for the rug and was filling out the required forms for shipping when Norma returned from the tour and stood next to the cash register and asked what I was doing. I said I had just bought the most beautiful rug and hoped Richard would allow me to put it in our dining room. If not, life was long. I had married an older man and I would let my friend Debbie use it in her home in Pennsylvania until Richard died, and then I'd put it in my home later in life. I never thought of divorcing, but I knew that some day he would die and release me from my vows, and I could live my life my way at last.

Mom glanced over at the rug on the floor that the workers had taken from its storage space on the far wall and laid out for me to inspect. I had already signed the back in permanent magic marker and photographed the rug to prepare for shipping.

She said in an off handed way, "I want that rug."

"I'm sorry, Mom. I've already bought that rug. Besides, don't be fooled by looking at it laid out in this large warehouse space. It's much bigger than it seems - fifteen feet by twenty feet. You do not have a room in your house big enough for this rug. There is an identical one only smaller on the far wall over there that I am sure they will sell to you. I paid six thousand dollars for this one. They were asking for ten thousand."

"I want you to buy this rug for me."

She stuck out her lower lip and stomped her foot like a child.

The owner of the factory became extremely uncomfortable.

"Mother, you have your own money. It you want a rug you can buy one for yourself. I've already given you your birthday gift - this trip to China, the pearl ring and the Ann Taylor clothes. That is enough."

"But, I want THIS rug."

"It doesn't make any sense. It won't even fit in your house. Besides, I am not buying you anything else."

She did not know that I had gotten her an exquisite opera length necklace of superior quality pearls for four thousand dollars that later in the United States appraised for ten grand. It was going to be her Christmas gift.

Things quickly changed for me after I returned home from China. December eighth Richard yelled at me because he said I had allowed too many newspapers to collect at the bottom of the driveway and ordered me to pick them up and then tried to run me down with the car, and I ran away. Norma prepared with Richard's lawyers to testify against me in court. I kept the necklace.

What else did I tell that gorgeous man that day in the park? I walked the trail this morning at dawn and found the precise spot where I had met him near the one mile marker. I remember he had run past me and suddenly stopped. He adjusted his shoe lace and stretched. As I walked toward him, I looked over. He seemed to be injured badly. He limped. We walked side by side without speaking. I walk incredibly slowly since both of my hips have been broken and one hip has, in fact, been broken twice. He was right at my side laboring with his leg. I didn't want him to think I was some weirdo walking right beside him so I explained that my pace was extremely slow and that it was likely we'd be walking together. I asked if he wanted some company on his walk and conversation or if he'd enjoy just being alone with his thoughts. I told him that I could understand it if he just wanted to walk alone. He said he would not mind walking with me. It was okay with him. I joked with him about my pace, pointing out that hunched over little old ladies in SAS orthopedic shoes could pass me like I was standing still.

I told him the story of my tendon injury. It was my first day back exercising at The Woodlands Athletic Center after having my third child. I had three children under the age of five and therefore qualified for a handicapped sticker for my car, but when you have three children under the age of five who can go downtown and stand in line and fill out all of those forms?

I had just gone swimming, lifted weights and used the stairmaster machine. I decided to clean my locker that day and had filled my swim bag with several old stinking towels, bottles of shampoo and lotions and swimfins. It was heavy. I also carried the diaper bag and the infant carrier with a fifteen pound child, and two full eight ounce bottles. I was weighted down. My four year old walked along beside me, and I held the hand of my two year old.

We were near the parking lot when the clouds opened up and buckets of rain slammed us. It was the kind of rain that makes it impossible to see more than a couple of feet in front of you when you are driving. My toddler broke free from my hand and ran into the parking lot. A car was coming. I ran after him and scooped him up carrying him like a football back to the safety of the sidewalk. There was a very steep incline I had to walk up carrying that load. The first step caused so much pressure on my planter fascia tendon that it ripped completely free of the round ball of bone at the base of the heel.

My podiatrist said he wanted to know how a housewife had managed to cause the injury because he usually saw that kind of an injury with professional football players or people involved in car wrecks. He thought the amount of relaxin levels in my body after having recently had a child, overworking the tendon doing forty-five minutes on the stairmaster and the weight I was carrying had all contributed. I did not tell the stranger, Calhoun, how that baby became very ill, and I had to struggle to keep him alive for months while recovering from the injury.

Calhoun was attractive. Cute rear, not overly skinny like many marathon runners, tall and muscular and genetically gifted with a natural V shape to his upper body. He was older, probably my ex-husband's age, fifty, but in great shape. You could tell he weight-lifted, but not in that obsessive way that overly vain men tend to do, just enough to stay scrumptious.

If I had been walking with my friend Becky that day we could have ranked him a nine and joked, "You trip him, I'll bag him and we'll drag him into the woods and take turns with him."

We were just awful, some of the things we would say about the hard bodied men we'd see at the track.

"Gay."

"Gay?"

"Definitely, Liberachi gay!" Things like that.

Calhoun asked how I had broken both of my hips. I seemed so young for that. I told him once a hip is broken it is vulnerable to break again. I had been running in the house playing soldier with the boys and I was trying to jump from the entry hall into the pit couch in the sunken den because I only had a count of five to get to safe base before my three year old nuked me with his nuclear weapon.

I only had an imaginary bazooka. There was a piece of white paper on the white entry tile and I didn't see it. My foot slid out of control and I went down in a Chinese split. The doctor said I was lucky that I didn't break both hips and my pelvic bone.

I told Calhoun, "I know, I know. Moms are not supposed to run in the house. They are supposed to warn their children about the dangers of running in the house. But, I'm just not that kind of mom."

I didn't learn my lesson and continued to play soldier even on crutches and learned how to really pick up speed on them.

He wanted to know how Mark, the baby, had a nuclear weapon, and I was only armed with a bazooka. I told him it was strategy. I did a lot of hiding early on in the game coming out only after others were killed and there were fewer soldiers. Each time you got killed you had to die loudly and dramatically and then slowly come to life making the sounds from the theme music for the Terminator. When you were alive again you had the next higher level of weapon. You had to stay down and count to sixty out loud. It was fun and good counting practice. Mark liked to get killed early and often to get better weaponry before everyone else.

I played with the children all day and watched cartoons with them rather than doing other things and using the boob tube as a babysitter. I'd sit on the floor and hold them in my lap and watch cartoons with them. They are only children for such a short time. I told him I had originally studied business at University of Houston and then got a masters in education. I used to teach Montessori school, then later I taught emotionally disturbed children in the fifth ward.

Calhoun asked how my hips were broken the first time. We walked a moment silently while I considered what to say.

I was violently assaulted by a group of black men in a courtyard. I was a minor and did not receive medical attention at all. My parents were not even called. I did not remember who I was, or that I was even a university student.

The attackers were wearing their school uniforms, basketball shorts. When I interviewed with the Houston Independent School District, I tried to get a job where they went to school. I found a job at the middle school that fed into that high school.

I turned to Ray and apologized if I had upset him. He said not to worry. I explained that I was certain that things happen for a reason to prepare us for the next step in our lives or to give us the life experiences to be equipped to help others. Sometimes we are just the tool for someone else to learn an important lesson in life. I wanted something good to come from a horrible experience.

I also needed therapy. I had anxiety attacks after the assault and was afraid sometimes in parking lots even though the attack didn't happen in a parking lot. I also sometimes would be very afraid of black men. So, I taught at an all black school. I loved my principal and he said I was proof that a teacher could turn a child's life around.

Calhoun asked if I taught now. I laughed and explained that I was retired and until recently stayed at home with my children. Now, I was retired from even that. Since I divorced, the children lived with their father and were being raised by their dad and his twenty-six year old girlfriend, my next door neighbor. I told him I was embarrassed for my husband, and I was writing my memoirs now and had titled that chapter 'My Husband is Having an Affair with an Embryo.'

I told him I was happy to be alone and, in fact, had started to get a little worried about myself because I enjoyed being alone so much. I had recently met an old woman at the plant store who had sold me my orange trees and she said I reminded her of herself when she was my age. Her husband had died and she loved being alone so much she never dated or remarried. She warned me not to be alone for too long, or I would never be able to remarry. I would learn to love being alone too much to be able to give it up.

I told him her remarks had frightened me into dating. I gave myself a month to find a boyfriend and had everyone I know fix me up. I had twenty-five dates and it was absolutely horrible. Ten minutes into the date, I would want to leap from the moving car. I would be nice to the person and try to make sure that they didn't have a miserable time. I just wasn't interested. I told him I should have married the love of my life. That was my college boyfriend. I hadn't married him because he was the oldest son of one of the wealthiest men in the world. I didn't want my children to be raised with that kind of money and turn out to be freaks.

I married an obese man with a stutter, a failing business and a home in foreclosure that had a broken foundation. We founded a software company and my kids ended up being raised with money after all. I might as well have married the one I really loved! I felt that the children had chosen me as their mother. Maybe the lessons that they were meant to learn in this lifetime required that they be wealthy.

Most people think it would be great to have a bunch of money, but I don't believe that it belongs to me. It belongs to God just like my life and my body belong to God. I just have custodianship for awhile and need to take care of what has been given to me to watch over. I get this philosophy from my American Indian grandmother, Inez.

I laughed with him that I didn't believe everything that the people in my grandmother's tribe believed. They, for example, believed that babies came from the breath of man too near a woman. God breathed the baby into the woman through the man.

I told him that I had never mastered birth control, so it was very lucky for me that I had been a 'good girl' as I conceived my first born using three forms of birth control simultaneously. At that time I taught a pregnancy prevention program. I went into class one day and told the students I was accidentally pregnant. Three different preventative measures had all failed. It scared them to death.

Calhoun chuckled as I disclosed this embarrassing fact, "Well, you know what they say. Those that can't do, teach."

I told him I thought Jonah was just ready to be born. Richard had wanted me to abort him because the prenatal testing had turned out badly. I told him that the prenatal testing just gave us extra time to prepare for the blind, deaf and disfigured child we were about to have. The testing was not permission to kill him.

I was already reading aloud to Jonah, age five months two weeks, inside the womb. His favorite book was *I am a Bunny*. He'd kick inside me as I read aloud to him in the bathtub, and I'd splash my belly with warm water to communicate back to him.

How could I kill him? He wasn't fetal tissue, he was a baby who already had a relationship with me. I stayed in bed with my feet up. I almost lost him at six months. I only got out of bed two times a day.

My mother and sister did not visit with me, and Richard withdrew from me, working until ten-thirty at night. I was very isolated and had always dealt with stress by exercising, and now that was taken away from me as an option. I was very depressed.

I prayed and I was sure that God had chosen me to be this child's mother because I was prepared. I had helped my mother when she was legally blind for four years. I had stayed home from school to care for her, my newborn little sister (who I refer to as the evil human pet, Terry Jo) and my retarded great Aunt Eula Lee who suffered from dementia. Eula Lee wandered into neighbor's homes, brewed a pot of coffee, and sat at their kitchen tables talking to persons that were long since dead. The sheriff's deputies would bring her home.

I also cared for my grandmother, Inez. Federal money cutbacks to the state mental hospital resulted in her early release. I got a call that she was on her way, so I called my Aunt Mabel and asked her what to do. She said to not answer the door. She'd find a nursing home spot for her and contact the authorities and have her sent directly there. She emphasized that I should not open the door under any circumstances.

A handful of nursing homes and a couple of weeks later, I was also caring for my grandmother. She had been violent and had also spit on nursing staff, so the nursing homes rejected her one by one. It turned out she was having a severe drug reaction. She was on inappropriate levels of drugs that were having a bad interaction.

For a long time, I had to change the diapers of both the baby, Terry Jo, and my adult grandmother. This was in the days before disposable adult and baby diapers were popular. I did laundry all day long rinsing cloth diapers in the toilet, cloroxing them and then washing them twice to get all of the Clorox out.

I remember one day complaining to my father that my sister, Lauren, was having a normal childhood, and I was just cleaning and cooking and taking care of people all day. I pointed out that Lauren could at least do a couple of loads of laundry each day. She claimed that she already did help. I asked her to show dad how to turn on the washing machine, and she didn't know how, proving my point.

My mother eventually regained her eyesight after a series of experimental laser eye surgeries. My grandmother returned to normal mental health after getting her medication corrected. I had four years of hell but the family pulled through. Great Aunt Eula Lee ended up in the nursing home after the television started to tell her to kill me. She had very, very long discussions with the television about killing me. After she was safely in a home, I left for college.

I had not attended high school except to pick up my assignments. I did very well on the SAT exam, so the counselor said I could leave high school early at age sixteen. My maturity level was far beyond the other students. He told me that I could get scholarships if I stayed two more years and took the SAT again after having trig and calculus. I had an A average.

I wanted to go to a local ivy league university, but my family had zero college savings and the admissions officer said they were refusing early admissions because of the number of recent suicide attempts among their younger students. This caused them to reevaluate their early admissions policies. So, I went to the University of Houston and was out by age nineteen with a double degree and a thriving printing business that employed five people twice my age.

I confessed to Calhoun that I had an IQ over one hundred seventy. I thought I would most likely live the rest of my life alone. Research shows that people who are happily married for twenty or more years have IQs within five points of one another. Demographically speaking that meant that to find a mate I was looking at one in twenty thousand people in the city. Of course, my match needed to be someone male, heterosexual and unmarried. I additionally demanded a similar moral compass and on that the bar was held very high. To make matters worse, political viewpoint was very important to me as well.

It is not surprising at all to me that the men I have dated have all had in common the fact that they are multimillionaires and have clearance to be alone with the president of the United States. So far,

I have not dated anyone who lived farther than three square blocks from my home. My money manager said he would put me on a budget if I was any other client, but he was sure that long before my money ran out I would remarry and marry very well. The wealthier the person, he had long ago discovered, the more lonely.

When we parted ways I probably hugged him, since I hug everyone.

I remember gently teasing him about not sharing his last name with me saying, "Goodbye, Ray, last name mysteriously withheld."

I told him I was one person with whom he could have shared his last name, since in the assault I had also suffered minor brain damage and would probably have absolutely no memory of having ever met him at all. I told him I really liked him, and that if he ever waved 'hello' at me at the park and I didn't wave back that it was not because I was trying to ignore him or be rude. I simply would not remember ever having met him. I asked him to come up to me at the park and remind me of who he was if he ever saw me.

At the 'after the hunt' party Calhoun tried to remind me, but I still did not remember. The dental hygienist at my dentist today told me she remembered me telling someone in the office I had met the most gorgeous man at the park. She told me that I was walking without my body guard that day for some reason and had walked with a man who had injured himself, and I had an anxiety attack and couldn't sleep for three days due to my heart racing. She said I had gone to the cardiologist and had a complete workup.

Oh, my God! Now, I remember. I had a similar reaction to him at the party. I felt faint. My heart raced. My knees started to go out from under me. Oh, my god. It is him, and I had the same physical reaction to him.

I'm doomed.

I just returned from Barnaby's restaurant with my friend, Taylor. He read the most recent chapter of my memoirs and gave his comments after reading my mother and my sister's court testimony. He thinks Ray will be at Lynn's birthday party tomorrow. He thinks Calhoun has to be interested.

Lynn said it seemed very suspicious that her husband Ted planned to celebrate her birthday on a day other than her real birthday since he has always celebrated on the actual day before. Now, he was planning a party for her, and she wasn't allowed to invite the people she normally invited in the past, the single girls who teach pilates with her. Her husband limited the guest list to only married couples. We were meeting at a restaurant that is notorious for its strong margaritas.

Lynn said the only problem is that both Rays are coming and Calhoun's close friend, Ray Malloy is also keen on me. She said Calhoun is the kind to step down if his friend expresses interest in me. I told her I'd have to make things very clear. I'd have to tell Ray I am interested in Calhoun. I'd have to tell Calhoun that I was interested without scaring him silly. I had already told him he was a very attractive man.

I began to wonder if he would even show up. Lynn invited him when she ran into him outside a restaurant the other day. Ted had said he'd invite him, but then Lynn just happened to run into him. He didn't ask about me, or if I would be there, he just said he'd come. My friend Taylor said Calhoun doesn't seem like the kind of guy to just go from party to party every night. Parties are not good experiences for him. He must be coming in hopes of seeing me again.

Lynn thought Ted knew something and simply wasn't telling her because she is a blabbermouth. I'll keep that in mind and be careful of what I say to her in the future. I asked her if Ted had a history of matchmaking people and she said, "No." The whole idea of a set-up made me squeamish if Calhoun was being dragged there and wasn't even interested in me. Lynn told me she thought guys never take it upon themselves to fix people up. That is a girl thing. Ted would only have a party to get two people together if Calhoun expressed interest or had out and out asked him to do it.

At first, Ted had asked me to dinner with him, Lynn and Ray, and I had said, "No." That put too much pressure on us and would be too uncomfortable. I'd only be interested in seeing Ray again if there were a lot of people there, as in more than ten. I felt a lot better about the dinner invitation thinking Ray had wanted to see me, but now that it looked like a set-up I felt very uncomfortable. The more I thought about it, the party was my idea. Ugh!

Maybe he won't show up. A definite sign he's not trying too hard to see me again. If he does show up it doesn't mean anything either as Lynn didn't tell him I was coming. I'm going to make myself absolutely nuts if I keep thinking about this.

Okay. In my heart, do I think he is attracted to me? Yes. Why would he stand so close to me? Why would he press his cheek to mine for a photo? Why would he remember me a year later after one walk in the park? Lynn says I'm gorgeous in the photo. She can't believe I haven't seen it yet. I don't know how to do email, so Ted couldn't send me the digitized image.

The day we met in the park, I told Calhoun I was proud of how I had raised the children. I thought they had a good relationship with money and knew the importance of giving. They went with me to hand out sleeping bags to the men who live under the bridges and to give food at the Nourishment for the Needy. I had exposed them to a world beyond the homogeneous white middle class world of their neighborhood.

I told Calhoun that one of my boys had taken the tag out of the trash can that I had removed from my Victoria's Secret bra and sold looks at it on the playground for twenty-five cents for three looks. He made eight dollars before he was caught.

Later, I questioned my son. He told me that he allowed the boys to look three times for twenty-five cents because they wouldn't pay a quarter for one look, and if you let them look five times they weren't interested in buying a look the following day. He was already a marketing genius! My own little Larry Flint!

Anyway, in Houston I live near a predominantly gay area known as the Montrose and took the children with me to a deli where there are as many gay couples as straight couples. The children are able to see gay couples holding hands and hugging and kissing. I hope that this helps them to be more understanding of a variety of lifestyles and accepting of others.

I looked to Ray to see his reaction. So many people are full of mindless hate especially on this subject. He simply nodded in an understanding way and laughed when I pointed out how this must have really fueled their father's accusations that I was a lesbian. I assured him that I was not. I had not left Richard for another man or another woman. I had left him for my own reasons.

I told Ray about the first moment that I ever thought I might divorce my husband. It was a rainy Saturday and the ice cream truck had just delivered our ice cream. As the man wheeled the dolly of ice creams up to the back kitchen door, he looked in through the window and laughed. I was dancing with my dog to Eric Clapton's "You Look Wonderful Tonight." The ice cream man opened the back door and commented on the smell of my gumbo cooking on the stove. He said what a wonderful, happy home I had.

Moments later, my husband came home to that exact same scene. I was laughing and cooking and dancing with the dog. His face contorted like wax exposed to a flame, twisting in an ugly way. He couldn't stand to see my joy because he couldn't have it for himself. He was an unhappy human being and nothing I could do could reach him. I began to consider leaving him. Mercifully, he gave me a guilt-free reason to leave.

I explained to Ray that I had always taught the children that there were only three reasons to leave a marriage – the three A's. Abuse – verbal, mental or physical, Alcoholism or substance abuse and Adultery. Richard didn't drink but he certainly had the other two bases covered.

Now, I had discovered another reason for divorce – betrayal. For years, Richard had led me to believe that he had filed the taxes when he had not. Now that we were both in trouble for not filing our joint return each year, he was taking the stand that he was completely innocent and unaware because I was responsible for the taxes! After I filed for divorce, Richard told the judge we were behind in filing. He assured me that the fine was only five hundred dollars and a class C misdemeanor. That didn't sound right to me because if the penalty was that small most of the United States would be behind on their taxes. I told him I didn't know who he was getting his information from but that just didn't sound correct. The penalty turned out to be millions.

At the time that I filed for divorce, our stock was selling for one hundred and ten dollars per share. Richard tried to stop the divorce using different ploys. He lied in court and told the judge he was behind 'maybe' three years on filing but would have it done by the time the divorce was final. He knew full well that he was behind eight years. The IRS had been sending threatening letters.

The divorce should have been final at the end of May. It was delayed due to the fact that the taxes were not completed. So, I offered that I would do the taxes for both of us and get it done. My tax attorney said Richard was extremely uncooperative.

In my memoirs, you will enjoy every word of the trial in which I was charged with contempt of court for hiring my own tax attorney. I decided to someday let you read every word of it. Keep in mind at one point the bailiff came forward to shackle me, and I stood to allow him to do so. My friends had told me a rumor, I don't know if it is true or not, that there was one woman who had been in jail for two years for contempt for doing something minor. She was to remain there until the divorce was final while her husband and the judge delayed indefinitely the finalization of the divorce. The rumor was frightening, true or not. Maybe, I will post the transcript on a website.

Anyway, tomorrow I might get to see Calhoun again, the man that has kept me up at night causing me to write this book that I've been intending to write for two years. I have not been able to sleep since I saw him at the 'after the hunt' party. I'm going to tell him that I remembered him and all the embarrassing things I told him at the park.

At one point in Malloy's kitchen, at the party, I had flirted with Ray Calhoun giggling and showing him my manicure (and doorknob ring, which escaped comment). I admitted that I had the lady at the nail salon keep my nails short and pink because I kept telling her that I was writing my memoirs, but then I never do because I'm lazy and having too much fun living my life to write about it. I batted my eyelashes (YES, batted my eyelashes!) and leaned into him, allowing him to support my weight on his chest for a split second while I looked up at him looking down at me.

He was so tall and wonderful. I threw myself at him in that moment. But was he catching? I told him that I had had a rather exciting life but had given up on writing about it. I was going to hire a screenplay writer that was a friend of a friend if he was interested in the project.

When he commented that I walked quite a lot, I told him that in my wild imagination I thought that I might someday walk the Camino. He asked what that was.

"It is a religious pilgrimage from the Spanish border in the mountains to the border with France at the sea. It is approximately five hundred and fifty miles."

"Wow! How long does that take?"

"A month or so, depending on how many miles you cover in a day. They give you a little book that you get stamped at each refugio along the way."

"What is a refugio?"

"Oh, people allow the pilgrims to camp out in their yards or sleep in their barns and give them a simple meal, fresh water and a place to take a shower. Of course, you can say you've walked the Camino and only walk part of it, and, of course, there is more than one way to walk it." Now I flirted heavily, giggling, smiling broadly, my eyes flashing. I explained, "You can camp out in people's yards, but technically there is nothing stopping you from checking into five star hotels. For that matter, a limousine can follow you, so you can take a break when you get tired. I kind of think I'm a being followed by a limo, staying at a five star hotel kind of Camino gal. Shirley McClaine walked all of it but stayed at a hotel a couple of times to get away from reporters. She wrote a book about it."

At least at the party I had something to say, some real conversation. I could make him laugh. Like I said, he didn't look like he'd laughed much recently.

I've hardly slept since I've met him, working myself up into an almost manic state. I had the kids the weekend of Lynn's birthday party, so I asked Yesenia to drive them back to their father's house at five in the afternoon. I napped for three hours and washed my hair at five o'clock, so it would be all shiny and sweet smelling of rosemary mint shampoo. I had planned my 'not trying too hard' outfit days in advance to be dressed down. I wore clogs and black socks with tiny blue flowers on them, very sweet. I wore my Escada navy blue jeans style pants that are extremely figure flattering and a big floppy pink chinchilla cowl necked sweater that retails at Neiman Marcus for six grand. Not everyone has that in their closet to just casually toss on. I had my nails manicured the day before in pink and wore my pink patent leather wristbanded diamond watch and twenty carat pink citrine ring.

At one point I saw him look down and admire my hand and nails. Nothing escaped his notice. He saw how perfect all the pinks were together. I wanted to touch him but didn't dare in public so soon before he filed for divorce.

I think he really likes me. He was fifteen minutes early for the party. When I arrived, there were only three people there: Ray, the recently divorced family law attorney, Robert Newhouse, and Robert's girlfriend. The girlfriend looked freakishly like the wife he just divorced if only the wife had ever smiled.

I drove my little champagne gold Mercedes convertible. From their vantage I am sure they got to see me pull up and park.

When I entered the restaurant it took a while for my eyes to adjust to the light because the restaurant interior was so dark. Robert and his gal called me over waving and Ray stood like a gentleman. I started to walk right past Ray to give Robert a hug and didn't see him until I was right up to him.

I stopped in my tracks and said, "Ray, I was hoping you would be here. It is good to see you again." I smiled encouragingly.

If he did set this up he was probably thinking all of the same things I was thinking, "Will she feel trapped into a set up date she didn't want?" He smiled back. I gave Robert a big hug and said 'hello' to the gal at his side. If she was going to be in the picture much longer I was going to have to learn her name.

I started to sit far from Calhoun just on the other side of Robert but Calhoun pulled out a chair next to him. What was I thinking? My knees were weak already. I had to sit immediately.

Calhoun asked if I wanted a beer and I joked that I wasn't sure since I had just woken up at five p.m. I explained that I had had dental work earlier in the week and at first had not taken the pain killers the dentist gave me, but I had finally given in that morning and taken one and it had knocked me out all day. I laughed and asked everyone present if it was a good idea for a beer to be the first thing I put into my body all day.

Robert raised his beer high and said, "Breakfast of champions!" I told Calhoun that I would have a Corona, the same that he was drinking. He walked over to the bar and got my drink.

He was acting very much like my date. I liked the way this was going. He had on a brand new belt. He hadn't been wearing a belt the first time I saw him. He had buffed his nubuck leather shoes and had a starched crease in his khakis and a starched shirt in a deep plum color similar to what he was wearing when I saw him at the 'after the hunt' party, only all gussied up. He had put gel in his hair that I swear was the same horrible stuff that Robert Newhouse used. It was sweet he'd made so much effort. It looked like he had shaved less than an hour ago. I was quite flattered.

Robert and his girlfriend had both asked to touch my sweater and commented on how soft it was, so I extended my arm and told Calhoun, "Everyone else at the table has petted my sweater. Don't you want to feel how soft it is?"

He stroked my arm three times. "That is incredibly soft."

I told him, "I'm hoping you are not an active member of PETA or anything horrible like that."

"Oh, no. Quite the opposite. On the ranch we have to monitor the animal populations carefully and keep their numbers back."

"Yes, people just don't understand that if you don't do that the animals die a pathetic death, starving. It is just awful. And you won't see the cow or the chicken on the endangered species list anytime soon. As long as there is a financial incentive for humans to keep an animal population alive, you won't see that happening."

Calhoun agreed. I told him my furrier loved me. He said he was sure that was true. I said, "No, he really loves me. I changed the entire way he does business and this year was his best year when it should have been his worst year since everyone selling luxury goods from custom golf clubs to boats was having a disastrous year. Richard Peters Furs was having his best year ever.

Two years ago at the Montreal International Fur Show, Richard had followed my recommendation and bought several small colorful fun pieces like vests and jackets. They sold very, very quickly. So the following year he devoted a third of his showroom floor to things he saw at the fur show that he thought I would like. He said he just pretended he was buying for me. He thought that he had bought enough to last the entire season and they just flew out of the store in a couple of weeks. I told him he had to give his customer something different and casual that they could wear as an everyday piece."

Calhoun was happy to add to the conversation, "Yes, that would make sense, especially with the warmer weather here in Houston, a vest you could wear more often."

"I told the furrier that once a woman has a full length mink and a stroller length other fur, she feels her fur wardrobe is complete. I told him to get some fun pieces and have them out when the women come in to pick up their furs out of cold storage to show them something different. He's thrilled. He's had his best year ever."

"Well, that would make him really love you."

Calhoun then asked me where I was born, and I told him, "Right here in Houston during Hurricane Carla." He said he remembered Hurricane Carla. He had been a teenager then. He looked a bit uncomfortable, no doubt thinking again about the age difference.

I told him my mother had interviewed the doctor that had delivered me to make sure that he was good enough. She had been wheeled out of the delivery room and was laboring in the hallway because the ceilings in the delivery room were bowing from the weight of the water. The nursing staff had poked holes in the ceiling to allow the water to pour through.

"Yes, that would prevent the entire ceiling from caving in," Calhoun added. I could see his engineer brain working.

"My mother was lucky to have a doctor help her deliver a baby at all because during the hurricane there were plenty of people who really needed emergency medical attention. A woman can deliver a baby on her own without any help, let's face it. This doctor was running past her in the hallway and stopped to offer help and she interviewed him! Where did he go to school, what was his class rank, how many babies had he delivered before?

Years later, she and my dad were eating at a restaurant in Galveston and she thought she recognized him at another table and she told my dad she was going to go over and ask him if he was the doctor that delivered me. My dad didn't want her to because, after all, he had probably delivered hundreds of babies since and wouldn't remember her."

"Yes, but not hundreds of babies during a storm like that."

"As she approached the table, the doctor turned to his wife and said, 'This is the woman I've been telling you about all these years, the one who allowed me to help deliver her baby during the hurricane.' He remembered her right away. Of course, having someone job interview you under those circumstances would be quite memorable," I paused. "I fired my doctor during the delivery, just as my first born was coming out."

"You fired him?"

"Yes, he was a speaker at an ethics seminar the following day and made it a topic in his speech. He said he thought he had seen it all. I fired him and had the nurse deliver the baby because he wasn't doing it the way we had agreed. He just thought when the moment came he could do whatever he wanted, but it wasn't what we agreed. So, I fired him. He delivered my next two babies, but he followed my instructions."

Just then, Lynn, the birthday girl, came through the restaurant door. We waved her over, and I gave her a hug. She whispered in my ear, "He's here! I told you not to worry." As other couples arrived Lynn very heavy handedly introduced Calhoun and I together, as if we were already a couple. I observed Ray carefully, and it didn't seem to be making him uncomfortable. In fact, it made him smile. Calhoun informed Lynn that his buddy, Ray, was caught in traffic but was on his way and was bringing Sharon. Sharon was the bitch lawyer who had asked me rude questions at the previous party.

Lynn said she didn't know that Ray and Sharon were dating. Ray said, "Yes, they've been out at least three, maybe even five times since the party."

"Oh, very interesting," said Lynn, "I wasn't aware of that."

Later, Lynn said she thought Ray had made a special attempt to make it clear to me that the other Ray was together with Sharon. "The boys have obviously had a little pow wow," said Lynn, "and Calhoun has told his best friend to back off."

Before, she had told me she thought Calhoun would be the type to bow out if he saw his best bud express interest in a girl. Maybe this time was different. Maybe he wasn't interested. Maybe he was extremely interested.

He had said when he met me it wasn't for the first time. He said that he recognized me. Those were the same words my Greek boyfriend had told me. He had recognized me. Ulysses also told his friends, "There she is. That is the woman I am going to marry." Then, the womanizer was too afraid to even approach me. Ulysses sent his best friend over as an ambassador who quickly returned with the news, laughing, that I was happily married with three kids.

Ulysses' reply was, "Then, I'll wait."

He didn't have to wait long. A couple of weeks later, Richard was trying to run me down with his car, and I was getting the hell out of Dodge.

As Calhoun returned from the bar carrying our second beers, I pulled off my floppy sweater to reveal the tight fitting, plunged neckline red cashmere Armani sweater with tiny little buttons that just beg to be ripped off.

As he walked toward me, he took it all in. I was being absolutely evil to this man.

I wore a huge diamond necklace hanging from a thick black silk cord at my throat. It was a Hamsa, an art deco piece from Turkey that was blessed to ward off evil spirits and protect me from the evil eye of other people's jealousy. The diamonds set in platinum covered a surface roughly the size of a tennis ball. Again, not every woman has this kind of jewelry wardrobe. A gal at the head of the table for twenty admired the necklace and asked if she could see it. I explained what Hamsa was and turned to find Calhoun standing very near looking down at me, smiling.

It felt good to have him so near. He was so tall. He looked down at me and asked me if I knew how old he was. I said yes, I knew how old he was. He said he was concerned that I might think that he was too old for me. I said I wasn't bothered by the age difference, not at all.

If a man just wants to bed a woman a couple of times and move on he doesn't talk about whether or not she thinks there is too big of an age difference. This was going very well.

He said, "I am fifty-five you know."

"I am forty-one," I paused, "and a half." He smiled again.

He served some food onto two plates from the buffet area and brought both of our plates back to our seats. Yes, he was acting very much like my date. I was starting to feel good.

Then, he got three phone calls in a row. Between the second and third calls he began checking his watch, often. Each time he got a call he checked to see what number was dialing him, decided to take the call and stepped away from the table towards the bar so I couldn't hear the conversation. I was polite and turned away not even looking or attempting to hear. I had noticed he had the cell phone in his pocket with the antenna fully extended. These were calls he was expecting.

He announced that he would have to leave soon as he had another place he had to go next. He asked Ted if he could buy a pitcher of margaritas for the table, but Ted said, "No, that's okay, but thanks anyway."

48

Ray said something to Ted I couldn't hear, and Ted replied, "I am Penelope's designated driver, no sweat."

I told Ray if he wanted a margarita that I would have one with him. He went to the bar and got us both a margarita. When he returned, Ted was standing next to me.

As I took the margarita from Calhoun I asked Ted, "You've never seen me drunk have you, Ted?"

"No, I can't say that I ever have."

"Well, you are about to, as soon as I finish this." Ted told Calhoun the margaritas were killer here, very, very strong.

"Oh, really?" Calhoun then checked his watch and said, " I've got to go. I should already have left." He dumped his margarita into a large Styrofoam cup.

"A to-go cup for a margarita? I didn't know that they would do that for you," Ted noted.

"I didn't tell them what the empty cup was for. I just asked for it."

I don't remember what he said to me in parting, but it wasn't much and it definitely wasn't 'I'd like to see you again' or 'Could I have your phone number?' I must have misread the entire situation.

Ted said, "Well, how did that go? You two seemed to be getting along."

Ray and Sharon could hear every word and Sharon made no attempt to conceal her open listening, so I spoke loudly enough that she would not have to strain her ears, "Well, THAT was a big dud!"

"A big dud? I didn't think so." Ted's voice had a note of confusion in it.

"Well, I was very disappointed. He kept taking cell phone calls all night. I was flattered at first because I thought he got all dressed up for me, but he obviously just stopped by to be polite and kill time on the way to a date. He was not dressed up for me, but for his date."

His buddy, Ray, looked distraught. The bitch at his side glowed. She was enjoying my disappointment so much. You could hear how upset Ray was with Calhoun when he asked me, "You mean he didn't tell you what was going on?"

"No. I think it is pretty clear he was on his way to a date, and I am not going to try to hide it, Ray. I am very disappointed. I had dental work this week and only dragged myself out of bed to come to see your friend. I have a big crush on him, and I am feeling very disappointed and rejected right now."

"I can't believe he didn't tell you. His ex (interesting she is referred to as an ex when he hasn't even filed for divorce yet) has two kids by her first husband and they have both been very sick all week with the stomach flu. One of them got so bad that she needed to take him to the emergency room and Ray promised he would take care of the other one while she was at the hospital."

At first I was angry. Well, isn't that just nice and cozy. She can call him to baby-sit a sick kid. That doesn't sound too 'estranged' to me.

Then, I thought about it. Those phone calls probably weren't too pleasant and they were awfully brief. If he was getting ready to file he had been warned to play it cool and be good especially in the couple of weeks just before he filed. She had access to some of his money, certainly enough of it to hire a private investigator even if on a contingency basis through her attorney. He was taking a big risk being in public with me, acting so much like a date. It had to really tick her off that he was in a BAR enjoying himself and not rushing over to lend a hand.

A few days later, I asked my bible study mom, Donna Reid, if she thought that made him a bad person that he kept a date with me if he had told her he'd help her with sick kids. He should have ditched me and helped with the kids.

She said, "It sounds like the man is a good guy and possibly feels very attached and responsible towards those children even though he is not their father." Donna said, "It also sounds like she is very manipulative and is using the kids and being very pitiful and helpless to keep him with her." She guessed that the woman was very young, and he felt sorry for her. "That is how she pulls his strings. Maybe, that was why he never filed for divorce even though he hasn't lived with her in two years," Donna suggested.

That night in bible study at First Baptist, one of the largest churches in Houston with an arena that seats thousands, the place was packed. Beth Moore stopped right in the middle of bible study and said that she was going to have to go off on a tangent. She closed her eyes in concentration and held her fingertips to her forehead deep in prayerful connection with God.

"There is someone in the audience," she said, "someone who maybe has missed a couple of bible studies, but is here tonight just to hear this message from God. This person is contemplating having an adulteress affair. You are fooling yourself if you are telling yourself this is not an affair because there is no intercourse. You are fooling yourself if you say we are just spending a lot of time together, and it is not hurting anyone and that it is not adultery."

I asked Donna if she thought that message was for me.

Donna said, "No, I don't think so at all. Penelope, that marriage is over. He hasn't lived there for two years, and she just somehow is manipulating him into not divorcing. You hang in there, he will file and then call you. Most men can't go through with a divorce unless they get something else going first. They just don't want to be alone. This man has been alone a long time now. Maybe he has a reason to file since he has met you. It may be a month or so but he's not going to forget you."

At Lynn's birthday party, Ray Malloy seemed delighted when I announced that I had a crush on Calhoun.

The bitch lawyer huffed, "A crush?"

"Yes." I didn't look at her because I didn't like her. I talked to Ray, "Yes. I've seen him at Memorial Park tons of times walking. He is gorgeous. He said he was worried that he's too old for me, but he's not.

The bitch's mouth dropped open. Ray laughed. He was going to be very pleased to relay this information back to Calhoun.

"You know the situation he's in right now, and you are okay with that? You'd be willing to see him under those circumstances?" The woman had nerve. I had no clue what she was talking about, but she was certainly asking things, again, that were none of her business. I didn't want to admit to her that I didn't know anything at all about his situation. I'm sure he didn't tell me because he was trying to be attractive to me and wanted to wait until he knew me more and was certain that he had my interest. Then, he would clue me in on the 'situation' and not frighten me off immediately. Was Calhoun's wife dying of cancer, an invalid, what? Was the situation just that he was 'about to file' yet unendingly never doing so? Was I never to be seen in public with him or ever acknowledged as a girlfriend? Did I follow one or more girlfriends that he had treated in this manner? What situation?

I answered her, "Yes, I really like him, and I haven't been interested in anyone for a very long time. What better girlfriend can he have than one who never leaves her house? I only came out tonight to be with him."

3

My Mother Is A Sac Of Dung

My mother is a sac of dung.

I may acknowledge that she had somewhat convinced herself, even if she convinced no one else, that her motivations were pure when she took the stand in family law court, swore an oath to the God she had for years told me she did not believe in and blew lies out of her ass for a full hour. I know her. She relishes being in the center of drama. The attention must be focused on her. She showed up a couple of times to 'help' when I had to take my first born to the emergency room, until I figured her out. When our turn would finally come after hours of waiting, the doctor would ask me, the mother of the child, about the symptoms. She would interrupt and demand that the doctor address her medical concerns first - a frozen shoulder, heart palpitations, et cetera.

My mother, Norma, was evicted from the delivery room during the birth of my second child by the floor nurse in charge because she acted like such a nutball. Norma demanded that I, the laboring, delivering mother hooked up to all sorts of I.V.s, equipment and monitors, leave my bed and go fetch her a glass of water. She told me she was sure that she was having a heart attack or stroke or both. Oh, and she also wanted a cold cloth for her head and a popsicle.

She had arrived at two in the morning with her large suitcase and laid down in an empty bed next to mine in the semiprivate room. It was after visiting hours. The room was dark except for the green glow of the monitors. She woke me up upon arrival with her demands.

I told her that I couldn't possibly get her water as I was all hooked up to the machines, and she said I was always only thinking of myself. She had gone to great effort to get there to be with me, and I didn't appreciate all she did for me. I told her I would use the call button for the nurse.

Just then, the nurse stepped from the shadows and said, "No need. I'm right here."

The nurse must have been in the room to check the monitors or change the I.V. bag or something. She had been completely silent during my mother's tirade.

She addressed my mother now, "This is not the place for an invalid or someone requiring emergency care. If you think you are having a stroke or heart attack, then you do not belong here. This is a labor and delivery room. Your daughter has been admitted and you have not. You do not belong here. You need to go immediately to the emergency care area and be properly admitted to the hospital."

"I think I'm feeling better now," my mother said in a pathetic squeaky voice like an abused toddler. She tilted her head to the side in what I have to assume she believed was an appealing way. I knew the moment the nurse left she'd turn right back into a grotesque demanding monster.

I was the one with the stroke level blood pressure. That is why they were inducing labor two weeks early.

One method of manipulation failing, my mother quickly mutated into an authoritarian power house accustomed to getting her way in the business world.

"I am Dr. Sherman and I know my rights. This is my daughter and she needs me here."

The nurse turned to me. "Do you want her here?"

I sighed, exhausted, "My mother, Dr. Sherman, is not a medical doctor. She has a doctorate degree, not a Ph.D., as many people assume, but simply an Ed.D.; a degree requiring far fewer qualifications and fewer math courses that my mother wished to avoid.

"You didn't need to tell her that," my mother snapped.

"Mom, this is a hospital. In a medical setting when you introduce yourself as 'Dr. So and So' people naturally assume that you mean M.D. I didn't want to give the nurse a false impression of your medical expertise, just in case you are in the room, and there is some sort of situation where you are telling the nurses what to do. They might think you are a doctor and think you know what you are talking about when you order them around."

"I would never do that." She was wildly irritated. "You are lucky I am even here at all. Your father insisted I wait until morning, and I had to argue with him before he would let me come. I would have stayed at home if I had known you were going to treat me so ugly. Home, where I am wanted. I really do not feel well."

"Then, I suggest you go check into the emergency room," the nurse said firmly.

"I am not leaving unless Penelope tells me to leave."

My mother gestured towards me with her arm snapping out in my direction, palm upraised and fingers flared, so the red tips of her sharp fingernails seemed like talons on a claw. Her face contorted in a menacing glare directed at the nurse, jaw set, lips thin, certain I would never eject her.

"Please, get her out of here. I need to sleep."

I had no energy for this. I had been admitted with an extremely high blood pressure. I shut my eyes and immediately began to fall back asleep. Maybe they had drugged me. There was no way I could stay awake another instant.

"Fine then. I am humiliated. You have humiliated me. I am leaving." The nurse gave her directions to the emergency room and asked if she needed assistance getting there. My mother hauled her heavy suitcase off the end of the bed with as much commotion as possible.

"Leave the suitcase, Mother. I still will need the shampoo and toothpaste and stuff."

"This is mine. None of this is for you. Richard can bring you shampoo if you need it. I'm never coming back here after this."

I remember wanting to say, 'Promise?' sarcastically, but I just wanted her out and shut my eyes again.

She was not allowed on the labor and delivery floor for the birth of my third child, either. I had the same nurse again. She remembered Mom and kept her away.

After my mother left, the nurse checked my pulse and blood pressure and brought me water with crushed ice for my bedside. She told me not to be embarrassed about the scene with my mother. She said she had a mother just like that.

Anyway, I am sure that a large ingredient for the sh** pie that day in court was the inner drive that causes my mother to demand attention. This is in part explained, but not excused, by the fact that my mother felt abandoned by her mother at the tender age of three years old. Grandma Inez was shipped off to the Texas State Mental Hospital by her in-laws, well to do upper middle class folk in Waco, Texas who were embarrassed by the uncouth, unsocialized wife their coddled, alcoholic, never-worked-a-day-in-his-life-son had chosen for a wife.

For many years, I suspected that grandma had never been crazy, just hated. But my mother's sister, Aunt Mabel, recently corrected me on that fact. Inez did lose her mind. Aunt Mabel said Inez was beaten so often that she forgot who she was. My grandmother wandered down to the train station in her nightgown after one really horrible beating and tried to get on the train with no dress, no purse, no money, nothing. When the train station manager asked her who she was, she said she didn't know or maybe just didn't answer. Someone recognized her and she was sent home. The next day she was institutionalized. She received shock treatments and all the latest experimental mind altering drug therapies, but they could never turn her into what they wanted her to be.

Grandmother told me that once her mother-in-law had turned on her in a rage and demanded to know if she had been raised in a barn because she didn't know how to properly set out the silverware for a formal table setting. My grandmother was too ashamed to tell her mother-in-law that a barn would have been a big step up for her family. She had been raised in a tent with a dirt floor that her mother would lovingly rake in a circular pattern starting from the center of the tent and winding around and around until she exited.

Inez was born on the Cherokee Indian reservation. Her mother was a red-headed Irish woman who had divorced the rich rancher who beat her. Great-grandma divorced back in the days when you had to look the word 'divorce' up in the dictionary because it was so unheard of. She then married a black-skinned Indian who was passing through town. He took her away from her misery to a new life on the reservation.

Great-grandma's skin was so white you could see all the veins through it. The Indian was so black his skin shined like a bowling ball. The family tree has some unusual litters. I had to warn my blonde-haired, blue-eyed Polish husband that there was a possibility that his blonde-haired, green-eyed wife could give birth to either a red-headed or a dark-skinned, dark-eyed Indian looking child.

This family history had always impressed me. It must have taken courage to leave luxury where you are mistreated and go off with a man who, in that day and age, some people considered the equivalent of a work mule or other farm animal, sub-human. The reason my great-grandfather was going to live on the reservation and not back in the foothills of Alabama with the other members of his tribe, was that he had been kicked out for sleeping with the wives of the other men. The United States government required the tribe to walk from Alabama to Oklahoma to live on the reservation with the Cherokee because they had similar languages. There were not enough surviving to populate their own separate reservation. Many eluded capture.

A friend of mine who wrote a textbook on the history of the American Indians once laughed when he found out about my origins. He said that that explained everything about me. He said my tribesmen were reputed to be an extremely willful, stubborn people who do not acknowledge the Unites States government's authority over them. Rather than give up their land, they slit the throats of their infants and children before turning their knives on themselves. They answer to the higher authority of God only.

The few stray misfits collected together on the reservation were outcasts or people with a strong wanderlust who happened not to be with the rest of the tribe when the army arrived to move them. They refused to give their names for the governmental records, unlike the Cherokee who possess an almost German zeal for recording everything. They did not take part in the reservation census or official recording of births as that would admit the United States government authority over them.

My mother said my heritage explained why I threw myself so fully and passionately into my fight against the annexation of my community by the nearby city of Houston. For a couple of years, I lived and breathed the annexation fight. I was Penelope Bernard, spokeswoman for the Citizens for Annexation Reform. I helped to coordinate other like minded individuals from all over Texas in the first effort of its size since the current laws had been written in the year of my birth, 1961. We patched together a motley crew of Texas motorcycle clubs, Black Baptist ministers and others and rode on Austin to make our point. We filled the legislation chambers to the rafters with people wearing our stickers on their jackets.

I was a scrapper. It ran in my blood. Of course, my mother was always trying to take credit for her children's achievements no matter how ridiculous the stretch to make the claim.

Anyway, my grandmother showed up at the train station and wouldn't tell people who she was. I have a theory. She was beaten, badly. Often. This time she was more afraid and ran for her life. She didn't care that she was only wearing a slip. She was afraid he'd kill her this time or very soon. So, she ran. She had no plan except maybe to ask for help from others at the station. She needed money, a coat, et cetera. She'd take the next train to anywhere.

Of course, she wouldn't admit who she was! She was not crazy! If she said who she was, then she would just be taken back home! Unfortunately, no one really helped her to escape. She was recognized, returned and drugged into oblivion.

Eventually, she divorced. Her next husband was a wonderful concentration camp survivor that she met at the mental institute. His wife had died, and he was suffering depression. They married and grandma moved into his beautiful home in Houston. The home had fine china, oriental rugs, elegant furnishings and a white picket fence covered in a rose vine called 'Old Bloom.' It was an antique hybrid rose and hardy and covered the fence so heavily it threatened to fall over. I later planted that same rose variety in my yard, in her memory.

Anyway, Norma, my mother, was bounced from one relative to another and had no stability whatsoever. She, to this day, has no core sense of self. Chameleon-like if you seated her next to a Republican at a dinner party she will talk on end about the virtues of free market capitalism. Later, at the same party if someone sat next to her who was say, a Marxist, she will speak in a very educated way with equal zeal embracing socialist ideas. It is horrifying to behold.

Who is she? Does she exist at all anywhere in there? Does she hold even one opinion, one conviction that is her own? She moves like flotsam on the sea. Certainly, this is some kind of psychological disorder. It is so weird. It comes from a desire to please, appease.

"I am like you, see? Like me, accept me, don't reject me," her every word and action an appeal for acceptance.

She has absolutely no close friends. She only has my horribly distant father and a few colleagues with whom she has worked for years at the community college, but they don't socialize at all outside of college functions. She has relationships with students who are momentarily mesmerized by the appeal of her professor facade but no solid friendships.

On the day she testified against me she had center stage. She had the approval of her son-in-law, Richard, approval she had always desired. Throughout our marriage he had always despised her for her treatment of me. Just prior to running away from Richard, my mother had come to me and asked me to pay off her home mortgage. She was tired of working overloads at the college and the previous year she had had significant health problems - a brain aneurysm that required emergency surgery. She asked me to write a check for the payoff amount.

I told her I'd have to ask Richard before I wrote a check of that size. I reminded her that Richard had embarrassed me at a meeting with our money management team claiming he had no interest whatsoever in planning for aiding his parents in their old age or for helping our children with their college education. He had done it 'on his own,' and they could also.

I pointed out to him that his father, a janitor, had spent a significant portion of the entire family income to send only one child to private school. He received this benefit as the bright hope for the family's future. This preparation, no doubt, had helped him in his brilliant academic career at Notre Dame where he studied psychology. He ran the rat lab and wrote several academic papers published in prestigious journals about behavior modification. He could manipulate people.

When we first met we went on a long eight mile walk together. He asked me tons of questions, good thought provoking questions, examining what I thought about life, God, my relationships to others, my life view and my perspective on all sorts of things I had never really thoroughly thought through before. After all, I was only twenty-five and a business major, not a philosopher. He was thirty-four and this was a two hundred question psychological inventory examination that he had studied and given to hundreds of people.

He later bragged to his friends that he had chosen me as a mate based on temperament testing similar to that used to test the Belgian Shepherd dog that his previous live-in girlfriend of seven years had taken to championship levels in dog shows around the country. He bragged that my genetics were great for childbearing. Little did I know at the time, in a few short years he would be like a broken record, expounding upon my obvious and unresolvable flaws, shortcomings and defects.

Constant exposure to a father treating a mother in such a way led our children to have headaches, stomach aches and rashes from the stress level in the household. Initially, I stayed 'for the children.' In the end, I left 'for the children.' But, I had learned from my grand-mother's flight to the bus terminal. I left with a plan.

After days of testimony from me about the horrible state of my mar-riage, my mother took the witness stand and determined the course of the rest of her life. She very shortsightedly chose to lie and say I was an abominable mother in extensive detail. Mark Twain, born in Cut-n-Shoot, Texas the son of the local English teacher, (I suppose he was lucky to not be named Huckleberry Finn-he missed that bul-let), questioned my mother. He was the local Montgomery county lawyer that my chief attorney, the famed powerhouse Pearle Wiley of Harris County, Houston, Texas, had selected as his co-counsel. Much case law on the books came from Pearle's landmark cases. In fact, his cases set the precedent for many fathers gaining primary or sometimes even full custody of their children away from the moth-ers. I brought the big city lawyer, nuclear weapon into a small town court run by a retired Marine, Nazi-style judge. The judge had nearly lost his spot on the bench due to gossip that he was just too much of an embarrassment to the Republicans because of his abusive behav-ior in court. When it was discovered that he had a brain tumor which required surgery, he won enough sympathy to slide through the last election cycle. His supporters speculated that the brain tumor caused all of those courtroom outbursts, not simply that he was an out of control jackass in a position of power.

Twain, referred to by Pearle Wiley as 'our local man in the county,' was paid a retainer of ten thousand dollars. I don't know how much he earned each year but I can assure you, not much. Ten grand was a hefty sum to pay for the three things required of him. One, he advised us on selection of a judge based on his knowledge of the lay of the land locally. Two, he was supposed to call the list of witnesses and let them know what time and day they would be expected to appear and three, show up in court. It occurs to me now that I should demand every penny of the money back as not a damned cent of it was earned. He failed to tell us about the judge's crazy temperament and the fact that the judge had just finalized his own divorce from a woman who looked like she could be my twin sister. The judge's ex-wife also spent a lot of time on and off over the past few years living at the women's shelter where I had volunteered helping women transition to a permanent environment away from their abusers. Oh, keeno! He got to hear testimony from me in court about my volunteer work, bits I might just as easily have left out if Twain had clued me in! It also would have been good to know that the judge was a bigot.

I volunteered teaching reading to Spanish-speaking children at a school for less fortunate children living on the other side of the freeway from our almost all white middle class area. Our neighborhood school had a hefty percentage of stay at home moms. Many of the moms at my second volunteer job worked two jobs. The moms at our school had to be scheduled on a volunteer roster there were so many demanding to volunteer. At the Spanish-speaking school, there were so few volunteers that I felt like the last living cell in a dead body. I could have kept silent about my volunteer work had I only known!

The KKK is very active in our county. I was warned by a Jewish neighbor when I first moved into the neighborhood. I am Jewish by blood. My Irish great-grandmother had immigrated from an Orthodox Jewish community in Wales. Also, grandmother's second husband was Jewish. My mother spent many of her formative years being cared for in the Jewish household of my great-grandfather by marriage, Pop Lyons. My new neighbor told me not to tell anyone else about my heritage. She also cautioned against putting anything out during the holidays that would attract attention to my house. A Jewish festival had been bombed and private homes had had trouble. She and her husband were moving as soon as they could.

I had always thought the judge was supposed to sit and listen except when called upon to make rulings. Pearle said it was like I was on trial for the crime of running away from my husband and the courtroom had two sets of prosecutors, the opposing counsel and the judge! When the judge found out about my volunteer work at the 'Spanish Kids School,' he asked why I didn't just volunteer at my own children's school? I told him I did also volunteer at my own children's school, teaching three hours every Friday in the Kindergarten. Volunteers were desperately needed at the other school. He couldn't understand why I would 'drive over there to teach a bunch of Mexicans.' He told me so from the bench. After listening to some of the things he said, my godmother, Donna Reid, suggested that the judge wore a white sheet to some of his evening meetings.

The nineteen days in court in Montgomery County would have taken one day's time in Harris County. Twain failed to call my witnesses, and the few I personally scrambled to call at the last minute late the night before they were expected to appear came at an inconvenience that could have been avoided if they had been properly notified. I found out, a year later, that key people like personal friends of the judge and his fellow church members, people who might have influenced the judge, were never called. Twain lied and said he had contacted them. He claimed they couldn't or wouldn't come, or that they had said bad things about me in his 'interviews' with them, interviews that never took place. He just dropped the ball and covered his ass or worse, took money from my husband to intentionally harm my case.

I found out the judge had a track record of giving fathers primary custody of all male children. He believed a father's influence was critical, and he was deeply impacted by the overwhelmed single mothers trying to rein in their boys who appeared in the juvenile criminal court he also presided over.

The judge shackled these children. Some of them were so small for their age that they looked younger than my eight year old, although they were probably as old as eleven, just scrawny. The juvenile defendants sometimes wore orange jumpsuits just like the hardened criminals, big men that lined the two back rows of the court awaiting their turn to plead with the judge. Pearle said he thought he was going to be sick one day when we arrived early for the start of our midday trial time. We had a chance to watch the judge in action lording over these poor souls. Pearle ran his hand across the top of his head several times. There were beads of perspiration on his scalp he had become so emotional. He was going to throw up. Mercifully, it ended, and our trial began. But, it gave Pearle a reality check regarding the judge and his frame of mind when determining the fates of others.

It has been speculated by many that the judge was paid off. He was not. I know in my heart he was not paid off. I believe he hated me on sight and had certain inclinations and prejudgments that were simply too ingrained to put aside even though he strived for impartiality when he made his judgments. He was a hothead and Richard's lawyers had worked with him so long they knew how to manipulate him like a puppet on a string. Meanwhile, without guidance from 'our man in the county,' we walked blindfolded across a minefield.

If I suspect anyone at all of being on the take, it is Twain, the man who lied and said witnesses who had volunteered to help had retracted their offers. He told me not to call them because I could be accused of tainting their testimonies. The year following the divorce, I ran into a pre-school teacher from the church school who questioned why my attorney never returned her phone calls when she tried to find out when and where to be there to help. She told me the school director had even postponed a very much needed surgery endangering her life in order to be available to testify.

But, it didn't matter in the end. My mother and sister, yes, my sister, both lined up to testify for Richard and the fact that the judge allowed me to see my children ever again at all after their damning lies shows me that the judge couldn't possibly have believed their testimony. I am sure that he was very upset at having to make the decision of who the children would live with, and who they would simply visit.

The story of my life, growing up and then being Richard's wife had been very sad. The judge had wept openly on the bench more than once. I am sure that the judge, for all his shortcomings, tried his best. But, most of all, I am sure that he prayed for God's help in making the decision, and I accept God's will and have faith in His grand plan for me and the children. For this reason, I suffered less and did not become bitter or depressed as you would reasonably expect. Instead, I accepted that God had released me from the life I had previously lived and had a different plan for my life now, His plan.

The judge called my attorney to the bench after he made his ruling that Richard had 'won,' meaning the children would live with Richard and visit me every other weekend. He asked Pearle if he had ever seen such a thing in his life - a mother testifying against her own daughter. The judge shook his head slowly back and forth in amazement. They discussed how even prostitutes and drug addicts have their mothers testify for them vowing to help out with the grandchildren and keep their daughters on the methadone program or whatever is necessary. Pearle said he had never seen it or even heard of it ever happening in his entire career.

The judge's parting words were, "God will bless your client for all the good she has done for others."

My mother knew exactly what she was doing. She was not a misled, innocent dupe. My good sister, Lauren, who lives in Florida and is a professional golfer (not to be confused with my unemployed evil sister who lives with my mother) called my mother and came to Texas to plead with Norma not to testify against me. She warned her mother. (Excuse me, reader, I simply cannot refer to her as my mother. I hope you understand. For the remainder of this book I will only refer to her as Norma, if at all.) Norma was warned by my sister, my Aunt Mabel, my attorney Pearle Wiley, my childhood friend Andrea Stephenson and by me personally that if she told her lies to help Richard, the judge might very well give the children to Richard and I would then cut her from my life forever with very good reason.

Norma was also warned by my attorney, Pearle Wiley, in my presence just moments before her testimony that temporary custody ninety per cent of the time becomes permanent. Richard would in essence become the new primary caretaker, feeding them, dressing them, taking them to school and to the doctor, doing the homework with them. It would put me, the prior caretaker, in a difficult position to win them back. After months of fathering, Richard could point out that that is now the life the boys had grown accustomed to and any further change would be traumatic. Norma knew for a fact that I was the current primary caretaker. She had, in fact, talked to her colleagues at work about my burden as a stay at home mother with little support from a husband who worked all the time. She bragged about my superior mothering skills. HA!

She had vomited into my kitchen sink in late November she was so upset by my devotion to my family. She had come over to pick up her red wool coat and cashmere sweaters at my home in The Woodlands. It was one of the four times she had ever been in my home. I had taken her to China for her birthday gift in a bizarre attempt to extract some drop of mothering from a cold stone. Even though it had been my New Year's resolution to try to form a relationship with her as an adult woman that had never been there before, I frankly was ready to give up the idea. In China, she decided to ship back her red wool coat so she wouldn't have to carry it on the plane. She had come over to pick up her coat after calling ahead to see if the freight had arrived.

While she was at my house, she picked up the cashmere sweaters she had special ordered and shipped to my address. She later claimed the birthday gift of ten thousand dollars worth of clothes from Ann Taylor was not her own special order but clothes that had been forced upon her by me. She claimed the clothes were not to her taste and too youthful. My gift, she testified, was too extravagant, proof I had lost all grasp of the meaning of a dollar and evidence that I was manic and out of control. The day she testified against me she wore a sweater from Ann Taylor that was one of her birthday gifts. Pearle commented to me that she couldn't even get dressed that day without pulling something out of the closet that I had given to her.

Anyway, it was a rare occasion for her to be in my home. It was also rare for Richard to come home early. When the garage door opened, I called out, "Kids, Daddy is home! Come downstairs and give Daddy a hug."

I explained to Norma that if the children delayed and did not rush to the door, I would take away whatever it was that delayed them - Nintendo, a computer game, et cetera. I told the children that nothing was more important than hugging Daddy 'Hello' because he drove a long way from work so we could live in this nice house. I also kept the rule, ending telephone conversations abruptly or turning down whatever I was cooking on the stove in order to greet my husband. At some point, Richard began pushing me away or walking briskly past me only returning the hugs of the children. He had developed an anger towards me for some unknown reason. I discussed it with him, but he denied it. This day, in front of Norma, he hugged us all.

Upon witnessing our family ritual, my mother rose abruptly, went to the kitchen sink and heaved. I rushed to bring her a sprite from the refrigerator. When I handed it to her, she looked away from me.

"You've lived your entire life in judgment of mine," she announced melodramatically and headed for the door. "I've got to get out of here. Where are my sweaters?" She grabbed her coat off the back of the kitchen chair and headed for the door, but I stopped her from leaving.

"Mom! Where are you going? What on earth are you talking about?"

"I tried to get you a job at the college, but you were not interested."

"Mom, I was seven months pregnant and had a two year old and a husband to take care of. I didn't need a job. I had a job taking care of my family. The teaching job was at night, a long drive from here and didn't pay much. The evening was my only time with my husband. It didn't make any sense. I already told you."

"It would have been a foot in the door. Oh, my God. I think I'm going to be sick again." She leaned over the kitchen sink and made loud belching and stomach gas hissing noises.

"Do you want some Pepto Bismol?"

"No."

"I have not lived my life as a reaction to your life at all, Mom. I have simply chosen what is best for me. That doesn't mean I expected you to stay at home. Not every one is cut out for this. It is hard work and sometimes you feel very isolated from other adults being with just kids all day. But it is what I want to do, not what I think you should have done."

"I wanted to stay home with you. I really did. I saved the money, but your dad spent it when he found out about it. He fixed up his car and bought that German shepherd dog. So, I had to go right back to work and leave you with other people."

Mom, thank God, had gone back to work, and I had been raised by a nice, normal woman who lived across the street, Betty Taylor, in Hidden Valley subdivision, Houston, Texas. So, I had a snowball's chance in hell of turning out okay, unlike my youngest sister, the evil one that did receive Norma's twisted affections, and who I refer to as the 'human pet.'

"You judge me!" She was raising her voice now, hysterical. "Your whole way of being is a judgment of how I should have parented you, but I didn't."

'Jesus Christ,' I thought, 'This woman is a lunatic.' The children were becoming frightened now.

"Mom, let me help you to your car. You can get your sweaters another day."

"No, I don't want to drive all the way out here again."

You should know, reader, she will drive out several times each week to meet my father for lunch, coffee or dinner. She just can't be bothered to drive out to pick up a few two hundred dollar sweaters that she special ordered the day I was in a supposed manic state and bought her too much for her birthday.

Dad worked as a realtor for Remax and officed nearby. I rarely saw either of them. That didn't stop Norma from claiming in court that Richard raised the boys with her help and that of Yesenia, a full-time maid. She said the maid came to my house every day to help, and that the youngest couldn't tie his own shoes yet because the maid dressed him. She said he'd never been taught how to dress himself.

In fact, the maid came only twice a month until the September before I ran away from home. That included the summer I had a broken hip, even though, by that time, we were already worth twenty-five million dollars. I *enjoyed* the company of my children.

One evening in September, I was up washing dishes at ten-thirty with a plan to sit at the dining table and pay bills and file medical insurance claim forms for a half hour or so until it was time to change over another load of clothes before I went to bed. Richard had been asleep since nine o'clock. He complained to me that I was always tired. He claimed he was a superior physical and genetic specimen because he didn't suffer from my ailments - tiredness, headaches, backaches, neck and arm strain from the children hugging on me and suddenly lifting their feet off the floor and wrenching an arm out of its socket. Well, of course, I was tired. I never got any sleep.

It was my fault for not hiring help. I was rich. We had built a company of twelve thousand employees and made millions. It was time to find better, more fulfilling things to do than scrubbing the toilets each morning and mopping the floor each evening.

The next day, I called Yesenia, hired her full time and told her to quit her other houses. I was happy to get her away from some of the houses where they mistreated her. She had some horror stories. She was always in a good mood when she came to work in my home. She and her sister called it the 'happy house.' I worked side by side with her, and we always tackled a project like closet organization, garage cleaning or washing the walls down with spic and span. Sometimes when her sister was depressed, she would come along and help Yesenia clean my house because it made her feel good to be with us.

I signed up for dance lessons and told Richard that at the upcoming company retirement party for our sales manager, Byron McCoy, I would be able to dance salsa to the music of the salsa band Byron had hired, Mango Punch. A friend who I had known since I was seven years old, Tessa Wilroy, met me three days each week at the dance studio that was equidistant between our two homes at West Side Dance Studio. We'd have our lesson from 2:00 p.m. until 2:50 p.m., and then I'd rush to my car and drive home on the tollway.

The kids got off the bus at 3:25 p.m. if the bus driver ran the route in one direction and at 3:45 p.m. if the driver ran the bus route in the other direction. I liked to be there to greet them when they came in the door. It was a thirty-five minute drive, so I would book it on home lickety split as fast as I could. Tessa and I would talk on the cell phone as we each drove home. It was our adult time, socializing outside the house time, SANITY time in an existence otherwise populated with only short people banging plastic sippy cups or begging for McDonald's.

Later, in court, these dance classes were held up as evidence by Norma that I had abandoned my family and no longer cared for my own children. She ignored the fact that Richard had never taken them to a single doctor's appointment or dental checkup and had never met the children's teachers. He complained that he didn't want to watch them play baseball because they were embarrassing to him. They were the worst on the field, he had said.

Each child had three baseball practices and one batting cage practice each week plus the Saturday game. That was fifteen required places I needed to take three boys each week. In addition, I had scheduled Tuesday and Thursday tutoring sessions with a private tutor, Kathy Baird. We had the tutoring spot and used it for whatever problem needed to be addressed that week. Adam had speech therapy two mornings each week at the elementary school at 7:15. I had to get him ready, pack all the boys into the car, go to speech, entertain the oldest and youngest for the forty-five minute lesson and return to pick him up at eight before school began at 8:05. On top of this I had pediatrician appointments, allergists, ear, nose and throat doctor appointments plus birthday parties, scheduled service visits for home repairs, and play dates at the park for the kids to meet their friends.

I wanted to buy myself a daytimer for sixty-five dollars at the Franklin Covey store like the one my friend Edna had. The baseball times were not set but ever changing and it was difficult to keep track of everything. Richard would ridicule me for ever being late or unable to be three places at once or having to chose between taking one boy to the doctor and another to baseball.

He once called me a 'cluster f**k' for taking Jonah to a makeup tutoring appointment. My son, Jonah, had missed school and didn't understand his math homework assignment because the teacher had introduced a new concept that day. Kathy had a cancellation and called to see if we'd take the time slot. I usually took the boys to karate during that time, but a child with a fever and strep throat doesn't belong in karate class so we went to the tutor.

When I say 'we' went to the tutor, I mean we all went. The two not being tutored would sit with me in the waiting area and read or nap on the couch while I petted their backs. Anyway, you get the picture. It was a grueling schedule with little or no help and a tyrant of a husband who criticized and namecalled. By the way, he said I *didn't* need the Franklin Covey daytimer for Christmas.

In our thirteen years together, he bought me three things. Birthday, Christmas, anniversary went unrecognized. Once, Mark was in the hospital, and I had to stay with him while Richard had the responsibility of caring for the boys. During this time, for safety reasons, I had hired someone to care for the children from eight in the morning until six at night. Richard couldn't work late, as was his habit. He had the boys in the evening and had to put them to bed, but the babysitter would feed them before she left. It was his first experience with childcare. He brought the kids to the hospital and they desperately needed a bath, so I put them in the hospital room bathtub and washed their hair. It was almost Christmas, and I asked him if he had put up the tree. He lied and said yes. He was shocked when the hospital allowed me to come home Christmas eve with the baby and spend Christmas day at home. Richard had to go from store to store to try to purchase a Christmas tree stand. He said at the fifth store, a local discount store, the worker laughed at him and said, "Good luck buddy," so he cruised through the store to try to find a gift for me since I'd be upset that there was no tree. He got me a navy blue cotton tunic, which was a good color for me and a flattering fit and still had the bright green eight dollar price sticker on it, unwrapped. I wore the tunic often and thanked him for it constantly, trying to encourage more of the same gift buying behavior, but he didn't love me.

I was a work burro. He lived his life exactly as he wished, without any change to assimilate a wife and children into his world. He received little pleasure from family life except during the thirty minute wrestling time he'd have with the kids each evening before I put them to bed.

Now that he has adjusted to parenting them, he even kisses them goodnight. The kids know what a good parent is supposed to do, and they have taught him how to do it over the past two years. He might have drifted away from the boys completely if the judge had decided differently. Now, the boys have a real father, a bond.

One of the first acts of independence I made was to buy the Franklin Covey daytimer. I deserved a Christmas gift from Richard and after years of getting nothing I bought something for myself.

My mother knew I was a terrific mom. Yet, she was willing to go into court and say I was a danger to my children, crazy, schizophrenic, abandoning, drug and alcohol abusing. You know that your mother is scum when the Sally Jesse Raphael show calls you and asks you to appear. I still to this day am shocked that Richard ever handed me that phone message. I guess he figured they'd contact me somehow, anyway.

He handed me the message and said, "I hope you're not considering doing this."

I didn't even take the number from his hand. I said, "Don't be ridiculous. I'm not trailer trash."

Someone at the courthouse must have tipped them off, or maybe my sister Terry contacted them to try to make some money. It sounds like something she'd do.

When my attorney and I arrived at the courthouse the day my mother and sister were scheduled to testify, we were lucky to get there before them and lay claim to the wonderful little secluded waiting room for witnesses that was comfortable. We posted a guard at the door. Pearle had had more than one client shot over far less than one hundred and ten million dollars, and Richard's behavior gave us every indication that a twenty-four hour armed guard was not a bad investment.

During the mediation which followed ten months later, the extremely intelligent, retired nun, Tarrant county family court judge who mediated our case spoke to my main guard, Dan Dealba, in the hallway outside my mediation room. She had just spoken to Richard for the umpteenth time that day and was crossing back and forth down the corridor between the two rooms. Richard had just explained to her his firm position that he had not loved me in more than four years. He wanted the community property split according to what we were worth four years ago. He figured a ninety percent and ten percent split was only fair since he was the only one who worked. He demanded that I absorb any and all penalties from our tax situation since he claimed that I, the household manager, had been completely responsible for the fact that tax forms had not been filed in seven years. (My tax attorney later discovered even one more additional year not filed making a grand total of eight. Seven years was the cut off point making it a felony carrying a twenty year prison term. You must serve every day, with no time off for good behavior.) In court, my attorney had directly questioned Richard about the taxes because I had told him Richard had run for political office prior to meeting me on a tax protest platform to abolish the IRS.

The day I hired Pearle I told him to immediately find the best tax man in the city to look over our filings for the entire marriage because Richard had done it himself and never hired a professional to help him. With so much money involved we might have paid more taxes than necessary without a competent professional's help. The money management team had recommended a list of local tax professionals to us at the meeting we had. Richard had been behind on filing for three years at the time that we took Kaliyuga Software public. The CEO hired to help with that transition and the team from Goldman Sachs had required that all of the top employees submit all their tax returns. It made Richard look financially irresponsible to be behind on the tax filings. He told me not to worry about it. We didn't owe the IRS any money since more than enough was taken out of his paycheck. They probably owed us refunds; he assured me at that time. It was just a little embarrassing to be behind on filing and he had to do it for the company to look like it was being run by responsible adults and not a bunch of flakes. He'd do it he said.

He spent hours upstairs 'working on the taxes' after sending me downtown to get the required old forms and down to the different county buildings to get records of our local tax payments for those years. I was sick with the Asian flu that day and delirious with fever. It was pouring down rain and I vomited into a large plastic ice tea pitcher I brought with me in the car for that purpose. Richard told me I had to drive there, even though he was not sick and I was half dead, because I had been to the county buildings before and he had not. He wouldn't be able to find the buildings especially because it was raining. He yelled at me. He said it was an emergency. He had waited until the last minute to do the tax work, and it couldn't wait until the next day. I had to go immediately.

Of course, I later found out he hadn't filed at all. I had gone into the rainstorm with a hundred and three fever and nonstop vomiting for nothing at all except to satisfy the whims of an ogre.

This was the perfect husband my mother could not believe I was leaving. She demanded to know why I was divorcing him, and I told her that it was private and she'd have to respect my ability to make decisions regarding my own life. I told her I had given it much thought and two therapists had met with Richard and I and agreed the marriage could not be saved. I told her the reasons for leaving him were not for the boys to know, and since she had a history of not being able to keep a confidence, I was not going to tell her or, for that matter, anyone else. That was the only way to insure with absolute certainty that the boys' relationship with their father would not be destroyed.

Richard had crossed the line, I told Norma. He had DONE something, and as a consequence I was leaving and that was that.

"But, WHAT has he done? I have the right to know!" She was perched on the edge of the bench in our waiting room area. The viper about to strike, to testify in court that I was not a good parent. She leaned forward in her dress for success business suit in what I knew from the research she had selected in power colors to make her testimony all the more convincing, all the more damning. It wasn't enough to come into court, she had to carefully select the attire that would best persuade the listener. She had been calculating my demise since the moment she woke up and selected her suit, hosiery and one inch modest pumps.

"Deserve to know? What makes you deserve to know? You've never helped me with the children. Even this year when I made a huge effort as my new year's resolution to make you a part of my life, you've hardly spent any time with me or the kids. Every year, you bought a Christmas and birthday gift for both of my sisters, very expensive ones and the same exact thing for yourself and never once given me a gift since I was fourteen."

"We already resolved that."

"No, we didn't. I just confronted you, and you admitted that you had kept all of my gifts for yourself each year. That is sick. That is not resolved. And now, this!"

"You don't need anything."

"I think that is for me to decide. You could have at least offered me the Coach bags or Brighton belts and let me have the chance to say, 'No, Mom. You can keep it for yourself.'"

Pearle, my attorney, could not help but interrupt. "Norma, am I hearing correctly? For years you gave her sisters expensive gifts and nothing to Penelope?"

"Pearle, you don't understand. Penelope doesn't need anything from me. She's always been on her own. She left home at sixteen."

"She needs you today, Norma. And you cannot pretend ignorance of the negative impact that your testimony for the opposition will have on Penelope and the boys. She's been a model wife and mother, and you KNOW that, Norma. Why would you testify otherwise?"

"She needs to go back to Richard. If Richard gets the boys she won't leave him. Besides, it is only the temporary custody hearing. It is not permanent. It's TEMPORARY."

"Norma, you are far too intelligent to hide behind that excuse. You know how it works. I've explained it to you. You will be putting Penelope through a huge prolonged legal battle, great expense and maybe even end up having those boys placed on the witness stand if we have to come back here and fight for them. Without gross negligence on the part of the father it will be practically impossible to reverse today's decision. Have you given any thought to how your actions today will impact your relationship with your daughter Penelope?"

"It will not impact my relationship whatsoever. I am doing what is best for the children. What is best for them is for Penelope to go back to Richard."

"Norma, do you not think that Penelope has carefully considered what is best for the children and that that has in fact played a major part in her decision to divorce your son-in-law? Do you not respect her decision making capacity as an adult? You say she's been on her own since she was sixteen, and she seems to have done pretty well for herself and seems to have been making competent decisions all her life. Is there any reason you think she has suddenly been rendered incapable of deciding this for herself along with the advice of marriage counseling professionals?"

"Pearle, if she would just tell me WHY!"

"So, then you would switch horses? That is the bargain? Penelope risks the children finding out the reason she is leaving their father and that puts you in the position of constantly threatening to spill the beans at any moment unless she does your bidding. I can answer for Penelope on this one. No deal."

I chose this opportunity to speak again, "Pearle, I have one thing to say to Norma. One last thing."

"Don't call me Norma. I am your mother."

"We've been asking you to consider how this will impact me and the children. You have little experience thinking about others. So, now I'm going to ask you to do something you have considerable experience doing. I'm going to ask you to think of yourself. With your testimony you are making a lifestyle choice. You are an old woman. Soon, you will not be able to work anymore. You could require medical attention, someone to drive you to doctor appointments, and help you if you ever have surgery. You have three daughters, and you know that I am the one you would have depended on to help you in your old age. You've got one daughter who lives out of state and her job prevents her from coming to Texas to help. You've got another daughter who is a psychiatric mess, who lives at home with you and can't even take care of herself. Who is going to help you? I'm rich. You are choosing between a lifestyle of private nurses, chauffeur driven limousines and lunches out at Brennen's or a state run nursing home with no visitors. If you can't think of me, think of yourself."

Pearle spoke, "Norma, I think it is clear how you are going to testify. I just wanted to know what motivations you had to destroy this wonderful woman who has been a perfect daughter to you her entire life. It is clear to me now that your motivation is pure unadulterated hatred. You have always treated her differently than her sisters and you continue to do so. You may leave now."

"I do not hate her."

Pearle stood and cleared the way for mom to get past his chair and out the door. She turned to him and demanded once more to be told why I had filed for divorce. He couldn't look at her. He studied the cold coffee in the bottom of his paper vending machine cup.

"You are about to do a terrible thing, and you know it."

"It is only TEMPORARY!" She looked from him to me.

Pearle responded, "You know exactly what you are doing Norma."

The only thing I might add here is to tell you, the reader, that at the time of this testimony my sister was having severe psychiatric problems. I forgive her for everything she said. She was vulnerable and easily manipulated by both my mother, upon whom she depended for all of her physical and emotional needs, and by my ex-husband who my attorney refers to as Hannibal Lector.

In court, my sister looked hideous and ghoulish, wearing one of my mother's suits in heavy wool that made her lovely figure appear matronly. The colors were all wrong for her. The suit fabric had a loud, large black and white checkered pattern with a dizzying effect on the eye. Her hosiery was white and her makeup paste colored, giving her the look of a badly made up corpse. Her pathetic motivations were clear to all present - the judge, bailiff, court reporters and lawyers.

Only one witness was allowed in the room at a time, so my mother was not there to monitor my sister's weird behavior. All I can say is that at one point Pearle turned to me and said, "My God, can't they see what she is doing and tell her to sit down?" I looked over at my sister standing very, very near Richard. Richard was uncomfortable and looking around to see if anyone else was watching. Pearle said, "She's practically humping his leg."

Poor thing. She was convinced that with me out of the way she could assume my role in Richard's life as wife and mother and just take my whole life, the life she had coveted.

My psychiatrist later apologized to me for wasting several of our sessions trying to convince me to rebuild the burned bridges between me and my family members. I came into his office for our regularly scheduled visit to find him sitting in an unusual posture. I was accustomed to seeing him leaning back in his leather psychiatrist's chair one ankle propped on his knee, leg bent and fingers laced together in a relaxed fashion, prepared to listen and advise. This day he looked like a picture of defeat. He was bent forward looking at a spot somewhere on the carpet between his widespread feet. He moved the flat palms of both hands across each side of his head as he burst into apology as soon as I stepped into the room.

Before I was even seated he said, "I just found out who your mother and sister are. I deeply regret having ever suggested that you reunite or ever have contact with them again. I treated them, or rather I treated your sister, but your mother would not let her be alone in the room and insisted on joining in all of the sessions and speaking for your sister. As a result, I have a history of five sessions with them both. I had recommended to your mother that your sister needed to be committed. But, in court, as a trained therapist, had I only known that THEY were your family, I could have stated unequivocally that I would recommend them both for commitment. That certainly would have damaged their testimony against you. I am so sorry. I simply did not know."

But God works in mysterious ways, and I truly believe everything happens for a reason. Dear reader, remember James 1:2.

Count it joy.

Count it all joy.

Sonya Bernhardt

Texas - Land of the Big Hair

4

Some People Just Need Killin'

In Texas, things are different. If you are coming here from other parts of the country you'd just better figure that out real quick, or you'll get into trouble.

Yes, I have tried my best to kill someone with my own hands. Yes, it did change me forever. Once you've crossed that line, you've crossed it. There is no going back. You realize you are an animal when it comes right down to it. Before you cross the line you have a fantasy of being something special, God's creature with some special ability not given to the other animals on the planet because you have His love. Then, you try to take another person's life, try with every ounce of strength that you have to kill, not just maim or stop. Kill. Then, you are different. Forever.

You can fall into a hole if you do not accept God's gift of forgiveness. You can turn away from good acceptable people and only associate with other low people because you do not feel comfortable, worthy of being around good people. That is how Satan gets his toe in the door, throws the door wide open and grabs you down. If you have done something despicable, trust God has already forgiven you. Accept his gift of forgiveness. You are deserving, and He will always give you another chance and another to be good from that moment forward. Just try your best.

I had many opportunities to kill my husband. People offered to do it for me. I had to beg a couple of people not to have him killed. It would be too traumatic for the children.

A neighbor told me that she had a cousin in the construction business in Chicago who 'knew someone.' She told her cousin what happened: my money cut off, threatened with twenty years in prison for a crime my husband committed, my children locked out of the house and lost in the woods miraculously finding their own way to safety, my middle child's asthma medication taken away from him resulting in him collapsing and his lips turning blue during baseball practice. My baby, age six, did not receive medical care for a month while I was in hiding after my security guard was assaulted, and I was sent away. When I returned from out of town, the emergency room doctor threatened to call the police on me for criminal neglect when I took Mark to the hospital. Once her cousin heard all the hell that I was being put through during the divorce, he offered to not only hire the killer but pay for it as well.

I had an ex-boyfriend who was basically a mobster who would have also arranged and paid for it. The husband of a friend said he'd do it himself. I had three police officers offer to kill Richard, two of them homicide officers! An old man offered to tie him up and throw him in an area of Louisiana where the alligators would eat him and there would be no bodily remains.

I didn't want someone else, someone I cared for, to suffer the knowledge I had. The knowledge of what it was like, really like, to cross that line.

You see I have crossed it. More than once. My security guard once questioned why a neighbor who owes me a lot of money, that I will not talk to or allow in my home, is the emergency contact person for my alarm system. I told him she was the person, years ago, that I had once called in the middle of the night because I had to get rid of a body. I thought I had killed someone. Let me explain.

When I was seventeen and living in the dorms at the University of

Houston, I was assaulted by a gang of five black men. They strangled me so badly I still have one vertebrae out of place. My neck, weeks later, was still black and blue and swollen. My head had been beaten repeatedly against the limestone surface of the dormitory building until I suffered brain damage. I was only aware of three men during the assault. If I had known that there were five, I might have given up and not fought so hard.

Of all of the women they attacked that month, fourteen, I was one of the lucky ones. I was not raped. They did not cut off any part of my body or hurt my face. I have been told that brain trauma is one of the most difficult assault injuries to overcome psychologically, even more difficult than rape. I was fighting for my life. I wanted to kill. I pulled an eyeball out of one of the young men, but he didn't even seem to notice. He was high, high, high.

His anger was so overwhelming I had felt the presence of these young men half an hour before the assault. Once exposed to one person with this level of anger, you become far more sensitive to it. You feel its residue after an angry person has left the room even if it is hours later. Your body, your entire being remembers and responds to the danger. This heightened level of awareness has saved my life more than once. I can thank these young men for my life.

I remember an apartment manager once trying to show a model apartment to me at Mariner Village Apartments. As we approached the newly remodeled unit, I felt a wall of foreboding that physically blocked me from moving forward any further to approach the general area in which the apartment manager was walking. I asked her if we were going to the corner unit on the first floor.

She said, "Why, yes! It has just been freshly repainted and re-carpeted."

I stopped and told her I could not go any farther. I could not make myself enter the apartment.

She asked, "Why?"

I told her, "I have a terrible image of a whole family being knifed to death and blood everywhere. There is rage emanating from that space."

She was shocked. She asked if I was psychic.

I said "No, I was assaulted and ever since the attack I have been sensitive sometimes to places where violence has occurred."

She said a couple of months before, exactly that had happened. An entire family was killed in the apartment, knifed to death.

I told her, "The husband killed the wife and children while they slept."

She said, "Yes."

The second time I was assaulted was one year after the first assault. I had just pledged a sorority and was wearing my little pledge ribbon. My big sis that had been selected for me took me along with her to a bar where we met up with other girls in the sorority and their boyfriends, most of them frat guys. My big sis asked another gal in the sorority to see me home so she could go out with her boyfriend, leaving me in the other gal's care. This other gal looked like a wild, drug-using skank. She didn't even have her car at the bar. She had to phone her boyfriend, an even worse looking creature, to drive us to the fraternity house, where she had parked her car.

At the frat house, she claimed she had to use the bathroom and went inside. It was a very rough section of town, and he advised me to follow them inside rather than wait in the car. The two disappeared into the bathroom together. When she came out, the door swung open wide, and I could see him hovering over the sink snorting something. She claimed she had to get her keys upstairs. Seconds later, I heard the tires of her car on the gravel parking lot.

She had left me there, alone with him. He was very high when he jumped on top of me. He threw me down in one motion and shocked me.

My boyfriend was a competitive weight lifter and the only way I could spend any time with him was to weight lift with him down at Gold's gym. He was there five hours a day. Frankly, I ran out of things to do after three hours. I was in very good shape.

Flat on my back, I was winded but in good defensive position. I just bent my knees into the same position I was accustomed to for the leg press machine. When he jumped on top of me I caught him with the flat of my feet on each side of his rib cage and pressed him off of me.

He flew hard against the wall. His head tilted strangely, and he slid down the wall in a sitting position, all limp and leaning to one side. He didn't move. I thought he was trying to trick me into getting closer to him so he could grab me. I watched him. He didn't seem to be breathing. I got close. He looked…well…dead.

Only her car was in the parking lot when we arrived. I looked outside again and the situation had not changed. I listened closely and could not sense the presence of anyone else in the frat house. I couldn't call a cab.

The list of people who you can call under these circumstances is very short. I thought of my childhood friend, Tessa. She's an incredibly beautiful fashion model, now married and living two blocks over from my home in River Oaks. She is not the brightest bulb in the pack, but she is loyal. I called her.

She asked only two questions. The first question, 'What should I wear?' seems silly, but it was true to her basic nature. She once called the police to see if it was appropriate to wear a fur coat during a flood evacuation. I advised her to wear jeans, sneakers and a t-shirt but nothing with any writing on it that could later be remembered by witnesses.

"The t-shirt should be loose and baggy so no one can tell if you are a girl or a guy. Put your hair up in a plain baseball cap. By all means, do not wear all black and look like a criminal."

Next, she asked, "Is it drippy?"

Just before she arrived, my assailant had awakened. He was apparently not as dead as he seemed. I made him drive me home. Tessa followed in a truck she had borrowed from a neighbor that was out of town who always left the keys on the hook just inside his garage door.

My attacker was afraid of me now and cried the entire way begging that I allow him to drive to the hospital. I told him I didn't care where he drove after he dropped me off. I saw him six months later in the dorm swimming pool and his ribs were still taped. They didn't know back then that taping broken ribs isn't the greatest idea.

I once told the leader of a rape support group that I felt I could recover mentally if I could just go two years without getting assaulted. She called me, years later, after a man followed her home and beat her brains out with a hammer, nearly killing her. It took her twenty-four hours to slowly crawl to a kitchen window, open it and hang her body half way out to attract the attention of her next door neighbor who saved her life. She told me that she had remembered me from the support group and our injuries were similar. It is hard to get on with life when you have a disability such as impaired memory, lack of time orientation and depth perception problems that are constant reminders of the attack.

She called to ask me how many years it had taken me to return to a normal life, able to live alone without constantly looking over my shoulder. I told her I had been assaulted twice more and I was sorry, but I had no good news for her. I still constantly monitored my surroundings and had a male roommate who stood on the back porch with his fiancé to await my return from school each evening to make sure I was safe before they went to bed. It had been ten years.

I told her heightened awareness was a good thing. It had saved my life. She said it wasn't fair. She felt like she was a prisoner in society unable to drive around at night and go wherever she wanted to go, whenever she wanted to go there.

I told her that now she lived in reality, deal with it. Fair or not fair was not the issue. It was time to grow up and acknowledge the big wide world existed out there and one per cent of the people made it a dangerous place for the rest of us. I told her I was dealing with the problem by working in the school with troubled kids in the poorest section of town. I was trying in my own way to make a difference. She decided to do the same.

I told her it had been a wonderful healing process for me to work with the kids. I like to believe certain events, negative though they may have seemed at the time, needed to happen in order for me to be able to help others.

Decisions based on love are rarely poor decisions. It is when your decision making is revenge, hate or fear based that you steer wrong.

The next time I was attacked, the police at first tried to charge me with assault! I was working for a secretarial service at the corner of Fannin and West Holcombe. I had been needing a break for hours, but I was trying to balance the books of three small companies my boss's ex-husband owned, so that she could bring the books to the CPA to meet a tax preparation deadline. The pressure was on. I was pounding away at the ten key machine and answering the phones for our fifteen line answering service at the same time. I had no patience that day. When the other worker, Pam, arrived to take the switchboard, I was able to run downstairs to the bathroom next to the Sandwich Chef.

When I got to the main lobby of the building, I felt a horrible wall of foreboding. I stopped and tried to sense where it was coming from. It seemed to be coming from the basement bathroom. I thought I'd just go up to the second floor bathroom, but as I approached the elevator the same feeling was radiating from the second floor bathroom. Impossible. There could not be two attackers simultaneously awaiting me in two different sections of the building, I reasoned. I decided to put aside my feeling of dread and go to the downstairs bathroom.

'I must be on the verge of another anxiety attack,' I thought. I certainly had the right combination of stress, extra caffeine and PMS.

I ran down the steps to the ladies room. I never used a public restroom unless someone else was also in there. This was rarely a problem in my office building due to the fact that the Sandwich Chef was so busy and the restroom was frequented by the customers of the restaurant. This time three ladies were at the mirror applying their midday makeup and chatting. Good. I looked for feet under the stalls. No bad guy feet there. Good.

My sense of dread increased. I heard the ladies leave the restroom, laughing and talking loudly. The bathroom door swung shut behind them. It was very quiet now. I looked under the stalls once more, thinking myself silly for doing so, but unable to control my strong desire to check again.

I saw him quietly stepping down off of the toilet seat where he had been standing, hiding. I kept quiet. I at least had the advantage of surprise. I knew he was in there, but he didn't know that I knew. I was also closer to the exit. I banged the stall door open sending it crashing wide against the next stall, metal against metal. He looked up, startled. He had been concentrating on tiptoeing while looking down at the knife he was opening. He froze.

I sized him up. We weighed about the same. We stood facing each other five feet apart in the narrow space between the metal stalls and the tiled bathroom wall. I had a sudden vision come into my head of grabbing him by the hair and slamming his head against the tiled walls and cement floor until the entire room was coated in his blood. I was not seeing in color anymore, but in a sort of black and white like an old television, but it wasn't black and white. It was varying shades of red and white. I later thought that this must be what is referred to when people say they 'saw red.'

I had a sudden need to kill him, obliterate him from the planet. I needed to prevent him from ever, ever hurting another woman. I didn't care how many times he cut me with that knife. I did not care. He was not leaving this room alive, and I frankly didn't give a rat's hind end if he killed me. I was tired of living my life in constant fear, having panic attacks. If I was going to die anyway, I was going to take one down with me.

I stated in an overly calm, controlled voice, "You are going to need a bigger knife than that."

Then, I screamed the primal rage scream I had often yelled in group therapy. A perfect line of horizontal demarcation crossed down the man's face as the blood drained from his features. Above the line he was ghostly, paste white and below the line, normal skin color. It started in the middle of his forehead and slowly went down his face crossing his nose and cheeks and finally his lips and then his chin. We stood frozen five feet apart for about three seconds. Then, we both ran for the door. My scream had been so loud that the metal paper towel holder was still reverberating slightly. We were shoulder to shoulder both shoving our way out at the same time as we spun out into the hallway.

The elevator door opened and at that moment a shocked man stood there taking in the scene. He saw the man close his knife, shove it back into his pocket and run for the stairs.

I ordered the stranger in the elevator, "Catch that bastard! Get him, get him!"

This man was a Richard Simmons look alike wearing a loud Hawaiian print shirt, jeans and tennis shoes. In his tennis shoes he could give chase. I was in strappy high heeled sandals. I have ever since always considered my ability to run in shoes when making my shoe purchasing decisions. The two men were already out of the front door of the building and on the public sidewalk when I made it to the top of the stairs. I ran outside and could see them running ahead of me toward the heavily trafficked corner of a major street intersection.

Directly outside of my building was a bus stop with several people standing awaiting a bus. Two of the men were big and tall and dressed like real cowboys. They wore plaid western shirts with pearl snap buttons, jeans, cowboy hats and work boots splattered with old caked mud. I walked directly up to one of the men and pounded on his chest with the tips of my index and middle fingers. Later, when he returned to my building with the police I saw I had left a couple of purple bruises there on his chest.

I looked right into his face and said, "Catch that bastard, get him." The two men looked at one another without speaking a word and ran off after the bad guy.

I tried to run after him also, but the heel of my shoe broke giving me a full three inch difference in heel height. I gave up and returned to my building. Pam was answering the phones which had become extremely busy. My boss, Nikki, was working furiously on the word processor trying to get out a rush job from that morning. So, I just returned to my ten key, relieved of the switchboard with Pam's arrival, and concentrated on my three o'clock deadline.

The outer wall of our office suite was glass and faced the main hallway.

Minutes later, the old black security guard, Tommy, arrived in the outer hallway with a large group of people: five oriental men with cameras, the guy wearing the Hawaiian shirt, the two cowboys, the little piece of human garbage that tried to attack me and a police officer that I recognized as the policeman who directed traffic outside of one of the buildings where I made frequent deliveries of tape transcriptions jobs. The building where that officer worked was pretty far down the street. That meant these guys had run a full three quarters of a mile.

The policeman entered my reception area alone, leaving Tommy outside with the group of men. They all watched us through the glass partition.

He said, "Pardon me, but we are looking for a woman of your description, early twenties, blonde and wearing a white dress. The security guard thought you might be who we were looking for to question about an attack in the ladies bathroom earlier today." I was still using the ten key as he spoke.

He continued, "I guess it wasn't you."

He started to leave, but I burst into tears, "Yes! That man had a knife!"

I told him what had happened. He asked me if I had said anything to the man in the ladies bathroom, if I had threatened him in any way. I didn't like his tone with me. Me threaten HIM?

Nikki had entered the room now, introduced herself and asked what was going on. The policeman said he had stopped the group of men in the hallway from kicking that gentleman – GENTLEMAN – there while he lay collapsed on the sidewalk from an asthma attack. I looked at the man now who had been tiptoeing towards me with the knife. He backed away from me a half step and then realized he was getting closer to the men who had been kicking him and thought better of it.

I told the policeman my side of the story including telling my attacker that he'd 'need a bigger knife than that.' I explained that was all I said to him. I wanted to get the heck out of there, not discuss the weather.

The policeman asked to borrow the phone and spoke to the prosecutor. After consulting with the D.A., he said he had some good news and some bad news. The bad news was that if it was indeed just as I had said, the knife was less than halfway opened and not yet extended towards me, and the man had said nothing of a threatening nature to me or touched me in any way, then the most they could charge him with was being in a public restroom of the opposite sex. He informed us that the sentence would be limited to a maximum fine of five hundred dollars.

He said, "However, if you thought about it for awhile, and remembered the knife being three-fourths of the way open or more or extended towards you, or if he said he was going to harm you we'd have a pretty good assault case with a bunch of witnesses. Maybe, you could help me identify the knife he used. I happened to find two knives on him." He put the little rusty, dull edged knife with the red handle down on my desktop that the man had been opening.

"That is it."

"Don't be so hasty. That knife has a four inch blade. You don't want to confuse it with this other one I took off of him."

He placed the scariest knife I had ever seen in my life down on the desk, a curved blade with jagged edge at the top and a deep blood run from tip to handle. It was one of those soldier of fortune magazine type military knives used to kill - kill humans in war.

"Now if, for example, this was the knife used we'd have a felony and be able to put this spic away for a long time."

I told him quickly that I was certain the knife was the little one. It looked very non-threatening like the knife carried by Timmy on the Lassie television series. It was a knife that a ten year old boy would be allowed to carry to cut fishing line or whittle a stick.

The cop was angry now. He told me the guy had been kicked on the public sidewalk and now needed medical attention. If I had incited the men outside in the hallway to attack this man, I could be charged with assault.

So that was it. Identify the wrong knife, or else. Nikki stepped forward and suggested that I talk to a lawyer before I speak any further.

She asked if I was being charged with a crime or not.

He was about to answer when Pam said there was a call from the prosecuting attorney and that it was for the police officer. His body language changed while he was on the phone. He glanced over at me with a new respect and shifted from foot to foot taking in all of the information being given to him. It seemed that the prosecutor now had the records on both the attacker and on me.

He said to me, "So, you fought off five gang bangers a couple of years ago." He sort of grunted, "Huh," and considered me for a moment before he continued.

"Well, it looks like we've caught ourselves a hardened criminal out here. He's only been out of state prison in New York for two weeks.

He's breaking probation being down here in Texas and he matches the description of the mugger who used a knife just like this one with the red handle to mug a lady doctor outside this building last week.

He also matches the description of a man who raped a woman in the second floor restroom of the bank building next door only yesterday. He stood on the toilet and grabbed her by her hair and banged her head against the stall until she passed out. Looks like we won't need to prosecute this 'being in the ladies bathroom' thing. We've got enough to go with." As he headed out the door he turned to ask, "Do you want to say anything to him before I take him in?"

I did. I first thanked the men in the hallway for helping me. Then, I spoke to the wimpy little man from New York. I told him that this was Texas and he was lucky that he had not been seriously hurt. I told him that I did not carry a gun, but that many women have one in their purses and if he kept attacking women he was going to eventually run into a girl who was going to just shoot him.

I told him, "Go back home, Yankee. You don't belong here in Texas."

I never would have lied about how open the knife was or lied to identify the wrong knife. There is a God. You are not supposed to lie. Everything takes care of itself eventually. Sometimes, we are meant to learn a lesson and move forward in life; sometimes, we are just

God's tool to help someone else grow.

"Some people just need killin', Mrs. Bernard," my security guard, sergeant of the robbery division for thirty years, has said numerous times.

My guard, Dan Dealba, admires me and that makes me feel good. He asked me one time when my ten year old almost died from medical neglect in Richard's care, if Richard realized how easy it would be for me to just have him killed.

He said, "Mrs. Bernard, you can only push someone so far and you have been pushed past the point that most people would have just taken matters into their own hands."

I told Dan I knew Richard would come around and begin parenting. He would learn or just give them back to me. Everyone told me that one day he'd just leave them on my doorstep and walk away. No one thought he'd still have them two years after the divorce. Soon, he'd give up trying to punish me by using the children.

My oldest asked to come to live with me when he turned twelve, the age when he is allowed by the state of Texas to go to court and request to live with a different parent. I explained to him that he was needed to help with the babies because he knew better than dad what to do in an emergency. Within a few months this proved to be true with Jonah demanding that his father take his younger brother to the hospital because he had an extraordinarily high fever. Richard just wanted to go to sleep and wait until the morning because he was too tired. My son, Jonah, threatened to call an ambulance and report Richard to C.P.S. - Children's Protective Services. Richard crawled out of bed and parented.

I bet he's tired all the time the way I used to be. I bet he gets headaches and back and neck strain. I know the children tore his rotator cuff in his right shoulder. What a shame. He has lots of hired help and only one child has remained in sports and he can barely handle it.

The other day my middle child, Adam, called at eleven thirty at night crying because he needed a poster board by eight in the morning for his social studies class.

In the background I could hear Jonah say, "Adam, what are you doing calling Mom? It is Dad's job now to buy poster boards. Let him wake up early and go do it. Mom needs a break now from taking care of kids. Dad needs to do some work, finally. It is his turn."

I enjoyed hearing the emphasis in Jonah's voice on the word 'finally.' He loves me and enjoys seeing me as a happy person now, on my own, throwing parties and having friends.

I asked the boys one day after skating with them at the Galleria ice rink, as we ate cheeseburgers and chocolate shakes rinkside at the Bennigan's restaurant, what they would think if mom remarried. Only Jonah and Mark were with me as Adam was at a friend's house attending a birthday party with the maid, Yesenia.

The boys both shouted in unison, "NO!"

My twelve year old, Jonah leaned forward and spoke in a serious tone, "Mom, why on earth would you ever even consider doing something as stupid as that?"

I said, "Well, Jonah, maybe mommy is tired of being alone all of the time. Maybe, I would like to have someone to take care of me."

He was quick to respond, "Mom, you are doing a great job taking care of yourself."

Mark was visibly shaken. His voice is already unusually low for a child his age, but when he wants to be taken seriously he lowers his voice even more.

"Mom, all that would mean is that someone would be mean to you every day, all day long for the REST OF YOUR LIFE." He paused and added, "And CRUEL."

Jonah jumped in, "Yeah, Mom. Don't do it. Please listen to us. Don't do it."

I said to them, "Maybe, Mom wouldn't marry someone who would be mean and cruel. Maybe, Mom will find someone who is nice to her all day."

Mark was enthused, "OH. You mean someone different then, not Richard." He referred to his father by his first name for the sake of clarity. "Oh! Well, that would be okay then." He smiled and picked up his cheeseburger.

"We thought you meant you and Dad were going to get married

again. That would be stupid. He is mean." Jonah thought for awhile and added, "And Mom, I've been thinking about it. I know you want to give him that DVD of his favorite guitar guy that you picked out with us at Best Buy. Don't do it. Don't do anything nice for him ever again. He doesn't deserve it. He's not nice to you."

Texas - Land of the Big Hair

5

And Now For The Grotesquely Sad

There are two people in this world who are completely devoted to one another, know they can depend upon one another no matter what and are very much in love. Yet, they will probably never be together. The time for that has past. Right in the middle of the nineteen day child custody court battle, Ulysses proved he was a true friend. Because Ulysses respected my marriage vows he would never think to make love to me or hold my hand, but he took me to the hospital and signed as my husband for exploratory surgery even though he had a phobia of hospitals.

Ulysses had to be given valium by the doctor because he was so nervous and panicked. The nurse asked me if my husband was okay. He was terrified, white knuckling the armrests of the waiting room chairs. When it came time to fill out the paperwork for the insurance I thought he would faint. He confessed to having a true phobia then, and I asked the nurse for help. He said he was sorry. He had thought he would be okay, but as things got closer to the actual surgery he lost it.

After the valium he was better. Loose as a goose so to speak. They opened me up and asked Ulysses to look inside as the doctor explained what had to be taken out. They probably had to give him another valium for that one.

When I awakened, Ulysses was sitting next to the bed. He had to carry me to the bathroom and hold me upright. Later, at home, he tended to me, carried me up the stairs, bathed me, held my head while I vomited and wiped my face. He brought Pedialite from the pharmacy to keep me hydrated. He was the husband I had never had.

But, he was in serious trouble. He owed millions to bad people; people who wanted him to go back to his old life, people who put pressure on him. He pretended to need money for a construction business, and I pretended to give it to him for that purpose. If the money had to be given through a shell to protect me, I could understand. He would not lie to me unless he had very good reason.

I waited for him to get to the point in his life where he trusted me more or was free to tell me the truth. My security guard, Dan Dealba, and I discussed this problem many times. Whenever Ulysses wanted to discuss with me my 'investment,' I would not discuss it. I cut him off and reminded him that I was not investing in a company to make money, but in a person, a belief in someone who deserved another chance in life.

It took awhile for him to understand that I had never been fooled. It took a lot of growing to see that one person can love another to help out to that extent and want so much for the individual to maintain their dignity.

At last, he confessed the truth. I was able to answer him in his native language, in a perfect Greek accent as I had been studying five days each week with a tutor. He laughed. He said he wasn't laughing at me or at my accent, but laughing because it was so perfect. I spoke as if I was a native born speaker, not someone who learned the language as a foreigner.

I told him I had chosen my tutor very carefully. She taught at the university in Athens. If I was going to learn Greek, I was going to learn upper class, university educated Greek, not the Greek spoken by the guy at the service station.

I asked him if he had anticipated that he would laugh at any point in the conversation with me, knowing the seriousness of what he needed to say to me. He said, "No," then took it back and said "Yes." As a matter of fact, he knew before he dialed the phone that somehow I would be able to make him feel better about everything. He knew that there was definitely a possibility that I would make him laugh, even now. Even telling me that the worst had happened, and the money I had invested was gone, all gone. I told him it was good to have the truth between us now because lies had been too much of a strain on him for too long. It pained me to see him go through it, lying to me, especially when I could be trusted with the truth. I would not abandon him.

So what? The money is gone. Our love for one another was completely unaffected and, in fact, deepened by the experience. Could any other two people on the planet go through the hell each of us had endured and come out on the other side of it all still trusting in one another? I wrote down exactly what I wanted Mr. Guillory to say to him the next time he called, and he has asked to hear it again and again since.

People have tried to interfere in my relationship with Ulysses, but it stands on its own. When he thought I was going to prison because my husband did not pay his half of the tax penalty (fourteen and a half million), he went 'bad' again. I don't know exactly what he did, but it was one more big payoff.

He didn't tell me, so don't subpoena me, I don't know anything. Call it a gut feeling. Call it knowing someone through and through and knowing what motivates him. He wanted to protect me and take care of me and never see me poor again. He was sustained by stories of my elaborate clothing and parties. He scraped by, hiding in the ghetto of a European city on only the money that Mr. Guillory sent to him by making small bank deposits here and there in an account set up under another name.

I had a dream one night that Ulysses was cold and hungry and begging for money in a foreign city. I demanded to know if this was true. Mr. Guillory confessed. He said Ulysses did not want me to know how bad things were. I told Mr. Guillory to come over immediately and bring the information with him, so I could begin giving him money to live decently. I gave three thousand five hundred immediately and another couple of thousand soon after that. He sent word to me to stop.

Maybe, he will find his way home to me. Maybe, he will make enough to get himself out of his hole, but I don't know how big the hole is. Maybe, he will be hiding forever. Almost two years ago, I told him I would wait for him for two years. At that time he thought this was more than enough time to see him through to the other side of his troubles. I soon will need to get on with my life.

At last, I have met a good, decent man that I respect and have feelings for. I am what you would call a bit skittish. I never thought I would ever, ever remarry and yet now, at that very end of the two year time period I have met someone. Someone I know Ulysses would be proud to see me marry.

When he told me the bad news and I told him 'I understand' in Greek, he said I was so much smarter than him and knew so much more about people than him. I was so much more grounded spiritually. He knew that I meant it when I said that I forgave him, and I worried that he would not forgive himself and be crushed under the burden of what he had done to me.

"Let it go and forgive yourself and know that I have forgiven you. What I gave you I gave to you out of love, not in hopes of making a profit, but in hopes that you would have a better life. I have achieved that, but not if you are crippled, worrying, 'Oh my God, what have I done to Penelope? I have taken millions from her.' Don't do that to my gift, don't ruin it like that.

Accept what was given in love and just make the world a better place each day for your existence. Every decision you make from now on just make that the basic criteria and remember me whenever someone is directly in your path and needs help. In this way, you honor the gift and make it all worthwhile. I have enough to live on for the rest of my life. I live simply and the things that give me joy don't cost much money.

I have only good friends now. All of the horrible people in my life I have put to the curb. Who else on earth can say that? My life is blessed. It is perfect and I know that we will always love each other even if we never see one another again. We will always know that there is someone alive on this earth who truly loves us."

My bible study mom and I had many discussions about this troubled Greek man. She said she would not question my decision to help him. She said some women try to buy a man's affections, but she recognized that was not what I was trying to do at all. My giving was complete and from the heart and not to the point where it hurt me or the children, but as much as I could possibly do. She said I gave in a Christlike way. She said other people would not understand, but she understood. She explained that she and I both operated on another level, far from everyone else.

She said I had always been this way even as a small child, age six, when she first met me. I was such a serious child. When she asked me then what I wanted to do when I grew up, I had told her that I wanted to be a botanist and develop a strain of high protein bean or rice that would not die in extreme flood and draught conditions, so that there would not be so much starvation in the world.

Later, she spoke to me on the telephone when I was age twelve, and she asked if I was studying to be a botanist. I had read the college textbooks from my mother's bookshelves. I told her I had decided that even if the perfect grain existed the problems of starvation are created because of politics and interference in free markets.

I had a friend who had been living during the summers with her mother and stepfather in Africa. They lived in a very elite neighborhood and one day there was a military coup and several of their neighbors, high level people in government, had been rounded up in the middle of the night and tied to docking posts down at the yacht club and shot. They did not die immediately and the sharks and other fish ate them throughout the day. Overnight, the country changed. Political interference in free markets starved people.

It didn't stop my interest in horticulture, but now my involvement is mostly in creating beauty all around me to share with other people. I'd like to leave a legacy of a beautiful garden for people to tour and the monies to maintain it forever.

I was able to talk to the people who had taken an interest in the Nicaraguan mudslide victims about my idea to have a joint project with a major university such as Texas A&M. Doctoral students could study the special properties of the local volcanic soil and develop new strains of grains using the area as a test site. They said A&M had previously had a project before the Sandinistas took over, but that the project had been abandoned. I encouraged them to recontact the professor in charge and try to renew his interest. The area had calmed down now. But, a lot of bad things happened when the Sandanistas took over. Some things can never be forgotten.

I met some remarkable survivors of that era. The only plantation owner to not succumb to the demands of the Sandanistas lost one of his sons, and the other two sons left for the United States as soon as they could escape vowing never to return. Now, he has no child to take over the plantation when he dies. The Sandanistas encircled the homes of the owners of each of the factories and plantations. One by one, in the middle of the night each family that held property was targeted for attack. Hundreds and hundreds of men armed with guns would chant and holler horrible things, threatening to chop off the heads of the factory owners and rape their wives and daughters to death.

Each family was given just a couple of minutes to come out of their homes and they were not allowed to carry anything with them. Then the homes were stormed. Many of the women were raped anyway. Some of the men were killed in the detainment camps even though they complied with all orders. The following day, Sandanistas moved into the luxurious homes, confiscating anything good for their own immediate use.

Large sections of the best property downtown rightfully belongs to the family of a Houston rose importer. He cannot convince his siblings to join him in his attempts to go to the new government in charge now and make application for the return of the family lands. I talked with this rose importer about the A&M project, and he seemed to think it was worth trying to resurrect. His siblings are bitter though.

They had to struggle in America to attain a middle class life style and believe the government in Nicaragua just wants them to work themselves into the grave, so they can confiscate everything all over again as soon as things begin to go well.

I had a wonderful five course formal lunch with the owner of the sugar plantation and his wife. During the war, they had refused to evacuate to the detainment center. Their home was built as a fortress, a compound easily defended. Their workers had worked for the family for generations and loyally defended them with machetes and torches as well as guns.

The Sandanistas kept returning night after night and then they no longer came. The family was trapped inside the compound. One son could stand it no longer and went out in the day and didn't return. The workers sent word that the young man's head was on a stake at the top of the road. The owner eventually gave himself up hoping the Sandanistas would keep their word and traded himself for the safety of his wife and other sons. The sons were imprisoned in a local detainment center, but not killed.

The story is notably missing what the Sandanistas did to the wife as she was detained within her own home by the local general. Even as an older woman, she is still stunningly beautiful. In war, men still value some things even if it is only to hold an object of beauty for a brief moment before it is sent crashing against the wall like so many porcelain tea cups against the walls in Shanghai. Once again repeated in human history, the class struggle between the haves and the have nots played out in that beautiful home. Brutes who demand more reason they 'have not' because others have taken their share view the world as finite. They do not know the world is so wonderfully infinite, and more can always be created. Never satisfied with any level of riches, they are always the most disappointed when they seize what they thought would give them joy. Joy is not within their reach.

When I first met my friend Nicole, a wonderful upper class woman from Brazil, the words I spoke to her she remembered for the year that passed before we had another opportunity to meet. I did not recognize her upon the second meeting. It took her months to realize I had memory problems, and she reminded me. I had taken the children after baseball practice to the mall just one hour before the mall closed to go to a one hour eyeglasses store. My son, Adam, had given me a note informing me that his eyesight was significantly nearsighted according to the school nurse's examination. This seemed impossible to me since I had all of the children's eyes examined each year before the beginning of school and that was only a couple of months earlier. I had the school's diagnosis confirmed by the mall eye doctor and waited for the glasses to be manufactured in the one hour as advertised.

The children wanted to walk around, and we ended up in a very expensive women's clothing store. My oldest dragged me inside to see a suit the color of my green eyes. He implored me to try it on and told me he thought I wouldn't look fat in it. My son had heard his father put me down about the clothing I wore, asking me to dress like the other corporate executive wives.

I wore long hemp dresses and Birkenstock sandals like a hippie. The children were instructed to hang on to the skirt of my dresses at all times during those years that I had three boys under the age of five. If one would let go I would stop and the other two would chastise the offending brother saying, "Why did you let go? Look at what you made her do. She stopped now! Hang on!"

Nicole came upon one of those mommy scenes that every mom has at one time or another endured.

Jonah was shouting at me from across the store, "Come on and try this on. You can wear it to go with Dad to get the entrepreneur of the year award."

Adam, age eight, was tired from his day that had begun with speech therapy at 7:15 a.m. and decided to lay down on the floor of the store just in front of the cash register where he would be the most in the way. He sucked his thumb when he was not telling us that he wanted to go home right now because he didn't want to wear glasses anyway. The baby, age six, hid himself inside a rounder of silk shirts and discovered if he held onto one shirt and ran, the entire rack of shirts would go whizzing around and around. I told Jonah to wait one moment, mommy is coming and begged with Adam to move to the dressing room if he wanted to lie down.

Nicole asked me if she could help me with the baby. When I said I would appreciate her help, she encouraged Mark to come out from under the silk shirts before he toppled the entire rack to the floor. I told the woman at the register I would take the olive-colored outfit in size fourteen and gave her my credit card promising to return the next day for a fitting.

I thanked Nicole and said, "Whenever we feel in life that we have any control whatsoever, we are operating in an illusion."

Nicole smiled. Little did I know that I was speaking to a woman who knew this much more than most.

I asked her, "Do you know how to make God laugh?"

She said, "How?"

"Just tell him your plans."

Nicole looked in her element in that expensive women's clothing store, an elegant refined woman, smartly dressed with gold knot earrings, stylish makeup and hair pulled back in a chignon. She had a heavy Brazilian accent, but I heard her speak both French and Spanish to the shop workers as she browsed the racks while I made my purchase. God is good and he put Nicole back in my life again months later when we needed each other.

My childhood friend from age seven, Tessa, almost died during the childbirth of her third child, Marie Claire. Tessa suffered from a condition called placenta previa and the placenta tore while she was alone in the kitchen unpacking boxes in the older home in River Oaks that she and her husband managed to scrape enough together to purchase for the value of the land as a 'tear down.' They were going to make the house as livable as possible and then sell the land again in a few years. It was a good investment.

Tessa is extremely creative and has very good taste. I was sure she could turn the house into a showplace on a shoestring budget in no time at all. Now, she lay on the downstairs couch surrounded by unopened boxes, unable even to walk upstairs to her own bedroom.

News of her near death hit me hard. I had taken for granted that she would always be there for me. Even though we lived in the same city, we only saw each other a couple of times each year. We saw each other usually at Christmas time and at my sister Lauren's birthday party in August when Lauren would come from Florida to visit. I had only a couple of months before driven a hundred balloons filled with helium to the Alice in Wonderland birthday party for Tessa's daughter. My evil sister, the human pet, Terry, was dressed as Alice for the event in a rented costume, and several other adults from her husband's side of the family came in costume as well. What if that had been the last time I had ever seen her?

I felt a little badly when I saw how many photos of the two of us were tacked to bulletin boards, stuck to the refrigerator and in silverplated and crystal frames all around the house. It struck me then, hard, that I was perhaps her best friend and I hardly ever saw her. The photos went all the way back to our flat chested days poolside in her parents' backyard.

I called my sorority sister, Gabriela, when I got home. I hadn't talked to Gabriela in more than a year and told her about the experience. She told me she didn't see her best friends that often either. "It is just the times. Everyone is busy trying to hold their own lives together, raise kids, go to work, keep the grass from getting so high that the neighbors complain. There just isn't time," she said, "for friendship. That is why we are such a mess nowadays," she believed.

She told me she had been so lonely the year before and her marriage had almost ended in divorce causing her to break out in hives for more than six months. She had quit her job and the family had moved to another house to get her away from the mildew that had made her so ill, but she told me that they had lived there for years with no problem. The hives began when her husband came home one day and announced that getting married and having children had been a mistake for him. He had simply changed his mind.

They were in marriage counseling, she confided, and she hoped it would get better. She thought she'd be back in Houston again soon, with or without him. She had applied for her old position in Houston and they were eager to have her back.

I told her I was having trouble with Richard. He was going through similar changes. We were on the verge of making some really big money, and it was going to his head. He had literally asked me why we didn't have a higher caliber of friends. The people we did associate with could hardly stand him! He also didn't like the way I dressed. I was experimenting shopping by catalog because there was no time in the day to take care of myself.

I told Gabriela that a girl in Richard's office had fallen for him. She was young and beautiful, and I had done something just terrible to her.

Gabriela laughed, "I need some pointers in this department."

I told her I had befriended the girl and sent her to my hairdresser.

"NO! Did they fry her hair with a bad perm?"

"It is much much worse than that. They convinced her to do one of those hair shows and paid her to model for one of those hair magazine layouts in a punk rock hairdo. They shaved off her long, beautiful blonde hair but only on one side of her head. They cut the rest of her hair three inches long and sprayed it hot pink with this stiff gel stuff to angle all the hair out into a jaunty little cap on the side of her head."

Gabriela was hysterical, laughing. "Oh, my God. Penelope, I am glad I am your friend because I certainly wouldn't ever want to be your enemy."

"The funny part is that she really likes it and has kept the hairstyle for months now, wearing it like that into the office and everything. Richard is just horrified. He keeps talking about it, but he says that most of the people in the office are very young and have tattoos and funky hair styles and studs through their nostrils, tongues and ears. So, how can he impose a dress code for one woman? She works on the phone and has no direct contact with the customer, so he cannot single her out and demand that she change her hair."

"Does he know that you did that to her?"

"Of course not. When he asked me what I thought, I just told him she was 'showing her youth.'"

I told Gabriela I was going to make friendship a priority for the upcoming year. I was going to evaluate my life and just make time for a couple of people I had been taking for granted. After much thought, I decided to drive into Houston two times each week and help Tessa, even if I could only stay one hour before I had to return to pick up Mark from halfday Kindergarten. I could unpack boxes, move rugs, hang pictures and just talk.

I was not as successful in getting my mother to spend time with me, but I made much effort. It was only after Richard and I struck it rich that we suddenly got a couple of dinner invitations and for the first time since I was fourteen my mother gave me a Christmas gift.

My maid warned me about my mother. She said in broken English, "When you looking, her face look like this," and she squeezed her face into an artificial smile, "but when you no looking she look at you very bad like this," and she mimicked Norma's facial expression, one of contempt and pure hatred. "I worker for you and I know this is no respect I talk to you like this but I see her do this too many times and I no like it. I think she jealous you because now you go to Ann Taylor and get cute clothes and exercise and now you have cute body and she old woman. She jealous you because you have thighs too skinny now."

I had to burst out laughing. Yesenia was so serious when she addressed me. I told her my mother had been jealous of me since the day I was born and it was sick, but I was trying to have a relationship with her, just trying. If it did not work then I had not lost much. I had never been close to her, and she had never been in my life before, so things would just return to the way they had always been. I just thought I would try as an adult to establish some sort of relationship with this woman before she died.

Yesenia asked, "You know she jealous you?"

I said, "Yes, when I was fourteen she had plastic surgery. She had a face lift to look younger and she was only thirty-eight years old and didn't need it. She was just terribly insecure. She took a photo of me to the doctor and asked him to make her look like me. He changed her nose. She also had her teeth crowned. Yes, she has ALWAYS been jealous of me. This is not news."

"Be careful, Penelope. I very nervous this woman in you life now. She do bad thing, I sure."

Later, after Norma testified against me in court, Yesenia just said, "Puta. I sure she do thing bad. She hate you too much because you thigh too skinny."

Pearle at that moment turned to me and said, "Your maid is a genius," and chuckled.

Anyway, Tessa was a good friend to have for the next year of changes that occurred in my life. When she got better, I took her on short outings to fabric stores. Her mother-in-law had a budget for the Christening and wanted Tessa to have a shin dig at the River Oaks Country Club. Tessa decided to take the same money and decorate her downstairs living area and have the party at home. She planned to have family and friends all pitch in and bring food. I took on the adjoining family room, front entrance hall and dining area as the spaces I would decorate.

We had a tiny budget, but that made it more fun. We found a deal on yellow raw silk. I am still sworn to secrecy to never reveal the price, but I will tell you to guess what you think we paid to have curtains made for one window and that was the cost for all of the downstairs curtains - including the labor! The expensive looking oriental rugs are not wool but olefin, and we got them at the hardware store. The knickknacks are all junkshop finds, and the most expensive lamp in the whole place was twenty-one dollars. It looks like a million bucks. Her friend is a picture framer, 'Jack The Frame Doctor,' and he framed tons of stuff for us.

My friend, Josie, who worked at the scratch and dent store for a local furniture company had helped me throughout the years find bargains for women who were setting up house for the first time after escaping from abusive situations. She had found lots of three hundred dollar couches for me. Now, she found six dining room parsons chairs covered in the most elegant color of brownish red. I think Tessa would probably want that price on the hush hush also.

The light in the home was exquisite and the home open to visitors of all sorts. Tessa has a big heart and has always taken people in and helped them out. Unfortunately, this often resulted in ending the relationship as it had with my sister in Florida, my friend Wendi and me as well. She didn't define boundaries in her relationships very well and didn't respect people's right to make their own decisions and choices. She wanted to chose everything for them - their jobs, homes, friends, spouses. Even a parent raising a retarded child would have given the child more respect and latitude in defining themselves than Tessa allowed her friends. So, one by one, she lost all of her friends, all except for the sad creatures who enjoyed playing by her rules or for whom the rules had been suspended for awhile for Tessa's short term interests.

She would go to extremes to break up couples that she didn't feel were suited for one another. She once told me that my Greek boyfriend was living with another woman and brought together two other people to lie and act as false witnesses. Of course, it had been so long since I had had much of anything to do with Tessa that she didn't realize I had just been with Ulysses in the homes of his relatives in Greece for several weeks just prior to their accusations against him.

My realtor had been the victim of Tessa's many schemes to break up her relationship with her fiancé. She laughed when she heard my story and then apologized and said she knew it wasn't funny. She knew because it had happened to her many times. She knew how distraught she had been when it happened to her.

"He must have a really long dick to be shagging another woman from all the way on the other side of the ocean. A really long dick!"

"Oh Becky, you're horrible!"

How sad that someone would go to such lengths to impose their will on other human beings and try to crush a relationship so brutally. I cried and Tessa thought that I was crying because she had been successful. My tears were for her and her sickness. This was madness, sick, sick madness.

I was penned into a booth table by her severely obese, drug and alcohol addicted, male friend with whom she had tried to partner me.

He had an emotionally disturbed eight year old that he needed help raising, and he was on the skids financially even though he had been able to keep appearances for Tessa. She thought we would be a perfect couple supposedly because he was so intelligent and had money. Let us just ignore that his tastes in women run to the stripper sort, like the stripper with whom he was currently living, and that he couldn't keep his nose out of the candy long enough to get down to the gym. I didn't want a man in my life at all, and I certainly didn't want this one. Now, he added lying to his list of offensive behaviors.

To entice him into this charade Tessa had told me to play a joke on him weeks before. We were polluted on bellinis and she called him on the cell phone to leave a voice mail telling him I wanted his body. She was going to do the same, but when I handed her the phone she reneged on her end of the deal. Oh, well. It was harmless fun. He knew I didn't want his body. But, I am sure the prank phone call was a factor in his decision allowing Tessa to enlist his aid. I felt sorry for Tessa's new neighbor, a cute divorcee with cotton candy for brains who had also come along for this sick ride.

I was saved by my friend, Wendi, who called and said she was sorry she had chickened out and not joined me. She and Michael had gone out to dinner with another doctor and his wife, and she was coming right now to rescue me. She asked if Tessa had said awful things about her in her absence. I told her not to come to the restaurant. I was going to join her at Michael's house. She said Joe was over at Michael's house and was asking about me. I told her to tell Joe I was on my way. Tessa was straining her ears to hear what Wendi was saying, and I am sure she heard every word.

She said, "Joe? Who is Joe?"

I said, "Well, Tessa, Joe is a doctor I've been seeing for about five months now. Not that I would ever tell you anything about any of my boyfriends since you take it upon yourself to do destructive things and interfere in people's relationships. I told you that you did not have to pay me back the money you owed me but that was based on your promise to never ever again interfere in any of my relationships."

She couldn't help herself. She immediately started asking questions about Joe, "What kind of doctor is he? Is he a Lasik eye surgeon like Michael?"

"Tessa, you are the last person on earth I would say anything to about any man I dated. You can't help yourself. You cannot stop yourself from telling other people what to do with their lives," The heavy man blocking my way out of the booth defended Tessa, "She only wants what is best for you, Penelope."

I looked at my watch. "It is nearly eleven o'clock, and Joe has been waiting for me since eight. I was supposed to go out to dinner with him, Wendi and Michael. Eleven o'clock would make that a booty call. Now get out of my way so I can leave this restaurant and get some booty."

Tessa had the nerve to ask me to call her the next day. I looked at her like she had lost her mind.

Joe took me dancing at the Mercury Room. They had a band that night. The stereo in his Porsche convertible was blaring when Tessa called twenty minutes later. He leaned over close to me, so he could hear what I was saying. It couldn't have been more perfect if I had paid my friend Joe ten bucks to do it. He asked in his very deep, masculine voice directly into the phone with a touch of territorial irritation, "Who the hell is calling you at this time of night?"

I explained to him it was Tessa. Tessa evidently had remained at the restaurant and pow wowed with her co-conspirators, and they had decided that there really wasn't a Joe. I was just making it up to get out of there and save face.

Whenever Tessa asked Nicole about me and my relationship with Ulysses, Nicole would always claim to know nothing. "We don't talk about these things, Tessa. We talk about art, music and politics, not low things like this. Penelope, she is not for talking about these things."

The world is upside down when an elegant woman like Nicole is the household help for a woman as unsophisticated and lacking in education as Tessa. They are both products of their choices. Tessa has a very kind heart and can truly no longer afford to keep Nicole.

Nicole was supposed to only work part time and be shared with a miserly, hateful woman who lived down the street and would have beaten Nicole with a whip as well as with her condescension if the law had allowed it. Nicole had reached a very low point in her life. Once the wife of an esteemed investment banker with several servants – housekeepers, nursemaids and drivers, Nicole's life circumstances had taken a turn. But, Nicole herself was not brought low.

I respect her for her grace and dignity under these deplorable circumstances. Her husband suffered a terrible clinical depression. For four years the bank kept him on at full salary even though he was incapable of working. Nicole had the best doctors at the private clinics treating him. None of the latest medications worked at all. Slowly, Nicole had to sell everything she owned. She sent her daughters to the United States to live with relatives. The daughters landed in a suburban area just outside of Houston called The Woodlands where I was living with Richard and raising the boys.

Her daughter, Christina, remembers seeing me there. She said she admired the way I had my own style of dress, wore no makeup and always had my children with me. She said I looked like a true earth mother and had imagined me baking my own bread and tending a huge vegetable garden. Even then, she wanted to get to know me. A couple of years later, she would be married to a young marine. While he was stationed in Japan, she lived in my garage apartment, and we would spend evenings writing poetry on the back patio.

I would be waiting for my man to return home as well. However, Ulysses' return was more complicated and included both a return from poor mental health similar to her father's battle and a war much more real than her husband would ever face in which the good guys and the bad guys were not so easily distinguished from one another.

In a world of shifting sands of loyalties I do not blame Ulysses for not trusting me with the full knowledge of what he battled. He hurt. I could see that. I am tender and nurturing, and I tried my best to help without causing him any harm.

Nicole finally ended up with absolutely nothing. She had the clothes on her back and one change of clothes. She sold everything to try to help her husband. He was not in a private sanitarium any longer, but in the government run facility for indigents where there was no hope at all for ever seeing him cured.

Nicole's eyes were opened to who her true friends really were. All rich people are plagued by false friends. But, many turned away from Nicole for the reason I also sometimes repel people. These weak people could not stand to see her steadfastness, her goodness. They could not lure her into thinking of herself and divorcing him and marrying better. She stayed true to her vows.

It is difficult to measure yourself against someone like that. It makes people feel uncomfortable when they look at themselves. Nicole would never demand that other people make the same choices in their lives as she does.

She has a loving heart and wants an easy life for all. I have seen photos of her with her maids. You cannot pay someone to look at you like that. My maid calls it 'Petrona.' Unlike 'jefe,' which means boss, 'Petrona' means someone higher, someone everyone respects like the woman I had the good fortune to meet in Nicaragua. There is a basic respect that she carries within herself. It can never be taken away by temporary circumstances.

This woman knows the bounds of human decency and respects those bounds. I am happy she is helping to raise my goddaughter, Tessa's little girl, Marie Claire, now three years old. We speak to Marie Claire in Portuguese, Spanish, French and Greek. She can learn English from her family.

Nicole is apart from her husband now but sends money for his care. He has gotten significantly better recently and is now employed. He just needs someone in the United States to employ him, and he can be reunited with his wife and daughters. It turns out that going into the hospital for indigents was an improvement for his overall care. There the patients were used in research studies for new drugs. The drugs that worked for him would not be used on the wealthier patients for years.

Tessa went on a binge once trying to improve Nicole's life. "Nicole needs a man," she kept saying.

"Nicole is married," I told her. "Respect that Tessa. I don't care how many years they are apart, there is a bond." I think Nicole had to finally explain things to Tessa to get her to stop trying to interfere.

"Just dump him and find a better one," was Tessa's attitude. I feel sorry for George, Tessa's husband, if someone better comes along.

"Tessa is like a butterfly," Nicole would always laugh when she described Tessa's latest interferences in other people's lives. "She goes flying about here and here and then over there. Like a butterfly, she can never stay still."

Nicole understands my bond with Ulysses. Sometimes there is just love. Once I was in despair over Ulysses' deep depression, and Nicole told me to just stand by him and pray. Ulysses didn't want to steal my life away from me. He wanted me to have a good life. His voice cracked the last time we spoke. He told me that no one would ever have believed that a woman would wait for a man as long as I have waited. No one would ever believe that someone could love another person as much as I had loved him and had had faith in him.

Many people have faith in him. Josie and Miguel have faith in the healing power of love and encourage me in all of my decisions and respect the way I have conducted myself. Mr. Guillory has faith in him and helps in every way that he can. Dan, my security guard, has seen many times how love of a good woman can turn a man's life around. He says he thinks Ulysses is going to make it, especially now that he is not burdened with lying to me about the money.

Pearle Wiley wants very much for everything to work out. He said, "Ulysses must have been in serious trouble, serious trouble with some very bad guys." He respects my choice to help.

My money manager knows as I have told him the money is all gone, and now I need to be on a budget. "The construction business is a bust in Greece, my boyfriend owed money to some guys who weren't willing to wait a year for the businesses to turn a profit. He was in a bad spot and gave them my money." At least I have someone I can tell that sort of thing without any embarrassment.

Can you imagine if I did not have real friends such as Nicole and my bible study mom, Donna, in which to confide? They make me feel good about what I have done. Any decision made in love, unconditional love, can rarely be a bad one. I have no regrets, and there was no harm done at all.

Sex In The City

I am always a bit slow to understand that a man has interest in me. It was the same when I met Richard. I had six months earlier broken off with John Waring, an Englishman who also went on to become a multimillionaire in the software industry.

Recently, John called me. After twelve years, he phoned to tell me the worst mistake he ever made in his life was not marrying me. I have to agree. We were a good team. I have no idea where that man is now, retired on a beach somewhere no doubt.

His wife was always accusing him of cheating, he explained. He had not had sex with anyone in four years. His wife was so angry with him, she had turned away from him. He stayed in that horrible marriage for four extra years because he loved his daughter and didn't want a broken home. His parents were still married after fifty-eight years. He had racked up two failed marriages and was just your normal, basic good guy.

He called me after the divorce was final. I lied and said I was happily married and would not see him. He said he would bring his best buddy, Peter, along, and I could bring my mother. He said he wouldn't mind seeing Norma again also.

I didn't want to risk seeing him again. People don't seem to understand that cheating doesn't happen all at once usually. You slide into it incrementally.

If you are turning outside of your relationship to share your problems, accomplishments or dreams with someone of the opposite sex and not sharing that with your spouse, you are cheating! Your relationship with your spouse has to be primary, before everything else, including the children, only behind your relationship with God. I could not cheat, not even the 'safe lunch with other people' kind.

John said that he had most missed the fact that I was so confident in myself, so independent. All of his friends had loved me, and we had never fought. What had broken us up?

I told him about his behavior the night I decided he wasn't the man for me. He had refused to walk me to my car in a dangerous area. I kept asking him to walk me to my car, and he kept telling me to wait ten more minutes.

I was tired, had a long way to drive and had to get up early to go to work the next day. After forty-five minutes or so his best friend, Peter, eventually got very annoyed with John and walked me to my car. I told Peter to give his friend the message that I had been given a taste of what the rest of my life would be like with him and had decided to break it off.

I wanted to be watched over, cared for, treated as something precious. His friend, John, lacked basic manners, and I wasn't going to take the time to train him. That was it. John went to Russia for several months on a job. When he returned, I was already married.

John apologized and said he had been a jackass if he had behaved that way. I told him to ask Peter. Peter would definitely remember. John had been playing darts with another woman, a cute little brunette who was flirting with him heavily. John apologized again.

He said, "You were not jealous though, were you?"

I told him, "Of course not." He wasn't a cheater. He was totally in love with me, that was apparent to everyone. He was not stupid.

He said he had battled his wife's insecurity for years but couldn't seem to patch the wounds that had never healed from her ex-husband's infidelities.

He said, "You know I never cheated on her."

I said, "I know that for sure because I know you." I told him to be more careful next time and find a woman who didn't need to be rescued, a woman who knew how to be happy on her own.

He said, "That is why I am calling you, Penelope. Peter and I were just talking about it this morning. Remember? He and I would go for a run in Memorial Park, and you'd make those huge breakfasts for all the guys. It was incredible. I was stupid to lose you."

"Too late," I said and laughed. "Three kids too late."

He said, "Only three? I figured you for six or eight."

"Yes, that is what I had wanted, but I almost died in childbirth with the last one so the doctor said, 'No more.'"

As I am enjoying this reverie of long lost loves, I am with my friend Taylor at his sister's beautiful lake house on Lake Livingston in Texas. Laura Lee and her husband Wally built this home with their own hands. Wally is a genius with woodworking and has a complete workshop in the garage here with every tool you can imagine for constructing anything your heart desires. The view of the lake in winter is so peaceful, and the sound of the lake lapping at the fringes of the property can be heard all through the home. It has the effect of lulling you into a restful state of mind. One day here is like a week's vacation.

Taylor is sitting at the kitchen table trying to use his computer, but I keep asking him to do things. In the past five minutes he has started a fire, brought me the ice pack the doctor ordered for the spasm in my back caused by writing my memoirs ten to fifteen hours each day, and also found for me two flat pillows and a book to place my Mac on so when it heats up it will not burn my thighs.

Now, he has put on music and sat down. I feel a bit guilty about asking him for a sweater, so I'll just shiver a bit. There. I just read the last section aloud and he said, "You don't have to feel guilty about asking me to get you a sweater, sweetie."

With male friends like Taylor, Bob, Parker, Mr. Guillory, my security guard, Dan Dealba, and of course, the friendly neighbor ever willing to renew our sexual escapades, who needs a boyfriend? It makes it very easy to be alone.

Taylor and I discussed this last night sitting all cozied up next to the fire in our favorite position in big wicker chairs facing one another with a single ottoman between us, our legs interlocked under the blanket in one long leg hug. The cold front blew in and we hoped for a big rainstorm like the last time we were out here.

I explained to him that I could always get hugs from him. For just general hanging out and companionship there is Taylor's neighbor who lives directly across the street from him, Parker, a ship navigator who works for a few months aboard a ship and then returns to Houston with my same schedule – the whole day open to do whatever pleases him. He has a few duplexes in the area of Houston known as 'inside the loop' which includes Montrose, which is the gay area of town, and River Oaks, my ritzy neighborhood.

The area has a lot of singles, so there is abundant night life. Parker always has something going on. He knows where to go and what to do at any time of the day or night if I want to leave my home and have an outing.

We are like an old married couple putsing around at the hardware store trying to find a new rolling piece for the bottom of a shower door or sharing a newspaper in silence. He automatically knows what sections of the paper will interest me and hands them to me as he reaches for the metropolitan city politics section, which usually holds his interest through his first two cups of coffee for the day.

I'll laugh out loud and he'll say, "What?" Then, I'll read aloud to him and he'll laugh. With the break in silence he'll fill me in on the latest shenanigans of our mayor and city council and repeat what he says every day, "Thank God for term limits, or we'd never be rid of them."

My friend Bob is a florist, but his Masters degree was in costume design for theatre arts. He worked in Beverly Hills with all the great designers of two decades ago, dressing movie stars. The stars would come in by appointment and Bob would completely outfit them head to toe for events or just everyday wear. They truly looked like stars when Bob was finished with them. He is an artist. What better man to bring with you shopping?

Bob made me buy this skimpy wrap dress at Armani last year. It is bright red and held together with a single button and a prayer.

I described the Armani dress to Bob this way and he laughed and said, "Yes, all the men sit around and pray for the button to break."

Mr. Guillory is a massage therapist but mostly serves the role of listening to me yell when I get angry with the world or cry when I am depressed.

He says that I am his favorite relative because he chose me to be his sister. He has never seen two people love one another like Ulysses and I love one another and hopes for the day we will be reunited. He has told me that he is an old man and knows that he has never been loved in his life the way that I love Ulysses, not even by his own mother, and he knows his mother loved him. He told me in his next life he wants to come back as my boyfriend.

He said, "Hell, I'd be happy to come back as your dog."

I suggested to him that he come back as Ulysses and Penelope's grandchild. He smiled and said, "Now, there is an idea."

The other night I felt such despair. I told him, "I am giving up. It is near the end of the two years I promised Ulysses that I would wait, and I just cannot take it anymore."

Last year, Ulysses said that it wasn't normal for me to go without sex for so long, and it bothered him that I was alone. He told me I could take a lover (as in *just one*) while he was away.

I yelled at him on the phone, telling him he was awful for suggesting such a thing to me. I loved him and wanted to wait for him. I cried. He told me that he was right and to trust him on this. He had discussed it with Father Stephen at the monastery.

I told my Greek tutor. She laughed and said my boyfriend was not like the American Greeks, but like the old traditional Greeks.

She explained. They want you to be pure. They put you on a pedestal. Then, they choose you for marriage, and they tell you to go sow your wild oats. "'Go be with the man you've always thought about.' They are so sure that you will come back to them. They will have won the prize," she laughed. "An American Greek would not take the risk that you might leave him for good, but a traditional Greek would take the risk and know for sure you really wanted only him."

I yelled at Ulysses. I cried. I hung up the phone. I waited only half a second and dialed the number of my neighbor, the man I called when the house had a mysterious gush of water pouring out of a pipe the first freeze last year, the man I called when my dogs escaped the gate and ran off, the man I called when the air conditioner made a high pitched squeal that couldn't possibly be good.

I called him and told him that I had an emergency. Could he come over? Could he come over and make love to me? There was a pause while he considered for a moment that I might be just kidding around. He said, "Sure, I could come over. But, don't you have the kids this weekend?"

I told him to come over in an hour and sent the kids out for the day with the maid, Yesenia, telling her if she returned for any reason I would fire her.

The next day, Ulysses called to tell me he was wrong to have said such a terrible thing to me. He regretted it deeply. I was different from all of the cheap women he had been around all of his life in the bar business. He was hoping that by telling me that I could have a fling he could prevent me from doing it, and that was stupid.

What could I say? I used the method all women use when in the wrong. I told him he was a beast and made no confessions.

All spring and summer the neighbor and I had swinging from the chandeliers sex every waking moment. I joked with my security guard that my lover had a daytimer and a work ethic.

The neighbor and I were in the same situation. He was technically married, although his wife had lived overseas for seven years returning home two weeks each year, one week at Christmas and one week in the summer. The last few years she had skipped the summer visit.

He supported her financially, and I respected what she did. She was a genius working for some think tank and was always going off to newly formed governments such as Kazakhstan and helping them to write their constitutions and banking laws. She wrote for a prestigious economics journal and did research. She traveled around being important. He funded it. But, that is not a soft place for a man to land at the end of the day. That is not a wife in your bed.

I was awful to him. I told him I just wanted him for sex. He wanted to go places with me, talk to me. I told him once to just shut up and do it. I was terrible. It was the worst I have ever treated anyone in my life.

The only problem we had was that he wanted to leave his wife and marry me.

I told him, "Why buy the steer if the beef is free?"

I told him when Ulysses returned it was going to end. It was perfect timing for both of us. His wife was due to come home just before Ulysses returned. That was the extent of the relationship.

He said it was the best anyone had ever treated him in his life. I didn't ever complain about him in any way, or make excessive demands on his time, always understanding of his busy schedule. He had someone to share his triumphs with, a life cheerleader of sorts and he had never experienced that before.

His previous relationships with women had been the sort where they were after the position in society they would have if they married him. He was wealthy, had a beautiful home in River Oaks and social and political position. All I wanted was to listen to him, make love to him and feed him.

My only complaint was that he was beginning to forget where he lived, and I had my own life. So, I went over to his house to see just what was going on. Why did he always want to be at my home? The conditions inside his house were shocking. In the freezer, a two month supply of weight watcher's frozen dinners. He owned no mop or vacuum cleaner. There were no cleaning supplies in sight. He was living like a college student, papers everywhere, on every surface. Six weeks worth of mail were unopened and scattered near the door. Files, magazines and old Wall Street Journals lined the hallways and covered the countertops, desks, couches and dining table. There were moving boxes from seven years ago still unopened.

The marriage must have fallen apart shortly after they moved into this home, I speculated and he confirmed. She never really moved in. They had been unhappy in Washington and it got worse when they moved to Texas. She became depressed not having her career and didn't want to teach at the university. He agreed to her first six month stint away from him because he had no choice. She'd made her mind up that she was leaving and announced her plans. The security guards that patrol the neighborhood confirmed his story. He'd been a bachelor for seven years.

Things went well for the neighbor and I until his wife had a fight with her lover with whom she worked and lost her job. She fought to keep her position, but she was terminated and came home suddenly. She was very upset and spent the first weeks frantically flailing about interviewing for jobs. She turned down something in Beijing, much to my neighbor's horror, holding out for something better in Washington, D.C. She continued to interview in D.C., making him feel very rejected. Meanwhile, I quit seeing him, of course.

He was married. He pointed out more than once that Ulysses and I were more married than he and his wife had ever been. Once, I had answered the phone in the master bathroom, and my neighbor had slept in so he was present for my morning call from Ulysses. I screamed and wailed. I slammed cabinet doors in the bathroom and came out throwing towels violently into the hamper in the bedroom.

The neighbor sat up in bed smiling like a Cheshire cat, "So?"

"So, what?" I asked.

"So, it is over then." He was gleeful.

"Oh, no," I said slamming the closet door, "He'll be upset for awhile, but we already agreed I am right. I am not going to have to decorate around those plain white rustic looking curtains they have everywhere on the island. I don't care how authentic they look. I bought hand silkscreen fabric from Milan in ocean colors, and we are using that."

My neighbor was momentarily confused. "You were fighting over curtains? I thought from the sound of it that you were breaking up for good."

"Break up? No. Pay Armenians five hundred dollars to break his knees if he puts up those ugly curtains, yes. Break up? Don't be silly."

It is just a different style of relating. It took awhile for me to understand. I never yelled at my husband during our twelve years together, but I'm allowed a complete range of emotions with Ulysses. If I am angry I can express it without being afraid he will stop loving me or go away. It is very freeing. I can really be myself.

"He already said he'd call back to check on me later after I have calmed down."

"You are not breaking up?"

"No," I told him, "We are just apart for two years. That is all. We will just see what happens when he returns."

Two years is a long time and I have changed so much in the first year. I am not the same person anymore. He was attracted to a pathetic, shivering little kitten in the rain. My life was at its lowest. I was sick, and the people I should have been able to depend on to take me to the hospital and stand at my side in court had turned on me after I had done nothing but help them in their lives. Ulysses was there for me. I told Ulysses the woman he had fallen in love with - the weak, pathetic one, was gone. Ulysses said I was the strongest person he had ever met. When his life was at the bottom he would just look at all I was having to shoulder: the level of betrayal, the loss of my children, the loss of my very identity, and count himself lucky to know someone as forgiving and strong as me. Weak? Never.

I told him I prayed at my prayer candle hundreds of times each day for strength and courage to endure what I must endure. I trusted God had a plan for me, a plan to place me in someone's life to help them through troubles like I was struggling through, or a plan to do something else with my life. Child rearing was my plan, and I had made God laugh. God had something else in store for me. I just had to open my eyes and recognize it.

Beth Moore, in her Bible study at First Baptist Church, has a lesson called 'Do What it is That You Do in a Christlike Way.' An example that she gives is that a woman hearing that lesson had been inspired by her and had gone home and knitted her some baby booties. She had a small at home business making fancy baby booties. After the Bible study, Beth's student no longer felt as if what she did wasn't good enough. What was important was that she conducted her life properly, treated others well and made her booties, did the thing that she does, in a Christlike way.

The woman was empowered, strengthened by the bible study lesson. Some people flip hamburgers, some people collect the garbage. Do what it is that you do in a Christlike manner.

When Donna and I left bible study after that lesson I told her, "Donna, you teach school. You do what it is that you do in a Christlike manner. That is easy to see. But, I don't do anything anymore except dress myself in elaborate clothes and go to lunch and play. Maybe I am not living my life in the right way. I have been so intentionally shallow for months now, making a concentrated effort to decorate myself and my home."

Donna was thoughtful and listened to me as she drove me home from church. "You know me better than anyone, Donna. Tell me. What is it that I do? I don't do anything. I have made an effort to not do anything!"

She said, "You bring love and calm to everyone that has the good fortune to come into contact with you. You listen. You communicate. You are a nurturer, a healer. You heal others with your joyful spirit. You rid them of their pain. You give hope. You live your life in a Christlike manner. Sure, you are not in a classroom anymore, but you continue to teach a message of love. You are living your life very well, Penelope."

Oh, if only my bible study mom knew the half of it.

A few days ago, last Friday, I had dental work. It was no big deal, just the second stage of a purely cosmetic procedure to get two of my upper teeth crowned to be as white as eight more of my upper teeth and all of my lower ones. I was striving for the All-American white toothed perfection that the dental brochures claimed was within reach for a certain monetary outlay.

For hours, I had my jaw wretched about, numerous injections to remain numb, and laughing gas. The dental hygienist laughed at many of the things I said under the influence of gas, remarking how it was like truth serum. No one told me to go home and go to bed. I guess that was just a foregone conclusion that a normal person would do just that after hours of dental work and gas.

Wrongo.

I drove home and got into the Jacuzzi bathtub and as many single women do, well, entertained myself with the jets. My buddy, Taylor, called and said he hated to disappoint me, but he had been social every evening that week, what with his new group therapy and all. He felt completely drained and in need of alone time at home to just chill out and pet his cats. Did I understand? Did I have plans for the evening or was he ruining my night?

I told him old Mr. Guillory had called to check on me and was going to be singing at the Argentine Grill that night with his friends, so I could just tag along for that.

Taylor encouraged me to go to the museum opening alone. "Lots of people go alone," he explained, "It is a big singles mixer. You will meet people to talk to. No problem. Go without me."

I said I was afraid of walking in the parking lot by myself. He said they have police in the parking lot and sometimes valet parking for big events. I told him I might go, after all, how was I ever going to meet people if I never left my house?

So, I dressed. I faced my closet, and my clothes were all too designer and rich bitch looking. I wanted to look sexy, cute, available but not slutty. I decided on short black boots with little corset leather lace up detailing on the heel of each boot, black and rust pinstriped pants, a tight rust top and my black leather jacket with rust stitching.

I wore my hair in a pony tail because my furrier had commented earlier in the week that I looked great with my hair pulled back away from my face. My hair was still a little damp from the Jacuzzi, so I clipped on my fake big hair piece, a super long blonde pony tail attachment that perfectly matches my hair color. It looks like I have waist length hair, many men's fantasy.

It was six-thirty in the evening before I left the house. The art opening mixer was only from six until eight o'clock. I got this information from the roommate of Drake, the professional mingler, who I had met only the evening before at the Vermillion Art Gallery. He published a book two years ago about rules and ethics of mingling at parties and is an 'inside the loop rat' to be found each evening at a different event that offers free or near free food and drinks.

He looks like the drunken hen pecked cartoon character I've seen in the newspaper for years, drink in hand and tie just a little loosened and askew. He had encouraged me the evening before to come to the Museum of Fine Arts opening. He said no one asks to see your membership card. If you have a membership card you get four complimentary drinks, otherwise you can just pay at the bar.

I worried that I would get kicked out, the first person ever to be asked to show their card in the entire history of museum cocktail parties. I was a patron, for goodness sakes, the year before. They had offered to put my family name on the wall, making me wonder if there had been some horrible miscommunication about the size of my donation, which I later forgot to check. My mind raced in all directions, and I realized that I was higher than a kite from laughing gas. I rushed to the event after calling the mingler's cell phone to say I was on my way.

Once there, I got my drink tickets - one soda and three mixed drinks, why not? My jaw was feeling bruised as hell. I met two lovely ladies instantly and had a wonderful conversation. They gave me ideas for clubs to join to meet men. They said Mensa would be good to meet smart, professional men, and the museum guild would be a bunch of good contacts willing to fix me up with the sons of their friends. I told them I really needed a running buddy my age who lived inside the loop who could attend events like this, so I wouldn't have to go alone. A man with bourbon on his breath sidled up and joined the conversation. He leaned on his cane and swept his dirty, long hair out of his eyes. His overly tight fitting white shirt was badly stained from perspiration. The ladies gave me their business cards and told me I really needed to have my own cards made, then went off to see the art show.

I never saw the exhibit. The man, after hearing the ladies suggest I put 'writer' as my occupation on my business card, asked what I was writing. I told him I was just working on my memoirs and hoped someday to have them published.

I added I was there alone because my friend had to stay at home and give his cats attention. He had recently joined a group therapy class that met so many days each week that his cats were freaking out from being alone too much.

The man seized on the topic of cats and said he had TWENTY-FOUR!

I said, "I bet you have them all named and know the habits of each one."

I was trying to be polite. I had just been dogsledding in Colorado with a couple who lived with fifty dogs inside the house with them, so this didn't seem as bizarre to me as it might have seemed just a few short weeks before.

The man blinked twice and said, "No, I just called them all 'cat' until recently when I had to take them into the vet to get them fixed. The vet asked me to give them names for the medical records." He said, "Cats don't come when you call them by name usually, so there is no reason to name them." He gave me an odd look, perplexed that I wouldn't see this as obvious and ask such a silly question of him.

He told me about his 'momma cat' the original, first cat he owned. She had a habit of running off to a dairy near his home and coming back smelling of the grease used to oil the machines. She was a good mouser and preferred to catch her food instead of eating the cat food he provided. Now that he had so many cats around the house, she had to go pretty far to hunt anything.

He asked what I was drinking since my glass was empty and informed me he was a bourbon man. He also offered that he was a writer as well. For years he had earned a steady living as a screen play writer for porno films. He rattled off the directors and producers he had worked with naming six or seven names I had never heard of before in my life. He said he didn't know why he was telling me since he usually didn't tell anyone what he did because people didn't understand.

I said my high school boyfriend's mother had written porno books and was paid by the word. The publishing company provided her with chapter plot outlines, and she turned in her work every few days, never even working on a complete book, just turning in the required number of words using character descriptions and outlines. She made it seem so easy. She once told me, "Just get from point A to point B and follow the outline you place in front of yourself. It doesn't have to be the great American novel, just finished on time."

Bourbon man laughed and said, "Exactly."

A man called to me from across the crowd that I recognized from a gallery opening months ago, "I just seem to be running into you everywhere." Then, before I could reply, he shyly turned on his heel and walked off. Darn. He was someone I could have talked to.

I walked over to the exhibit only to discover a guard planted by the sign which announced NO FOOD OR DRINK PAST THIS POINT. Rats. I wandered back into the main hall and sipped my drink, pretending to read about the artist for an absolutely horrible painting taking up a grand amount of wall space. 'Hmmm,' I thought, 'I'll remember never to buy anything by this guy.'

A man in a nice pair of suit pants and a leather jacket sidled up to me while I was reading, came to his senses and decided not to risk talking to me and walked off. I watched him out of the corner of my eye. He seemed to be mentally kicking himself for not talking to me. He stood alone several feet away gazing off at the crowd and nursing his beer. I walked up to him and took the same stance, gazing off idly in another direction sort of facing him.

I asked, "Are you here alone?" I was pretending to just notice him.

"Yes. Are you?"

"Yes. Me too. I feel a little awkward."

"Well, we could just be alone together then. You can hang out and talk to me."

"Thanks, that would be nice. I was supposed to come with a friend, but he cancelled at the last minute and told me lots of people come by themselves." He extended his hand and introduced himself with a name that sounded made up, the joining of two drink names like a serial killer would use to lure a hapless young victim into his trap.

"I'm Jack Smirnoff."

"Nice to meet you. I'm Penelope Bernard."

"What do you do?"

This is always tricky for me to answer. I remember once my money manager enjoyed watching me answer this question at a dinner party with a big smile on his face awaiting my reply. I had asked him why he was smiling like that, and he had said he was just waiting to hear how I answered that one. I had turned to the other party guest and said, "My personal assistant tells people that 'Mrs. Bernard takes care of herself,' it consumes all of my time and requires an amount of hired help that sometimes amazes even me. I'm exhausted at the end of every day, by exactly what, I've yet to figure out since I do nothing all day."

I turned to the money manager for his approval and received a big laugh. "That's a pretty fair description, but I wouldn't say that you do nothing."

Anyway, with four hours of laughing gas and two gin and tonics under my belt I had no difficulty rambling on about how I was retired, writing my memoirs, divorced, the kids lived with their dad, rarely left my house but had decided to go out tonight to meet people at the encouragement of my friend, et cetera, et cetera, et cetera. He told me, although I didn't ask, that he was a civil law attorney, had attended Texas A&M undergrad and University of Texas law school. He had graying hair, nice blue eyes and seemed intelligent. He carried himself well. He asked if I had plans for later that evening.

"Have you had dinner yet? I'm going to the Argentine Grill later to watch a friend of mine sing. He's an older black guy who took singing lessons for a year before he turned sixty-five, so he could sing in a night club for his sixty-fifth birthday. He only has a few songs, but he is singing tonight and I thought I would go over and watch him and get some dinner. I had dental work all day, so I haven't eaten."

"Sure, I'd love to join you. Just where is the Argentine Grill?

I know I have passed it many times; I just can't remember what street it is on."

I offered to call on my cell phone and get directions for us both. He noticed that I had another drink ticket and told me the bar was closing. He tried to buy another drink, but they had stopped selling tickets. I got another gin and tonic (as if I needed one, HA!). I sipped it, but it was so strong I couldn't even drink it. I think the bartender was trying to help the fella out a bit.

Jack asked me for my number, and I gave it to him. Hey, I was thinking, this is going really well. I've met two lady friends and now a cute lawyer has asked for my number and is going to go to the Argentine Grill with me. Then, the evening took a turn. I stood there and talked and drank half of that double gin. Suddenly, I felt that if I didn't have sex with this man, I was going to die.

I have been in this state of mind twice before. The first time, I was married to Richard and we were at the Houston Country Club for a tax protest lecture given by Jacob Hornberger that ended up costing us twenty-nine million dollars in penalties, thank you. I was served by a bartender named Mark. When we arrived at home, Richard was exhausted, but I wouldn't take no for an answer. Nine months later baby Mark was born. I named him after the bartender, I confess, not the book in the Bible.

The second time, I was out at the F. Scott Social Club, owned by a real slimeball Arabian who kept a stack of hot check notices on his desk for all the world to see and paid his contractors slowly, if at all. The manager was my friend Andrianna's little brother, Ulysses.

I had left my husband and gone out to get drunk and get laid. I targeted a sharp looking guy with a great build and an artsy look. He wore a black turtleneck sweater, nicely tailored jacket and cool Armani glasses. He was a great dancer, and I was all over him.

Every time we sat down, Ulysses would come over to the table and join us. It was weird. A security guard I hired the following year, when told this story, laughed and told me that Ulysses was running interference, and this was known as a 'c**k block.' It was appropriately described with this terminology.

We would ask to be left alone. We would return to the dance floor and exit the other side and find a different table and there he would be AGAIN.

At one point Parker asked Ulysses, "Who the hell are you?"

Ulysses had said, "I'm her body guard. I am here to guard her body."

I told Parker he was the kid brother of my good friend and was the manager of the club. Parker said he found his behavior to be quite odd for a bar manager. He had never seen anything quite like it before in his life.

He said, "So that is not YOUR brother, just your FRIEND'S brother."

"Yes. And he is being really weird."

"He is not going to try to beat me up or anything like that is he?"

"Beat you up? I don't think so. I'm pretty sure not. He's gay."

"Oh. He's gay." Parker found something reassuring in that, a reduced likelihood of a broken jaw or something along those lines and asked if I would like to leave this place and find a place to talk where we wouldn't be disturbed. I said great, I just needed to use the ladies room, and I'd meet him at the front door.

When I exited the ladies room, Ulysses was standing outside in the hallway as close to the bathroom as you could possibly get without coming inside to wash your hands. "You are going to my sister's house," He announced, "I've already called and she is waiting for you. My mom has cooked and they have dinner for you." He spoke very gruffly.

It was decided. I looked over his shoulder at Parker, who pretended not to be eavesdropping when he caught my eye and averted his glance as if surveying the dance floor.

"What do you mean?"

"You've had too much to drink and you are going to my sister's." He sorted through the keys in his hand until he located the correct one off the ring. He placed it in my palm and then looked warily over at Parker and rethought the situation.

"I'll follow you."

He took me by the shoulder and turned me toward the exit away from Parker. I escaped his hold and walked over to Parker with Ulysses right behind me. Ulysses glowered at Parker over my left shoulder.

"My mother is waiting for her at home," Ulysses told Parker firmly trying to intimate that he was my big brother and, therefore, had some authority in the situation.

Parker would not be dissuaded, "I'd like to call you sometime. Can I have your number?"

Unfortunately, I really did not know my phone number as I had just moved into my lease house. I couldn't even call directory assistance. It was not listed. Rats!

I met Parker again years later, and now he is my good friend. He said it worked out for the best. He would have slept with me, not had a phone number and then shipped out for six months and I would have thought he was slime. It is better being good friends. Especially since I ended up being so in love with Ulysses, who turned out after all to not be gay, just impeccably dressed and with an extraordinary amount of Ferragamo shoes for a straight man. Go figure.

So, I sipped just a few more sips of my drink as Jack and I continued to talk while people began leaving the art opening. We walked to the parking lot. I am afraid in dark parking lots, especially with so few people out and about. The crowd cleared quickly when the bar shut down. I asked if he could walk me to my car and allow me to drive him to his. He said yes.

Once inside my car he leaned over and gave me a very nice kiss. Very nice. Let me just emphasize this for the record. Very, very nice. I told him he was a great kisser. How could I say otherwise? I was loaded on truth serum. He said thank you, that I was a good kisser too. I told him I was afraid my breath must be funny from all of the laughing gas and pain shots I had had all day at the dentist. He said not to be concerned it was just fine and kissed me a couple of more times and very boldly reached for the zipper on my pants!

I guess this is a very accurate way to get your message across if you are a guy. If a gal is going to say no, she will pretty much be loud and clear about it when you reach to unzip her pants, for goodness sakes!

I pulled away from him and zipped up my pants which must have been a very negative signal to the poor guy. Then, I shocked him by saying, "You know, I've been in the dentist's chair all day and my jaw feels too bruised to even think about chewing food. What I really want to do is have sex with you. How would you feel about skipping the Argentine Grill and just following me back to my house? I live near here."

I don't remember exactly what he said, but it added up to, "Sure!" I backed out of the parking place and took him to his car, a cute little M3 BMW convertible just like the one Richard wanted to buy that Ulysses said was a decapitation machine. Ulysses wouldn't allow me to even test drive one because he felt it was so dangerous.

When you grow up building and racing cars you look at a vehicle differently. Ulysses wanted to know how far a car could travel on the roof at a speed of over a hundred before the roll bar failed. Lawyers buy cars to impress babes and look successful and to remain within speed limits. He had his alma mater, University of Texas, sticker on the bumper. I wondered if he was an organ donor. You really cannot control where your thoughts wander when you are this high.

I exited the parking lot and became immediately unfamiliar with my surroundings. I pulled over and got out of the car and walked towards his stopped vehicle behind me. He probably was thinking that this has been too good to be true and that I had come to my senses and changed my mind and with good reason. After all, a girl could get her throat slit with this kind of behavior or AIDS, or if he was truly reasoning things through - KNOCKED UP ON PURPOSE AND SUE. I was in the age range to be concerned about that if I were him. Maybe my biological clock was ticking. I was living in an area of lesbians and aging professional women who look around at age forty and realize 'Oops! I forgot to have a kid, and now it is almost too late.'

When I related this story to Parker blow by blow he kept saying, "Geez! Why doesn't anything like this ever happen to me?" He said he and his buddy were talking the other day and had decided that ten percent of the guys out there must be having all the sex while the rest of us poor bastards are sitting around twiddling our thumbs for months hoping for something to develop and then getting shipped out again.

I reminded him that I knew for a fact that three years ago he had a chance to get lucky because it was the last time I had had that much gin and tonic, and I knew because I was there. I was the girl throwing myself at him.

He laughed at the memory and said, "Oh, yeah. Right. I remember. But that guy there kept stopping things."

I said, "Yes, that guy who was in love with me, but I didn't know it. 'That guy' who I spent the next couple of years waiting for, 'that guy.'"

Parker then recalled he had had a similar experience recently. "Things were going really great and this girl took me back to her house, and then her neighbor came over and told me that I would, 'Have to go home now.' Her neighbor! I have those kind of experiences like you sometimes. I guess only in my experiences some interfering guy or NEIGHBOR shows up to ruin everything. I guess things worked out pretty good for me in your case though," he said this very sweetly and sincerely. I told him he was a good friend. I asked him if he wanted to hear what had happened.

I told Parker I wanted to know if I had done anything wrong or socially incorrect because I really didn't know how to act.

He said, "It sounds like every guy's dream come true so far," and laughed heartily.

I told him I told the guy I was turned around and didn't know how to get to my house after leaving the parking lot on the other side on a street I didn't know. He said he could get me as far as San Felipe and Kirby and then I could pass him and he could follow me.

"When we got to my house I started to show him around, but when I was having trouble starting the player piano..."

Parker interrupted me. "What do you mean, 'Had trouble starting the player piano?' All you have to do to the damn thing is hit the play button or start button or something. Just how much did you have to drink, anyway?"

"Just two and a half gin and tonics. But, it was the laughing gas. It made it hard to press the tiny little button, and I think I was nervous."

"Okay, I could see that. Okay, then what?"

"Well, he came over to the piano where I was crouched down, and I looked up at him and said I had to confess that I didn't know the etiquette of how I was supposed to act when you bring someone home to have sex with them."

"You said THAT! How come I never have things happen to me like this? Holy Toledo! You just came right out and said it like that?"

"Well, I had pretty much already made myself clear before I invited him over."

"Yeah. But, Penelope, you've got to understand. A girl saying 'yes' doesn't mean anything. It is like walking on a razor's edge. One wrong move and it changes to 'no,' and you never even see it coming. You are just watching for signs that things are turning in the direction of 'no.'"

"Really?"

"Pretty much, yeah."

I thought about that. I remembered the first time I was with Ulysses. He kept asking me about a thousand times, 'Are you sure, Are you sure?' Even after my underwear was off I had to yell at him 'NOW or no!'

Which is about as clear as you can get except for the time my French-Algerian beau couldn't understand my English (it being his fifth language, poor thing) and had stopped to make sure that I didn't want him to stop. I told him if he stopped I would kill him. He told me he was a little afraid of me that night.

I told Parker that I thought I had done something wrong because this guy had not called me. I joked that after going down on me for three and a half hours I thought he was probably in traction in a hospital somewhere in the Houston area. I couldn't imagine anyone going to so much trouble to give a woman that much pleasure and then not calling unless he was married.

Parker asked if I had called him, "Maybe the guy just thought he'd gotten lucky with a one night stand and that is all you wanted."

I said, "I don't think so."

Parker said, "Why not?"

I said, "Well, first off I think he was a little taken aback when we came in the front door, and I automatically did a half kneel and crossed myself in front of the prayer candle. I always do that the first time I come in the house after being gone for the day. In fact, I would have gotten down on both knees if I had been alone, but I am not going to do that in front of someone."

"Well, sure, I've seen you do that bunches of times just walking around inside of your house, but I've never seen you kneel. That would make me feel kind of weird. I see what you mean."

"I think maybe that was the reason he didn't, you know, 'go all the way' with me after seeing that."

"Yeah. Just hours and hours and thousands of orgasms! You've had your quota for the year!"

"I just don't see why a guy would go to all that trouble to give me that many orgasms and get hardly anything in return only to not have sex with me. Unless, he just got off on me begging him."

Parker was laughing hysterically, "This absolutely never happens to me." He laughed more and then got himself under control. "One thing I can tell you is that if you were doing all that screaming and stuff and giving him all of that positive feedback that probably made him just want to keep going because it made him feel like superman or something. Guys just aren't used to girls being so responsive, and if you were screaming and begging he wasn't going to stop."

"Wouldn't he want to have sex too?"

"Not if it was like you are describing, not necessarily."

"It was. The lady next door was even standing on a little footstool by her kitchen window looking up at my bedroom window trying to see what was going on or to hear better, I don't know what. I sat up to turn off the light after about an hour, and I saw her looking up at the window. I pointed her out to him, and we both died laughing."

"She could hear you from next door? Good Lord! She probably thought you were being murdered or something."

"Oh no. I don't think so. I wasn't screaming like that. I was screaming things like 'MORE, MORE!'"

Parker chuckled, "Like 'Don't!' 'Stop!' 'Don't stop!'" We giggled and giggled.

"Seriously, Parker. Why hasn't he called?"

"Hell, I can't figure out why that guy you went out with this summer never called you back. That is the weirdest thing I ever heard of in my life. Things were going great and then he doesn't call you for a week and, of course, you get mad. ALL WOMEN would get mad about that. He had a great thing going with you and he really screwed it up. I'll never figure that one out, never. But this guy, if he's not married, and like you say, you've got to consider that possibility, if he's not married, he'll call you. He just is trying to play it cool."

"But, I called him."

"Well, call him again."

"I did. I called him Saturday and voicemailed, 'Come join me and Wendi at your least favorite restaurant, the one that food poisoned you, we are meeting for a drink.' Then, I called him Sunday and left the message, 'This is Penelope 555-555-5555. I'd really like to get to know you, even with your clothes on.'"

"That is pretty cute. He should call you back after that one. Hell, even if I had been horribly embarrassed and had some catastrophe like not being able to get a hard on, I think I'd call back after that message. But, don't call anymore. That would make you look like a psycho chick or something."

"Oh, don't worry about it. I won't. Soon his phone number will drop off of my cell phone. It will be gone forever, and I won't be able to scroll back and hit redial."

"Well, hell, write his number down before that happens. You may want to call him in a couple of months."

"Whatever for? Call a guy who doesn't call me? Why? If he is not interested he probably has very sound reasons and that is that."

"Huh, just like that? After thousands of orgasms?"

"If he doesn't call me by tomorrow, that is it."

"Well, give the guy until Wednesday."

"He acted like he was going to call. He asked me for my number, and when I said I didn't have a card, he asked me to write it down. He held me, talked to me, stroked my hair lovingly and kissed me good night. Maybe, he is afraid he does have some horrible disease. After I told him my sexual history, which is comparatively short, I told him, 'I could show you a copy of my Quest blood test report.' After all, I am a rich lady with recent blood work. If he gave me something, that could be serious trouble. He is a litigator. They think like that."

"Could be. I think he'll call. Unless, like you say, he's married or something, but I don't think so."

"So, what are you doing now?"

"Watching TV."

"Could you click around for me and find something I'd like? You are so much better a clicker than I am."

"Ain't that the truth! By the time you find something and click around and come back to it, it's over! Here. Two things for you. The world news report on cable or that new show, 'I'm a Celebrity'"

"Oh, I love that show."

"Well, there you go. I'm going to watch an old Barnaby."

"What are you doing tomorrow? Have you seen that *Bowling for Columbine* movie yet?"

"No, not yet. We really should see that before it leaves the theatre."

"And Tuesday, if Kit says she can't go, I think she will but I've already asked her, I have a table for four reserved at Tony Mandenelli's for Fat Tuesday. They are going to have a jazz band."

"Oh, that sounds great. Sure."

"Also, this Wednesday, I've already invited Taylor to go with me this time, but I've become a patron of the Alley Theatre and they have dinner parties throughout the year. Would you be interested in going with me next time?"

"Is it laa dee daa as in do I have to get dressed up?"

"No, no one does. Just your usual black turtleneck inside the loop artsy chic look that you do so well."

"Okay, then. Tell me when the next one comes up. I'll go with you."

Dear reader, as I have told you, with all of my good friends – Josie and Miguel (I went to dinner with them Saturday and they called three times last week just to check on me), Kit (she is organizing a girls' trip to Mexico for sometime soon and we spent the day together doing a tour of homes in River Oaks, hashing out backyard landscape design ideas and eating dinner at Barnaby's), Parker (see above for examples), Taylor (has had so much therapy, who needs to hire a therapist? just ask him, good for hugs too), Mr. Guillory, Nicole and her daughters, Ulysses' family and Wendi, and Pearle Wiley, who needs a man? Well, according to the truth serum potion of four hours of laughing gas and two and a half very strong gins, obviously I do.

I screamed and begged this man. I got dizzy to the point of vertigo. I got dehydrated and could barely get to the sink in the bathroom to guzzle water and then lean against the wall in the hallway on the way back to the bed and say, "I'm about to pass out, but I want more." I finally had to tell him I couldn't take any more. I asked him what it was that prize fighters do when they think if they go another round that they would die from a concussion.

He asked, "Do you mean throw in the towel?"

I said, "Yes, I need to throw in the towel. I can't take any more, and I feel guilty because I haven't done anything for you at all."

I passed out on his chest and napped for a few minutes and then he got his turn which I will not describe. Sorry, Charlie. I get to keep some secrets. If that guy doesn't call, well, he's dead or married.

7

No Boundaries

I just averted near disaster. I thought I had dropped my cell phone into the mailbox at the River Oaks post office over on West Gray. I'm tired. This morning I woke up early and drove out to The Woodlands to deliver acne face soap and special finely milled clear zinc that absolutely will not clog pores to my pre-teen, Jonah, age twelve. I had given some thought to the fact that he was adamant about not cutting his hair, even though his brothers had gotten haircuts that week. Thursday evening, when he reached to brush the hair out of his eyes, which he now needs to do almost constantly, I could see acne on his forehead.

At first, I thought he was being rebellious to not cut his hair, but it dawned on me that the extra length succeeded in covering up the near solid rash of pimples stretching across his upper forehead. The pimples would surely cover his entire face by the end of his Spring break vacation with Richard. They were going to St. John's in the Virgin Islands, and if he used the grocery store brand sunscreens on his face it was going to make the problem much worse.

Knowing that a boy would not likely go to too much trouble with a beauty regimen, I delivered two choices to simply wash his face

- Proactiv of infomercial fame and a black mud soap by Borghese that is very drying. I told him to try them both and see which one he liked the best. One had little scrubby stuff inside and the other was good at drying up oil.

He tried to act disinterested, but he grabbed the plastic Ziploc bag out of my hand and only half turned away, too cool to be receiving acne advice from mom. He was listening intently though. I know my child.

I told him the sun block was very expensive and to use it only on his face to not waste it because it would not cause pimples and the other sunscreens would make his pimples worse.

Each baby came outside and gave me a big, long hug on the driveway. Richard came out dressed only in loose gym shorts. I think he's become proud of his new, leaner body. I suspect that he might even have succumbed to liposuction. Why not? He's battled his weight forever and this new gal with her perfectly toned figure probably makes him feel like he has to keep his body in equally good shape. It made me feel good for him that he could walk out in front of me shirtless and not feel embarrassment. This new woman is good for him and the children love her. Everyone is happier.

I hope he doesn't repeat the mistake he made last year, when he told all of the women in the children's lives – the school teachers, baseball moms, school principal, his girlfriend, the maid and the babysitter that I was an awful abandoning, neglectful parent. He claimed that he had shouldered the complete burden of childcare while I was an alcoholic, drug abusing harlot out all hours of the night hanging out in clubs, salsa dancing and picking up strange men.

Good grief! Talk about exaggerating a one hour midafternoon dance class with your best buddy, Tessa, just a tad! Sure, we went out on Wednesday nights and did ballroom dancing.

I could have brought my dance partner into court as a witness for me, an eighty-five year old retired engineer who always wore a cream colored linen suit and panama hat with a thin black hatband and a huge kerchief cascading out of the front breast pocket of his jacket, if he had not DIED of old age, thank you. Oh yeah, I was out just painting the town red!

Ulysses offered to call in all the employees from his bar as witnesses that all I drank was water with lime. My table was pretty memorable. I would tip one hundred dollars up front and ask for a plate of limes and to keep my water glass filled. I would order food and one bottle of champagne for everyone else at the table to share and close out the tab. This served to keep the overall bill down. I was the hostess and spent my time on the dance floor.

Once, I returned to discover everyone had ordered one or two shrimp cocktails. They were thirty dollars a pop! I pointed this out to Tessa the next day at dance class and she was horrified. She had ordered one and it was so good she ordered another and had encouraged everyone else to get one as well. No one knew they were that expensive.

She was incredulous, "What a RIP OFF! Thirty dollars for those little tiny things! I was thinking maybe eight or nine dollars tops." She was too vain to wear glasses and readily admitted that fact with a laugh. Also, the type on the menus was in curly script and tiny, making it nearly impossible to read in that darkened environment. From then on we drove through Whataburger on our way to go dancing if anyone had not eaten.

Anyhow, Richard should have learned by now that such lies will certainly backfire. Some people were happy to be informed that 'Little Miss Perfect Penelope,' who had always made them feel inferior by comparison, had a dark side that she had managed to conceal from the world with poor, victimized Richard's assistance. At first greedily eating up any negative gossip about me, they eventually had to deal with the cognitive dissonance of all that their own eyes, ears and direct personal experience with me and the children daily threw against that wall of untruths.

When the moment arrived, and it always did, and the person who had been persuaded to believe that I was downright evil concluded on their own that I fell more towards the end of the spectrum deemed saintly, they hated Richard. Hated him!

I do believe that is why he pulled the kids out of the public school and put them in a Catholic School in Conroe and then pulled them out of there before the term even began and entered them into a new private school just opening its doors for the first year. It is a lot of money to spend on a school with absolutely zero track record when the public school is perfectly fine. Unless, of course, you've made a jackass of yourself with everyone. Then, you need a fresh start.

Being a stay at home martyr required some effort on his part. He'd have to wake up and drive them to school. Martyrs don't have tons of hired help to do everything regarding childcare. It didn't help his martyr image that I was down at the school three days each week having lunch with first Mark and then Adam followed by reading circle with the first graders followed by reading circle with the third graders.

I had always been at the school with the kids. Now, I just had a bit of a drive. It was a tough one trying to paint me as the substance abusing, neglectful mom. I showed up for the parent teacher meetings, and he wouldn't even return the school's phone calls.

I knew my days at the school were precious and numbered. Kids grow up. It is uncool for a fourth grader to have mom seated at the lunch table. I had already been through that heart wrenching experience with Jonah towards the end of third grade. One or two teases from his peers about being a mamma's boy, and I had to fade into the background or harm him socially.

I watched for signs of that with Adam. He was a full year older than Jonah had been during the third grade, so I thought the guillotine blade may fall even sooner, but it didn't. Adam is my sweet one, Jonah my serious one and Baby Mark, my honor student.

My neighbor, Laura, was Richard's personal trainer and was seated across the cafeteria table with her little boy when Adam dropped the bomb on me. Richard was having an affair with the little twenty-six year old neighbor who lived two doors down from me but directly next door to Laura. I tried to conceal my shock at the news for my son's sake, but it was like a piano had been dropped on my head.

I had just arrived in the school cafeteria and slid into the bench seat next to Adam trying to give him my usual big hug, but he shied away from me. He held his body tight with his shoulders drawn up peculiarly as he leaned away from me, his voice robotic.

The first words out of his mouth to me that day were, "Dad is not ever going back to you. He is with Robbie now."

I had helped Robbie when her husband walked out on her shortly after their child was born. The baby had terrible colic, and I had much experience in that area and shared with her all of my tricks. The doctors don't know much to tell women suffering without sleep about how to deal with a screaming newborn.

Women are so isolated from one another now, moving away from family and friends and then sometimes moving every few years due to job transfers. In the old days, women were surrounded by other women who shared the common childbirth experience and offered their wisdom through day to day casual contact with one another. I told her she could call me if she started to feel desperate, even if it was in the middle of the night.

"Don't be embarrassed," I said. "Don't let yourself get to the point where you feel like you could snap and lose it. Keep my number taped to your telephone."

I guess as soon as she saw I was moved out; she moved in. It hurt me, but I wasn't going to ever take Richard back. Maybe it would at least divert his attention away from me, and I could live in peace without his harassment.

I caught the startled look on Laura's face as she absorbed my reaction to this news. I tried to behave as if it was old news to me. I hoped my cover was good.

Adam added, "I'll hate her if you want me to."

Adam was my most fiercely loyal child. Jonah, at first, didn't know who to believe. He kept saying over and over again each time I saw him, "Mom, I don't know who to believe." He asked me once point blank if Richard had ever hit me. He was constantly searching for clues and answers. Why had his entire world been shattered? Why had mommy moved out?

Could I tell him Mommy is fighting for her life, has all kinds of health problems and needs to live close to the medical center and daddy thinks people cause their own health problems and therefore deserve no help? Could I tell him that when I told Richard I had had a bad report on a breast lump that his father had pulled the car over to the side of the road and told me, "Get out of the car! You disgust me!" There were many, many reasons to leave their father, but in order for them to ever have a relationship with their dad I couldn't tell them.

The biggest reason, the tax problem, I was not even yet aware of. At that point, the Spring school term after I had moved out over the Christmas break, Richard had testified in court that he was three, maybe four years behind on the taxes. He had reassured me on the telephone that he would do the taxes, and his friends said there was only a five hundred dollar penalty because it was a class C misdemeanor. I told him that his loser Libertarian friends who earned next to nothing and lived in their mothers' garage apartments weren't the best source of information. He should hire a professional tax man.

With Laura and her child as audience, I pulled myself together. I told Adam that mommy wanted daddy to be happy and now that Daddy was with Robbie he wouldn't be sad and crying all of the time. I told him that he could decide on his own if he liked Robbie, but I was sure that if Daddy liked her she was probably a very nice person.

Adam had been holding his breath and now took a deep breath in and out and his shoulders relaxed somewhat. Good. I had somehow risen to the occasion. After all, I had liked Robbie, and Richard could drag home much worse than a young, small town girl with a good college education. Of course, as soon as she matured and an ego developed there would be trouble in paradise, but until then this was a nice woman in Richard's home.

I told my friends I feared he'd end up with a stripper with a rack and a cocaine addiction. I had tried so hard to shield the children from Richard's mistreatment of me, but I wasn't certain another woman would go to so much effort to protect my babies from seeing abuse.

Maybe, I had taught Richard a lesson, and he would treat the next woman better after losing me.

Ulysses said, "Not likely."

In fact, he didn't believe Richard had ever been that good to me, even the years before the fabric of the marriage began to fray and tear. He said I always looked for the best in people and had wanted so desperately for Richard to be good. He said a man does not suddenly wake up one morning and behave as he had seen Richard treat me without having a general hatred of women his entire life.

The psychiatrists told me in no uncertain terms to run, not walk away from Richard. One doctor told me that Richard was the angriest man she had ever had in her offices in eighteen years of practice, and as a mental health professional she could not in good conscience put me back into the car with him. She glanced at her watch and told me that there were twenty-five minutes remaining in the appointment, and she was afraid he might return early.

She shoved papers into my hand that I did not read for several months, partly because the post traumatic stress was so great that it was months before I was able to focus and read, and partly because I didn't want to sit around with a group of whining women who wanted to go to a group therapy to talk about their problems a couple of times each week as a Band-Aid to allow themselves to remain in their bad relationships. I thought the papers were to inform me about support groups.

I didn't need a support group to convince me to leave Richard or to convince me to stay away. I had body guards to keep me from ever having contact with him. The guards made good money. It was an easy gig following me around for my walk in the park, and they weren't going to allow me to go back to him. Richard hated the body guards, and the feeling was mutual.

This therapist had met with Richard once, and she was afraid of him. She said she would not take us on as clients and told me to contact the support services on the list she gave me. She was very nervous and stood waiting for me in the hallway, so I would begin exiting her office. The doctor nervously looked over her shoulder in the direction of the reception area and told me that it would be a better idea for me to walk out the fire escape stair in the back of her offices and then cross over to the next building and call a cab from there.

Richard had the children with him, and his behavior the evening before had been so bizarre that I was truly afraid he might kill the children and commit suicide. I told the psychiatrist I was concerned that Richard had the children, and she told me to let the police get them back.

In a bold move that came from left field, Richard called the Sheriff and had me charged with assault or something. Pearle was so upset he never even let me read the charges. From then on there was a notice posted on the doors of my home with the restraining order, and I suffered without my babies.

My sister in Florida, Lauren, took me seriously when I told her how frightened I was. Her ability to be there for me was constrained by the fact that she had never healed from her experiences with a severely abusive husband. She told me later that she had talked to mom about it.

She asked mom why she refused to believe that there was anything wrong in my relationship with Richard. What was so startling? Terry Jo, the evil human pet youngest sister, had been shot five times by a teenaged hit man as she tried to back her car out of my mother's driveway on the way to her mediation hearing. Lauren was beaten in the parking lot of the airport by her husband just as they arrived for their honeymoon.

Why was it so difficult to believe I might have an abusive husband? Because I had never complained? Neither had Lauren or Terry Jo. Why did they deserve family support in their hour of need, and I got cast out?

It was the family pattern. I didn't deserve gifts, food, clothing or later as an adult, family support. I could take care of myself.

"She doesn't need anything from us, Pearle," my mother had hissed when my attorney, who knew the members of my family, pointed out that I was treated differently than my siblings. Maybe that was my crime, not being needy enough. Whatever the crime was, I had apparently committed it the moment I was born.

I don't know how I got off on that tangent. Many, many months and opportunities for tears have come and gone since I first heard about Robbie, the twenty-six year old neighbor. Richard now has a new love, a more mature woman. I hope Richard has had the sense to not try to fill this new woman's head with all kinds of ugly hateful things about me. This one was paying close attention. Richard had asked her to marry him, and her eyes were wide open for any possible red flags indicating trouble on the horizon. She could see the love between me and the kids. Thursday, when I brought the kids back to the house early, she was in the kitchen cooking dinner. She saw me talk to Mark about wearing sunscreen. I knelt down and placed the flat of my palm on his tummy and chest and looked him directly in the eyes.

"Mark, you are going to the beach with Daddy and the last time you came home all sunburned. This is your body and your body is your responsibility. You have to take care of your body. Promise me you are going to get help to put on sunscreen and put it on more than one time each day."

He promised. I hugged him and stood up to catch Richard's fiancée, Tammee, soaking it all in. Mark slid down the stainless steel, modern stair rail that is precariously near the stream of water that flows through the home with a loud whooping sound. He was very proud of himself at the bottom of the rail.

He shouted, "Did you see how fast I could go?" beaming proudly.

I shouted, "Yeah, Mark! That was fantastic. MUCH FASTER than mommy's stair rail."

Mark ran off down the hallway but from his glance in the direction of Tammee, who was joined by Richard in the kitchen, I could tell that he had just gotten away with behavior that was not allowed in Richard's house. Just add encouraging children to slide down stair rails to my list of dangerous crimes. Richard and Tammee looked at one another open mouthed. 'Yeah, Tammee,' I thought, 'I just let the kids run wild.' In a world of 'No,' someone has to shout 'Yes!'

Richard said he was going to have a glass of wine and disappeared into the wine cellar in the dining room.

In the second that he was absent from the room Tammee leaned forward across the bar where she had seated herself and began to whisper conspiratorially, "I've been wanting to tell you…"

Richard returned in a flash. I wondered if he was nervous about leaving the two of us alone for too long. As he removed the metal outer wrapping from the neck of the bottle and fiddled with the corkscrew with some difficulty, I told him that I wanted to talk to him about the couple of weeks just after he returned with the children from Spring break. "Mr. Guillory, the old black man who plays chess with the children," I explained looking at Tammee, "is close to Shirley McClaine, and Shirley is feeling kind of low and wants to recharge herself at her ranch home in New Mexico. She is bringing the people closest to her that are her support people to be with her, and Mr. Guillory was invited and he is bringing me along."

I told Richard, "I don't know if you are aware of this, but I've been writing a book. I'm hoping Shirley will know someone who can turn it into a screenplay and maybe even get it made into a movie. I don't know exactly when Mr. Guillory will be leaving, but when he goes I'm going with him. I am afraid it will be right around the time you are returning from St. John's with the kids."

I walked over to his side of the bar where he stood struggling to open the wine bottle with a cheap corkscrew that just wasn't doing the job. He smiled as I gave him this new information about my life. I was enjoying seeming so free and exotic in Tammee's eyes. He shook his head a bit like life never ceased to amaze him, or more accurately, I never ceased to amaze him.

I remember my father telling Richard that there was one thing he could be quite certain of and that was that he would never be bored being married to me. I had had difficulty getting my father to attend the wedding because it was a beautiful day, and he had a tee time. I guess my mother had waited until the last minute to tell him the time and date details of the invitation and he had already made plans. I could imagine what my dad had said when she told him that he couldn't keep his golf date, "A daughter's wedding? OH, Penelope's wedding. Well, that is different. Penelope will understand."

I had to tell mom that she could not attend unless she brought dad with her. I told her I knew it was within her powers to force him to come. She should just do whatever she needed to do to drag him there, or I would embarrass her in front of everyone and tell her to leave.

The wedding cake was never baked by the bakery. I discovered this two hours before the wedding when I called to check on the delivery time. I told them not to worry, just take the display and put it on top of a sheet cake. We'd decorate it all with fresh flowers, and no one would ever know the difference. The manager of the bakery was in a panic. 'Just who was the bride here?' I wondered.

He said, "That's an excellent idea. How did you ever think of that?"

I said, "I grew up in the restaurant catering business, and I have seen my aunt do it before."

One day, I had been standing next to my aunt in her kitchen as she cooked hotdogs for a houseful of kids. She had wiped her brow and stared off in space and said she just had the feeling that she was supposed to do something that day. She told me to finish taking the hotdogs out of the pot for her and handed me the long metal tongs she was using. She walked slowly and with a bit of a limp from sciatica down the long hallway to the back bedrooms of the house to check her calendar, which she kept in her purse.

"OH, MY GOD!" she shouted from the bedroom to the front of the house, where she had about a dozen kids running around literally screaming like wild Indians. "I forgot I have a wedding to cater today."

She was hustling now down the hallway to the kitchen to turn off the burner under the hot dog pot. She turned to me.

"Feed everyone and get Suzanne home, pronto. She's got to baby-sit. I'm taking you with me. I'm going to need your help carrying things."

I didn't have any shoes on. I don't even think I had any shoes with me to put on, no matter. I shoved a hotdog on a bun in the direction of every child there and ran into the front yard to begin looking for her teenaged daughter. I don't know how old Suzanne was, but she must have been under sixteen because she was still living at home. She got married when she was sixteen. She was wearing blue eye shadow that day. I remember being absolutely mesmerized as I watched her artfully apply it using the mirror above her white French provincial dresser that matched her canopy bed.

That same eye shadow was running all down her cheeks when I found her. As soon as I came out of the front door she began screaming. She had for some reason climbed into the tree in her front yard, upset a bee hive, and they were swarming. The next door neighbor hosed her down to get the bees off of her. Mabel, my aunt, was in the bathtub and could hear her screams.

By the time we got Suzanne into the house and gave her benadryl and rubbed her down with Calamine lotion, Mabel, who had been shouting nursing instructions from the back bedroom as she pulled on panty hose over damp legs, came hustling down the hallway searching for her keys in her purse.

"Get in the car," she said to me with a glance over in Suzanne's direction. She asked the neighbor if she could stay for two hours, as she had a crisis and would explain later.

That day I learned how to crisis cater. Mabel pulled together a wedding in a few minutes and arrived with her makeup on and looking as if she was on the ball and hadn't skipped a beat. I've thought of her often as I've pulled together last minute parties and had one hell of a good time doing it too. When trouble arises, JUST DEAL WITH IT! I learned a good survival tool that day.

After leaving Richard and Tammee in their kitchen at their seven million dollar lake home in The Woodlands, I went to see Mr. Guillory sing at the Argentine Grill. I was all excited to tell him that the sex god I had met at the museum had indeed called me on Monday morning. Mr. Guillory had predicted that he would call unless, just as I had wondered, he was married or dead.

"It was so funny," I told Mr. Guillory in the bar as we ordered our food and waited for Jean-Paul the piano player to set up, "When he called me using what he probably thought was a sexy, provocative voice I answered back in a sing song 'Oh, nice to hear from you' voice." He immediately sensed I couldn't talk in the social setting in which he had reached me and asked, "Where ARE you?"

I said, "I'm in church," in a hushed and kind of embarrassed way.

He said, "OH! I'll call you back then."

I told him, "No, no it's fine. I was just leaving." I told Bessy good-bye in Greek, and he could hear the woman kissing me on the cheeks and saying loudly and lovingly in Greek thank you and goodbye. I spoke to him as I walked quickly down the hall telling him I was almost to the courtyard where I would have privacy to speak.

The next time I talk to him I plan to say, "Hey Jack, how is your beanstalk?" But I didn't think of it yet at the time of his phone call. Anyway, he made me feel desirable and talked to me for forty-five minutes. I would say something and he would laugh and then I would say something and he would laugh. It was a great conversation. I told Jack that I had told my buddy Parker about our encounter. He was surprised saying, "I thought you told me you weren't going to tell anyone!" I told him my closest friends all know and want to meet the sex god who bedded me within minutes of meeting me. He seemed pleased with the sex god moniker.

I told him as soon as I had reached the church courtyard, "Whatever it is that you've got, I want more of THAT baby!"

From a guy standpoint, I don't see how the phone call could have possibly gone any better. I told him how I had worried that he might not call, and thank God he had called because he really knew how to treat a woman in bed. Of course, I wanted to see him again.

He had to have left that conversation feeling really good about himself. He said he would call me later in the week. I was psyched. He had explained to me that he had a situation.

I said, "Oh, my God! You ARE married." He emphatically over and over again said, "I AM NOT MARRIED," with great laughter.

I grilled him in a funny way like he was on the witness stand, "Have you been living in recent weeks under the same roof with a woman with whom you are romantically involved?"

He said, "Boy, do you want to come practice law with me? You leave no wriggle room in that one at all!"

I said, "Non-responsive. Have you been living under the same roof with a woman with whom you have been romantically involved?"

He laughed and said, "Yes, but I've been trying to break up with her for months."

I said, "Do you have children with this woman?"

He said, "No, emphatically no."

I said, "Is she carrying your seed at this moment?"

He laughed and said, "No, but whatever happened to no questions asked, just hot sex with a total stranger?"

I told him that that was the other day, this is a new day. I was not looking for a boyfriend and had just written in my book at great length about why I didn't need a boyfriend. I told him he came along and reminded me that I needed a man.

He laughed a very comfortable laugh. I told him I didn't want to go around stealing another woman's man. I didn't want to hurt anyone.

He said, "No, no. It's not like that." He had broken it off; he just couldn't get her to move. I remembered him talking about local property values, and that he was house hunting. We discussed the huge difference in crime rates, and that he could look forward to a burglary per year in his area as opposed to zero crime in my area. Was she house shopping with him or was he moving to get away from her I wondered but did not ask. I would have to assume he was moving to get away from her, if what he was saying was true.

When I relayed this conversation to Pearle he told me that he had had trouble getting away from a woman like that before. He had moved into the high security building, the Four Leaf Towers, for that very reason. He said it can be a very real problem. Anyway, I told the guy that I was writing my book and then going away with Mr. Guillory for a couple of weeks and really wanted him to meet my friends.

"Call me when you have extricated yourself from your situation, and I will be free. I am very happy alone, and I am not going anywhere. I'll be around and unattached. I am not out there looking for someone. I am home writing my book at night and sleeping during the day."

I still thought he would call at the end of the week and was terribly disappointed when he did not. You have to respect people's choices and decisions in matters of sex and bonding with others. I think he truly was attracted, so I was going to try not to feel too rejected. I just wanted round two in the sack as soon as possible.

I told Pearle Wiley that I was ready now for a boyfriend. I had not been before. It takes time to heal. I need more than just sex. I am ready now for someone to be good to me, to share my super yummy life, someone who looks at me and thinks I am the cat's meow, someone to fall head over heels in love with, someone who thinks I am the answer to his prayers, someone who has his life together to the point where he can have that kind of relationship with me.

Two people can have the potential to have a great relationship, but there is luck and timing involved too. Just look at the situation with me and Ulysses, it is March of 2003 and we've been trying to get together for almost three years now. He got all choked up on the phone saying he couldn't believe that a woman would wait for a man the way that I have waited for him. I told Mr. Guillory that depends on what form the waiting takes. I have been intentionally involving myself with men that would never threaten the relationship, so when Ulysses returns I can be available. It is a different waiting than he imagines, I know.

Mr. Guillory told me, "No more confessions. If you tell him about another one it will kill him. It would make me look really bad if you told him about a new man I had not told him about. You need to just be cool." I told him if Ulysses asked me point blank, I would have no choice but to tell him the truth.

Mr. Guillory said, "Oh, don't worry. He'll never ask. He does not want to know, I assure you."

We had a pact of silence about the French-Algerian guy when Mr. Guillory went to Paris to see Ulysses. When he returned from his trip, he greeted me in the hallway of my home and hugged me tightly for a couple of minutes without letting go. Tears ran down his cheeks. I had no idea Mr. Guillory was going to get so emotional about his homecoming. He told me that that was the kind of hug Ulysses, 'Mr. P.' he calls him, the kind of hug Mr. P. had given him.

"He's all alone over there, Penelope. He's so lucky he has us, so he has something to hang onto. He's going to work his way through this, I just know it. It is just going to take time."

We sat in my tiny kitchen nook, and I teased Mr. G. about saying earlier that he was not going to suffer jet lag. He laughed at himself for boasting like that before he left. He explained to me that he was trained in the army to get up at any time and just go and to stay awake for hours and hours. He rationalized that this training would enable him, decades later, to get off the plane in Paris and enjoy the city without wasting a day recovering from the flight like mere mortals such as myself.

I told him, "You just wait. It is going to kick your ass. I drink Nyquil and sleep on the plane, so it is not so bad and it still hits me on day two. I go down for fifteen hours and there is no hope of waking me. It hits Ulysses immediately. He barely makes it off the plane and into the hotel room and he is O-U-T, out."

Mr. G. related his jet lag story and then tried to tell me about a nightclub he had gone to, but I wasn't interested at all in his adventures, only in details about my baby. He said Ulysses had grown a beard, and it looked great on him. He said it was his disguise. He said you wouldn't know him, even his own mother wouldn't know him.

I said I would know him by the way he moved his body. I know every hair on the backs of his fingers. I know the arch of his foot. I would know him by the way he looked at me, that would be the dead give away.

"That it would be, Cherie, that it would be. You are right there."

I said, "When Ulysses looks at me he falls into me like he is falling into a very deep well."

I asked how the clothes fit. I knew the beautiful expensive clothes in his favorite designers would help to lift his spirits after living so poor for so long. I had tried to ship clothes the year before, but whoever was allowing him to use their address had opened my care packages and stolen the clothing.

Mr. Guillory said the clothes fit perfectly, especially the shoes, and Ulysses had been amazed that I knew his size in everything that I sent. He kept saying again and again, 'How did she know?'

When he saw the socks he said, "Socks!?!! Why would she send me so many socks?"

Each sweater had a companion pair of socks that were exquisite and expensive that complemented the sweater. He laughed when he saw I had sent over hand and foot warmers.

He asked, "What does she think, that I am going hunting?"

He had been pleased with the thoughtfulness of everything. Mr. Guillory said, "And then he found, you know, that special item you sent."

I laughed, "What did he say? Did he think I was just nuts?"

"Well, let me tell you exactly how it happened. He was trying on everything in the suitcase and when he tried on the vest he was zipping and unzipping the main zipper and the side pockets - oh he loved everything you sent him."

"I bet it made him feel loved and cared for. That is what I wanted to do was to make him feel loved and cared for, not just that I would help him with money, but that I loved him and thought of him."

"Oh, yes. Believe me he knows you love him. That is what is keeping him alive, Cherie. It is what keeps him from just giving up. He won't go back to his old ways, now. He's got you."

"So, tell me. What did he say? Did he laugh really loud?"

"No, just settle down, and I'll tell you exactly like it happened."

I insisted that Mr. G. act it out. He stood up and pretended to be unzipping his vest and reaching in the pockets to see how they felt. Then, he got a quizzical look on his face and looked down at one pocket without extracting his hand immediately, feeling what was in the pocket with his hand just a second before he pulled it out, looking at his hand intently to see just what was that strange something he had discovered. Mr. G smiled slowly and held the imaginary little black string bikini panties up between the thumbs of each hand, drawing the string wide.

"Mr. P. said, 'The only thing that would be better would be if she were in them.'"

I said, "Did he sniff them?"

"No, no, no not right there in front of me, but I am sure he did later when I wasn't around."

"He said, 'I have just the place for these.'"

"What do you mean 'just the place?'"

"Honey, I don't know. I'm just telling it to you like it happened. He held them up and said he had 'just the place to keep them.' I don't know what he meant."

"Did you tell him about my business idea?"

"No, I figured you could tell him about that."

I pounded him with questions to the point that he couldn't tell me things like he had imagined he would upon his return. At one point he said, "You are just as bad as him, neither of you will let me speak. 'Tell me this, now tell me that.' You don't give me a chance to think of what to say. 'Tell me, tell me, tell me.' I could have told Mr. P. I was sick in the hospital dying, and he would interrupt me and say, 'Did Penelope come to visit you in the hospital? What was she wearing?' He was so mad at me for not being able to remember about your clothes. I did tell him about the American flag dress and that picture you had taken for the newspaper with the Elvis impersonator. The only outfit I could remember was that brown one with matching cowboy boots and vest and the sleeves on the shirt really big with pieces of brown suede sewn all over. He liked hearing about that."

"I have a question for you. Then, I promise I won't interrupt you. What kinds of questions did Ulysses ask you about me?"

"Oh, that is a very good question, a very good question." We sat in my little kitchen nook in hand carved mahogany chairs that Ulysses had never seen, had never yet rested the palm of his hand along the smooth curved lines at the top of the chair backs. I knew that someday, maybe not this year, but someday he would. He would walk through this little room, admire the paint color, remember the oil painting of the bare oak tree standing alone in a north central Texas field, strong and sturdy and ready to bear leaves again in the change of the next season, resting and gaining strength for Spring. He would pause and rest the palm of his hand on the chair and run it slowly along its curve and know he was home.

When Mr. Guillory told me one of the questions Ulysses had asked was, "What color nail polish is she wearing?" I knew that man would find a way home.

Pearle Wiley

I just drove over to Mr. Wiley's office to give him a big hug. I called earlier in the day and his new secretary, Cynthia, told me he was in depositions all day because he had been out of town. He was booked solid with appointments. She told me she had permission to interrupt if I called. He made that very, very clear to her on the first day she began working there.

Just then Pearle came out of his meeting and took the phone. I could hear a muffled "Is that Penelope?" even though he covered the receiver with his hand.

Next, I heard Pearle speak in his very deep, masculine voice, "Penelope, Honey, I'm sorry. I'm in depositions all day. I'll call you when I can break free."

I said quickly, "I just called to tell you that I love you, Pearle."

He made the sweet half laugh half exhalation of breath sound that he frequently makes if he thinks I've said or done something cute and said, "I love you too. I'll call you back."

Later, I called to tell Cynthia that I was headed over. Pearle would have too many calls to return to ever call me back, so I drove to his office after leaving him a voice mail to describe the cute little Escada red leather jacket I was wearing. I told him that since it was a terrible waste to look so great with no one to appreciate it, he should meet me for a drink. When I arrived, the security guard let me in the building, and I went up to the sixth floor.

I will always remember what I was wearing the first time I went to Pearle's office – jeans, a pale blue cashmere v-necked sweater, clogs and a short sheared black mink coat my children call my 'fruit loops' coat because it has circles of brightly colored dyed mink inset in a pattern covering the bottom third of the coat. It is fun. I bought it in Beijing. The photograper, Jan England who I befriended on the trip, was somehow related to the organizer of the tour and came along on business reasons to photograph Beijing's renowned acrobatic team for *Time Magazine*. Jan could bargain in Chinese and was able to get the owners of the fur store to come down on the price by fifteen hundred dollars.

When I returned to Houston, I found a wonderful cape trimmed in colored fur that reminded me of the scarf that Jan wore every day on the trip. It was her favorite scarf, and she said she practically couldn't get dressed without it. It gave her a real artsy flair. I envisioned her entering a similar wintertime relationship with this fabulous cape. I shipped it to her office. It cost fifteen hundred dollars wholesale because my friend in the fur business had paid an arm and a leg for it at the Montreal fur show and couldn't extend anymore of a discount than that.

When Jan called to say she couldn't possibly accept so expensive a gift, I told her, "We are even now. I wouldn't have been able to get the store owner to come down on the price of the coat in China if you hadn't known how to bargain in Mandarin. It's a fair trade. You have to have the cape. It is perfect for you!"

She agreed, "It is absolutely perfect." She said she had never seen anything so wonderful in her life. She said it was difficult for her to accept gifts from people. She was always the one giving them. It was hard for her to even buy anything for herself.

I told her we both had to be good to ourselves that year and give more to ourselves and accept more from others as well. In Beijing, Jan and I had spent two evenings talking about whether or not to divorce our husbands. In her stories about her husband, I could clearly see my relationship with Richard. Jan and I were always giving, giving, giving.

When I entered Pearle's office I could sense the tension hanging in the air. I stopped at the door of the deposition room and could feel the heavy sadness of Pearle's client who had described to a room of strangers blow by blow the tragic unraveling of a marriage. Even without the evidence of the used tissues wadded up and twisted into different shapes laying about the tissue box placed there lovingly by Cynthia, you could sense something very sad had recently happened in that room. Pearle must have been seated across from his client from the placement of his ledger sheets and reading glasses that remained on the conference table. I wanted to bring them to him, but there was writing on the ledger sheets, and I did not want to trample on the privacy between client and counsel that Pearle fiercely protected.

I waited at the glass door until Cynthia and Linda saw me. Pearle's assistants were sprawled on the floor searching through a box of legal documents for a file. When they found it, they looked up, noticed me, smiled and waved me in. Pearle was dictating at his desk, so I leaned against the short half wall that divided off a part of the room which served as a reception area for Pearle's inner office suite. A grander, posh reception area was in the outer offices just inside the heavy mahogany entrance doors where Linda usually manned the phones and greeted the clients. I told them I didn't want to disturb him during his dictation. I would just hang out until he waved me in.

As soon as he noticed me, he smiled and motioned with his index finger that he would be one minute. When he finished, he stood and opened his arms wide for me. I went into the office, and he came around to my side of his huge glass desk. The room was furnished in 1970's 'Jewish Modern' complete with white leather sofa, sleek mahogany Eames style high backed leather chairs and lighted bookshelves filled with memorabilia from clients throughout the years. The walls had framed newspaper articles, tributes to many famous paternity suits and groundbreaking cases. Pearle had created a whole new world of law for other lawyers to navigate.

Women were a bit safer in the world of men because of Pearle. How he absorbed all that pain and didn't bail out and find a new career, as brilliant as he was, mystified me for some time. Over the years I began to understand that he was a big, loving teddy bear. Always the alpha male in the room with a huge muscular chest and broad shoulders to carry the burdens life demanded, a fighter in the ring for the underdog, Pearle enjoyed helping others.

Once, he gave me an engraved paperweight from his memorabilia shelves to keep in my own home. It had been given to him by a heavyweight boxing champion, client and personal friend. Pearle told me that the words carved into it reminded him of me. "A champion is someone who gets up even when they can't." I keep it in my den on the side table next to my brown leather cigar smoking chairs. During my divorce I had done just that, getting up when I couldn't, day after day, sick as a dog. I hid my illness from everyone, including Pearle, because we had not yet established a trust like we have now.

For nineteen days we battled for custody of the boys in that ugly small town courtroom. Until Richard told some horrible lie to the Montgomery County Sheriff's Department, I woke up at five a.m., showered and dressed for court. The security guard drove with me to Richard's house and waited outside while I entered the kitchen and made breakfast for my babies, did homework with them at the dining table and dressed them for school. I had to cautiously stand only in the hallway outside of their room while they stepped into their school clothes.

Richard requested, according to temporary orders decreed by the judges, that I was only allowed to enter the 'service portions' of the household, no bedrooms, living areas or study. Once, Baby Mark, age six, had begged me to spend the night when I had stopped by on my way home from court in the evening to give them all hugs. He told me I could sleep on the towels on the laundry room floor with him and lock the door. He would sleep in there with me he said.

"You are allowed in there, Mommy. It is a service portion of the house."

I cried all the way home. To think that Richard had openly discussed the restraining order with the children to the point that my baby would speak in such legal technical language was too much for me.

Pearle said he has never had a man treat a woman as badly as Richard treated me during the entire divorce process. In large part due to landmark cases won by Pearle, a husband can no longer threaten to harm his wife and children, deny medical care to the children to the point that it endangers their lives or cut off financial support without risking severe repercussions. There are many points to prove to the jury, and Pearle said Richard had done all of it and then some.

I did not want battle. I wanted out. I wanted to feel safe. Then with time, I dared to dream of actual happiness. That is where I am now. I am ready to embrace happiness again.

Pearle came around the desk and gave me a big bear hug. I held him and held him. He told me he loved me, and I told him I loved him. He sat back in his desk chair and said he had twenty-seven messages to return because he had been in depositions and seeing new clients all day after returning from his vacation.

He had to call the airline and check his flight to Vegas, and we smiled with each other while he talked to the airline reservation lady in the most vulgar, provocative way. He somehow got away with acting like that. He has a tremendous charm and a well-earned reputation as a womanizer. I am lucky to know the real Pearle, the soft underbelly of him, or I might misunderstand and despise him. He wishes absolutely no harm with this behavior, no harm to anyone at all.

Once, when he was broken up with Becky, he and I had gone for one of our regular walks in Memorial Park, and he asked my advise about a woman that he was chasing and why she wasn't responding to his advances. I explained to him that a woman couldn't really take his advances seriously because he flirted heavily with EVERYONE, so it didn't seem so special when he flirted with someone that truly held his interest. He thought about it and decided that he wasn't going to flirt anymore. He was going to give it up. I laughed and asked if he was going to give up breathing too because flirting was like breathing to him.

He said, "Just watch. I am not going to flirt anymore."

He broke up and made up with Becky several times during the past three years. I had often wondered why Becky wasn't jealous of me because she was intensely jealous of almost every woman that Pearle came into contact with. Never once had there been a drop of jealously towards me.

She didn't know that during one of their break ups, Pearle had invited me to fly off to Paris to celebrate the finalization of the divorce with an affair. She didn't know that he said I was the only woman as intelligent as his first wife, Laura, who also had an IQ over one hundred seventy. He said I was the only women that he had ever really thought could 'handle him.' What a line!

We truly loved one another. He told me once we could have made it as a couple if only he had been fifteen years younger. After he heard the war stories about my affair with the neighbor, he concluded that he couldn't handle me. He was too old, and I would break his heart.

The truth is we could have made it as a couple except I wasn't emotionally prepared to be with any man at that time in my life. I needed time to heal, to regroup, to remember life without pain. I told him once when he had had a little too much to drink and had told me we should get married, that he just needed to give me two years to heal. I told him he would certainly get back together with Becky by then and the moment would be forgotten, which I am sure it was by morning.

He never made a sexual advance or behaved inappropriately, he was just Pearle. He knew Ulysses had my heart. He told me on the beach in Cancun, when he joined my friend Kit and I for Memorial Day holidays, that he had never seen a love like I had for Ulysses.

One night, Pearle got to observe me in his own words 'in action.' My target was a gorgeous man who I met at a resort hotel. The hotel had a reserved area for guests that had the best rooms. The restricted eighth floor had complimentary bar and enough waitstaff for each guest to have their own waiter. No kidding. It was wild. Kit, Pearle, and I settled in for a little relaxing time and soaked up the atmosphere. We were entertained by this gorgeous man's friend who joined us at our table in front of the fireplace in the V.I.P. area. We had four waiters bringing us drinks from the bar. The friend was a little guy in a Tommy Bahama silk shirt and man, oh, man was he wound up tight! He was anxious for his buddy to hurry and join him because they were going out drinking and dancing.

Mr. Tommy Bahama shirt told us his wife had just left him. His best friend was a workaholic who shocked co-workers by taking the first vacation he had had in years to help him decide what to do with his life. He could either file for divorce or move to Hawaii to live with his wife's folks. The runaway wife had grown up in a tiny village in a remote area of Hawaii, and she missed her home and family. She was unhappy living in the city of Miami all alone with her two year old while her husband worked long hours and neglected her.

He told us he had been a terrible husband. He earned a lot of money, but money didn't mean anything to his wife. She just didn't want to be alone all the time. Now, she was gone. She was threatening to file for divorce if he didn't join her back in her little town in Hawaii.

When his friend joined us at the table Kit said out loud, "OH. MY. GOD."

I think Kit pretty accurately sized things up. Mr. most-gorgeous-man-any-women-has-ever-laid-eyes-on was tall and tan and muscled all over. He wore a tight fitted black t-shirt, a big elegant flowing overshirt and blue jeans.

"Where do men that tall get blue jeans that fit so perfectly?" I wondered among other things that are unprintable here. Let's just say I noticed that his heavy leather designer beach sandals were about a size fourteen.

Little Mr. Tommy Bahama hopped up from the table and headed for the elevator button in a manic frenzy, calling out to his friend, "Come on, come on, I've been waiting on you for twenty minutes!" He pressed the elevator button quickly at least five times. I stood up wearing my little red Armani wrap dress and told the manic man that his friend was going to sit down for a minute and get a neck massage from me first. Pearle's left eyebrow went up.

The big guy looked over at his friend who was now holding the elevator door and swinging his arm in an overly broad way like you would beckon an animal that didn't want to go to the vet into a car. Mr. Gorgeous looked over at me. I pulled the chair out and told him that his friend could wait one minute more, so he could get a wonderful massage.

Pearle devilishly peered over the edge of his martini glass looking from the muscle man to me and back again sipping his vodka and enjoying what was developing. Kit and Pearle were struck silent. The man turned his back on his friend and sat in the chair.

His friend just about jumped out of his skin and shouted, "Oh, man!"

Gorgeous George settled into the chair, and I dug deep with my fingers immediately. He rolled his head back to look up at me and sighed deeply with pleasure. He asked how I knew he needed this. I told him he had been on the plane all day. Of course, he needed this.

His friend threatened to go without him and punched the elevator button with a loud slap of his palm. The doors instantly opened again as the elevator had not yet gone anywhere, and he got in. He held the door and leaned out, calling to us all, "Okay! I'm going now!"

His friend moaned loudly in response to my deep tissue massage and replied in a very disinterested way, "Okay. Have a good time." Then, he looked up at me and said, "My God, where did you learn to touch someone like that? It is like electricity is coming out of your hands."

I told him to just relax and enjoy, I was going to melt him into a puddle on the floor.

"Oh, please," he groaned. Kit said later she got turned on just watching while I did just that. I massaged first his neck, then his shoulders and down his arms and his hands and fingers, then his scalp and face and calves and feet. Finally, I had him lean forward onto the table and did his back and lower back and lower, lower back, then his feet again. He moaned and moaned not caring how it sounded to Kit and Pearle and his friend who eventually returned to our table, after hailing a cab and changing his mind about leaving without his buddy.

A band started playing in the dining area of our V.I.P. floor. The singer was great.

Pearle laughed when he heard the man lean over to me at one point and say, "I promise I will be very good to you."

I told the man that I wanted to go listen to the band.

His buddy nearly flipped out. "That is not fair! I have been waiting forever."

Mr. Gorgeous took my hand and we led the group into the dining area and sat on couches near the dance floor. There he pulled me close to him with his arm around me and started to ask me about myself, my kids, my life in Houston and told me about himself, his education and his work. He asked me to dance. He was a great dancer and knew more dance moves than any man I've ever met. I learned in dance classes that most men only know five dance moves and use them over and over. The band kept changing the style of music from salsa to swing to waltz.

Pearle said we looked great together. Pearle leaned over to Kit and said, "I knew she had been taking dance classes, but I didn't know she could dance like this." Other couples joined the floor and left the floor, but we kept dancing. As we danced, Mr. Gorgeous' friend, Kit and Pearle all negotiated the sleeping arrangements since the hotel was full and that is why Kit and I and the gorgeous man and his friend were sharing rooms.

Pearle offered to let Kit stay with him joking that he would love to share his king-sized bed. The friend said he would just stay out all night. We returned from the dance floor and drank and talked on the couch, oblivious to the negotiations that had taken place while we were gone. Everyone had concluded that this was going to end in the bedroom.

At eleven o'clock, I surprised Kit by looking at my watch and announcing, "Well, it is eleven, and I've been up since five. I'm going to say goodnight to everyone now. Are you ready to go Kit? These guys are going to go out and paint the town red."

I turned and extended my hand to the little manic guy and thanked him for being so patient and allowing me to dance with his friend. The huge guy stood and hugged me and asked if he could join me on the beach the next day, and I said, "Sure, I'd love that."

The next few days we all ate our meals together and had a great time. The wired little guy going through the divorce was still undecided about what to do with his life situation but had calmed down significantly. Pearle hit on every woman in the area, so his appearances and not so mysterious disappearances highlighted our afternoons. Pearle even picked up a little business. He met a River Oaks couple one day at breakfast who were fretting over what to do to help their son who was in a bad marriage separation situation in Dallas.

Ulysses flipped out when he called the hotel the first day, and I wasn't in the original room that the travel agent had assigned to me. On the beach Pearle made the comment about Ulysses and I loving each other the way it was in the movies and like he had never seen before in real life. Mr. Guillory reached me on the hotel phone that morning and told me about Ulysses' anxiety over not knowing where I was. Pearle had joked that Ulysses must be wondering whose hotel room I was in!

I said to Pearle very seriously, "He doesn't worry about that Pearle, not anymore. He is worried because I was so sick before. He is afraid when I travel that I will get sick, and he won't be there to take care of me and get me back to a U.S. hospital. I am his delicate little doll." Pearle said it was beautiful and renewed his faith in love.

He asked if I worried about Ulysses finding someone else and never returning. I told him that if Ulysses was happy then I would be happy and that he felt the same way about me. "Even if I found someone and married, Ulysses would be honored to come to the wedding to see me on the happiest day of my life. It is a different kind of love, Pearle. One where you only want what is best for the other person." Pearle said he was kind of surprised when I didn't go off with that big hunk the night before.

I was incredulous. "Please, Pearle. Don't be silly. I am a lady."

He told me how his first wife Laura had changed over the years. In the beginning sex was something special to her, something sacred. Then, it deteriorated into something just to be enjoyed like having a good meal and then forgotten. He hated to think that his stupidity in satisfying his own ego needs as a young man and neglecting her desire to have a real family life had led that beautiful, perfect woman down that path. He never should have divorced her. She tried everything to save the marriage, and he destroyed it all.

Sometimes Pearle will get a bit drunk and weep silently except for one word, "Laura."

As I've been writing these past few weeks I've been sharing the new chapters with Bridget and Sean who work as the hostess and bartender of La Griglia, an upscale Italian restaurant just a few blocks from my home. I eat lunch there so often that the cook begins preparing my red snapper in white wine sauce and julienned vegetables as soon as he sees me come through the doorway.

I sit at the table by the kitchen entrance where the waiters and manager often stand to survey the restaurant floor. The chef prepares the food in an elaborate open kitchen. Here everyone can talk to me and man their post at the same time. Everyone gives me a hug each day, so I never have an excuse to be hug deprived.

I like to eat when lunch is over, after they've stopped seating guests at two o'clock. I come in at two thirty and can be out of there and back at valet parking in fifteen minutes flat. "It is the best fast food in town," I joke.

I often see a couple of high profile movers and shakers doing the same thing at this hour of the day. One regular customer from the family that developed a nearby coastal area into the tourist attraction that it is today calls ahead on his cell phone to order and is served at the bar near the door, so he only has to take a couple of steps before he sits down and begins eating. The workers have the timing down perfectly, so he doesn't have to wait one second. He often steps through the door conducting business on his cell phone, eats and leaves without ever interrupting his business day. We all have our own space at this hour.

I potty trained this man's oldest daughter, Sophia, years ago when she was a toddler at the Montessori School of Houston.

I taught at the school for a couple of years while I got my Masters degree in education.

I had only worked there a month before Jacob, Sophia's big brother, age five, died tragically in a freak accident. The father was standing on the dock and the mother was standing in the boat with both of them holding onto Jacob by his waist while the father lowered his son into the boat. A speed boat came by going way too fast for the channel and created a wake so violent that it lifted the line and retaining hook free from the docking post high into the air. The hook descended and landed in Jacob's skull cracking it wide open and causing the child's brain to fall into the water.

"It was instant death," both parents kept saying over and over. "He didn't suffer. It was instant death." They both seized upon that one thing about the tragedy to sustain them through the weeks following the funeral. Maurisa, Sophia's mom, once told me that she had learned in grief counseling that most marriages end in divorce after the death of a child because men and women grieve so differently. Women want to talk about the child's death every second of the day and men want to get back to the way things were before as soon as possible. This will often anger the wife because it seems to her an insult to the memory of the child. The husband wants to put away photos and live without any painful memory that the child ever existed.

The wife becomes the cause of tremendous pain as she reaches out to him to unload, unload, unload her heavy burden. Anger storms around inside the wife because the person who should be able to share her grief withdraws, not there for her.

"Most marriages end within the first year, eighty percent. Almost all others end within a year of that," she announced to me one day when she dropped Sophia off at school. I wondered if that was true. It seemed so awful.

When I first saw Ralph at the bar wolfing down his food and talking angrily with his business partner on the phone about a clause in the contract for their latest business enterprise, a seafood restaurant, I thought that he seemed stuck in his grief still after all of these years. After Jacob's death, he dealt with his grief by working, working, working. A moment of rest would be rewarded by a flood of grief rushing in to fill any small space of time not occupied by work. I wonder how many empires have been built by grief.

I didn't mention his deceased son, Jacob, when I approached him and reminded him that I had been Sophia's teacher years ago.

He surprised me by asking, "Did you know Jacob?" I said yes, that I didn't know how he would respond to me saying Jacob's name so I had not mentioned him to avoid causing him any undue pain. He waved his hand and said, "No, no, no that is fine. Jacob was a wonderful child."

I asked about Sophia. She was still having trouble even as a young adult all stemming back to Jacob's death and the subsequent divorce of her parents. She was in college now but currently upset with her dad for buying her a car that was black instead of allowing her to come with him and chose the color car she wanted.

"I was too busy," he explained, "I didn't have time to spend half a day picking out a car. She should just be grateful that we are financially able to provide her with a brand new car."

He shook his head in disbelief and said his parents had not been able to help him like that. He would have loved it if his dad had bought him a brand new car no matter what the color. He said he worried about what would happen to Sophia with the next stage of her life. She would soon be finishing college.

I offered that she could live in my garage apartment, and I could keep an eye on her and offer her my support. I had done that for the newlywed daughter of a friend. The young woman was married to a marine stationed in Japan.

"Sophia may remember me from her childhood," I told him, " I certainly remember her. Did you know that she potty trained herself the day of Jacob's funeral? She said Jacob told her she had to be a big girl now. She talked to Jacob as if he was still alive for weeks after he died, carrying on conversations so real that it gave us all goose bumps. It was enough to make us believe in ghosts. One day Sophia said Jacob had to go, and she never played with his ghost again."

It was the first Ralph had heard of Sophia's behavior in the days following Jacob's death. What a thing to deal with, my God, I thought. I can't even begin to imagine that level of pain.

The bartender listened to part of the conversation and then moved to give us privacy. Later, he said, "I didn't know you knew Mr. Fortuno. I explained I had been his daughter's teacher.

"For a big city it is a small town," he noted, "especially around here."

One afternoon, I was seated at my usual table with Bridget, the hostess, after all the customers had gone and the manager came over and told me about the Tomassi wine tasting dinner coming up. They didn't know the exact time that the event would take place, but they had just gotten the date from the vintner, Tuesday, March fifth. He wanted to know if I would be interested in attending the event.

It was January and I was still living with the French-Algerian guy, so I felt certain I would have a date and said, "Sure." I was the first name on the list and the first to pay.

This is precisely what irked me the most when the event rolled around. It was March fifth. I had called earlier in the day and found out that the event was to be held at Tony Vallone's finest restaurant, Tony's, and would begin at six thirty with seating for dinner at seven thirty.

I no longer had a date even though I had called Pearle once each week since I broke off with the French-Algerian guy to invite him and kept getting excuses, 'too much work,' 'might be out of town,' 'I'll get back with you.' Wendi thought she might be able to go but then went out of town with Michael on an eye surgery outreach mission to Mexico. When I went to pick up Nicole, she was standing in Tessa's garage doing laundry. I told her, "Don't worry Nicole, you can just borrow something from my closet. I am sure I can put together a cute outfit for you."

Nicole had agreed to go but then the day of the event forgot and told Tessa that she would baby-sit that night.

I called Pearle again since he works just down the street from Tony's. I hoped that maybe I would luck out, and he'd be able to swing by and meet me there.

That is when he finally told me that he could not go with me because he was already going and had a date.

He told me, "I have to inform you that your mortal enemy will be there."

"I have no enemies that I can think of," I told him, "Do you mean my mother or Terry, my sister, will be there?"

"No," he said, "your enemy, Becky Bugle."

"She is not my enemy," I said.

Pearle tried to explain Becky's emotional state but it didn't make any sense to me. For some reason, she decided that I am her enemy. I don't know why since all I did was sue someone who had injured her. I brought the suit forward at Becky's request. I ended up footing the bill for one hundred and fifty thousand dollars worth of legal bills that would never be reimbursed by her employer's insurance company. Then, Becky cancelled the birthday party she was throwing for me because she was embarrassed about what was discovered during the depositions.

I had never gone around bad mouthing her like almost anyone else on the planet would have done. I had just discovered the truth along with everyone else in that room that afternoon. The only difference was that I got stuck with the bill.

"So, is this the reason you have been avoiding telling me if you could go with me to the wine tasting dinner all these past weeks? You knew you were going with her?"

"No, I didn't realize you wanted me to go to this. I just accepted the invitation the other day. I was offered some comp tickets as a gift. This was very last minute for me. You wanted me to go with you to this?"

"I've asked you at least five times in the past six weeks because I knew I didn't have a date, and it was a very posh event at your favorite place. I thought you would love to go. I was going with Shelia but she forgot, and I'm all dressed up in this wonderful custom Zang Toi designer outfit from that Malaysian designer from NYC and now I have no date. I am going to look ridiculous seated all alone at a table for two.

I feel like I've been run off from my own event because Becky is NOT a lady when she has had too much to drink and you know it. She cannot be trusted to not come over to me and create a public scene once she gets a few glasses of wine in her. I'll be seated alone, the only one in the restaurant seated alone for the event, and look like a social pariah. Great! And what really irks me is that I was the first person in the city invited and the first to pay. Now, I get run off from the event because Becky does not know how to act.

Tony has requested that you never bring Becky back into his restaurant again because of the way she has acted in the past. Doesn't it insult him to bring her after she's been kicked out, especially on a comp ticket? I was going to go alone. I figured I would attract a lot of attention being dressed so cute and being alone, and I was going to just ask to sit with the vintner. Now, I cannot go. I am all dressed up and in the car driving there, and I am going to turn my car around."

"I am really sorry, Penelope."

"It is wrong and you know it, Pearle. All I can say is that I can be depended on to behave like a lady, and she can be depended on to not be a lady. I should not be run off from my own event. I am going to see if Wendi's mom can go with me. Wendi's mom is a class act and can handle any social situation that Becky might create. I just want to tell you one thing, I can be depended on to be a loyal friend and I am ending this conversation now."

I closed my cell phone and drove to Wendi's calling first Taylor and then Parker as I drove. Wendi's child opened the door and let me know grandma was upstairs asleep.

There were many cars parked in front of Taylor's house and a note hanging on his front door, 'We are in session, please return at nine o'clock.' All I could do was stomp my foot for no one to hear and mutter, "This is unbelievable," under my breath.

I caught my friend Parker at home when I phoned again. He said he was dressed in his sweats and on the way out the door to go jogging, but he'd bail me out. He'd jump in the shower and would leave the door open for me to wait in his living room.

We discussed the situation very animatedly all the way there with frequent use of the word, BITCH!

Parker and I looked like we had coordinated our outfits. He wore a navy blue blazer over a red turtleneck, I wore Zang Toi's navy satin pants with matching navy satin over-blouse with white star cut outs edged in sparkles. The little under bustier had spaghetti straps and also had sparkly star cut outs.

I bought five outfits from Zang Toi at a trunk show at Joseph's in Houston and spent eighty-five thousand dollars in fifteen minutes. I told them I had no time to stay for my credit card and left the card there. The security guard would pick everything up when it was ready. Jonathan said he had the guard's cell phone number from last time and would safeguard my credit card for me personally. When delivery was made absolutely everything was perfect.

Zang called to check with me and gave me his cell phone number. What a professional man. My friend who used to work as a stylist for movie stars in Beverly Hills said he saw an Arts and Entertainment special about Zang Toi touting him as the new Armani, one of the next big name designers to come on the scene. All I can say is that he truly has his act together.

I just recently threw clothes out the window and onto the dirt in front of the shop of a local designer. I had gone to pick up the clothes countless times, each time being told on the phone by her assistant that they were ready only to arrive to find they weren't ready at all. Or, the clothes were ready but not what I had ordered or had a zipper that would not zip or had not been hemmed, et cetera. Don't call and tell me something is ready when it is not. It is a pain in the ass to make all those unnecessary trips.

I had accepted delivery in mid-February for Fall season clothes I had ordered and paid for in early September, that in itself is disgusting. Then, when I put the outfit on to go pick up my kids at school, the maid stopped me from going out the door because the back of the pant was sewn so poorly that she even noticed, a woman from the jungles of El Salvador who grew up in a cardboard lean-to shack. She noticed the clothing was unacceptable. How had it escaped the notice of the designer?

I called the designer's showroom and spoke to her assistant saying I was late to pick up the kids at school but was going to swing by to drop off the clothes and was now making the turn onto her street. She said she could step to the front door and get the clothes from me. I did not have time to get out of the car. I told her I had just bought summer shoes for goodness sakes, her employer already had her spring line hanging on her store racks and this was a despicable way to run a business. When I pulled up she was not at the door waiting for me as promised, so I just threw the outfit onto the dirt.

I called later to say, "Cough up the clothes or cough up the cash."

Anyway, at the Tomassi wine dinner, I was wearing my perfect, carefree Zang Toi outfit and had Parker on my elbow. Pearle was already standing in the bar and flirting heavily with two women. He smiled broadly, and I noted the surprise on his face that I had dug up a date so quickly. I introduced Parker. Pearle kissed my cheek warmly. I gave him a quick hug. Parker and I walked to the far end of the room so I wouldn't be standing near Pearle when Becky Bugle came in the room.

I had checked with the hostess when we arrived to see where I was seated explaining that I was involved in a law suit with another one of the guests and wanted to make sure I had not been placed at a nearby table. We scanned the seating chart and found my name at table twenty-one. Pearle was placed at the back of the room far from me, she assured. Good. That little situation addressed, I felt more relaxed.

"Good thinking," said Parker.

The wine was delicious. I had been told that this was Tony's best wine event of the year. The people at our table were a delight. It turned out I would not have been seated at an isolated table for two if I had come alone. The restaurant was at capacity with only large rounds in use, seating six or ten at each.

Two women seated at the table with me had come together. One was the owner of a retail store near my home and the other an attorney who had recently worked on a case with Pearle. Also at the table was an internal medicine doctor and his Irish-Puerto Rican wife who had been the oldest of nine children. Our table had a blast. Everyone told stories and laughed. I invited them all to my upcoming party on Tuesday March eighteenth. I told them the invitation read, 'A celebration of twenty-five years of music, Jean-Paul pianist, Musicians and Freaks only, casual attire.' I had a party each month, I explained. Each party was different from the next.

The Tomassi wine dinner was a kick ass time. Becky was absolutely nowhere in sight. From my table I could see the entire room. Parker at one point leaned over and asked me, "So where is that bitch realtor who pretended to be your friend and cost you a hundred and fifty grand?" An entire glass of ice water suddenly landed on Parker's head splashing down around his shoulders. I handed him my napkin. Tony's waiters were there in a flash with more napkins and then faded into the woodwork just as quickly. No scene was made attempting to clean him. The waiters just rushed forward and then receded. The others at our table didn't even notice.

I could see the back of Becky's smart dark suit jacket and long brown hair highlighted with golden highlights as she headed to the ladies room. I looked over at Pearle, and he was involved in a conversation with a man to his left. He could sense me looking at him and got up and came over and gave me a kiss on my forehead. He noticed the attorney seated with me and made her promise not to tell me any bad stories about him. Then, he sat down again at his table.

"Well," chuckled Parker. "I guess now we know where she is sitting."

He turned and looked behind him warily, "Jesus, they couldn't have seated her any closer if they had tried."

We didn't see her because her chair back was right up against my chair back facing in the opposite direction. She sat at Pearle's right with Pearle at the head of an extremely long table. When I eventually got up to go to the bathroom and returned I could see her clearly.

She had her arms crossed in front of her angrily, moping. Pearle was dynamic and expansive, charming the guests with a story in his deep booming voice. I could see all of her glasses were still placed in front of her, eight in all, for the wine tasting. Everyone else had only two glasses remaining. Pearle had brought her to a wine tasting and not allowed her to drink. Amazing.

On the way home, Parker thanked me saying he had had one hell of a good time and asked me if he could bring about four friends to my party on Tuesday.

"Sure," I said.

I wanted to meet the gal that he was renewing a romantic affair with after twenty-four years. I hope Parker and this gal, Joanne, make it as a couple. He is too sweet to be alone.

9

Gucci Leather

I do not know what has happened to my sleeping patterns. I woke up before dawn with a sore throat and took Nyquil thinking I'd sleep in until ten in the morning or so and go for a walk. I woke up at 3:45 p.m.! How on earth did I do that? It was a gorgeous day outside too, and most of it I had missed. I showered and put on my Adidas running shorts and was heading out the door when I got a call from Greg, my cousin Carrie's husband.

When I was going through my separation from Richard, Greg and Carrie had borrowed seven thousand dollars from me and never repaid it. I had asked them several times. It did not stop me from being generous to their daughter, Elizabeth, and last summer when I discovered she was not practicing driving because she was so afraid of being killed in a car crash like her half sister, Greg's daughter, I gave Greg twenty-five thousand dollars to help him buy a car that was safe for Elizabeth.

I wanted her to develop normally and not fearfully. Every teenager looks forward to learning how to drive and the autonomy that driving brings. The family did not need any more human pets like my youngest sister, Terry Jo, who at age twenty-eight still lived at home without a job, convinced by my mother that she couldn't even hold down part-time employment.

Terry Jo's main function was to accompany my mother to lunch and to not have any sort of life in case she was needed in that capacity. I remember once when Terry was a teenager, I was living at home for six weeks as an adult and got a chance to see the family dynamics as they had evolved during my absence of nine years. My sister got a phone call one weekend afternoon from another teen down the street, a normal young woman who had left home at the age appropriate time of eighteen upon her high school graduation. Terry's friend was sharing an apartment with two other girls to make ends meet and working as a waitress somewhere to help pay her college expenses. My sister, on the other hand, had not gone on to college, even though she had very high SAT scores and unlike that same period in my life, my parents had more than adequate funds to send her on to the university of her choice. She lived at home and did not work.

My mother was in bed with a 'spell' and was moaning as she handed my sister the phone. She made it clear that the agony of even such a small movement was overwhelming for her. Her voice was weak and shaky as she asked my sister to 'keep the call short' because mom was not well. Terry was very excited to hear from her friend who grew up just down the street from her and was home on the weekend to visit with old high school buddies. Terry was invited to the dollar movies with the old gang. She asked Norma if she could go.

My mother laid such a guilt trip on that young woman it was obscene. She said she would 'honor any decision' Terry made using overly formal language, but Norma felt it was wrong of Terry to leave her all alone, alluding to her 'spell.'

I took the phone from Terry and told Terry Jo's friend Barbara that Terry was on her way over and hung up the phone. Terry then insisted that she wanted to stay with mother.

I told her, "NO way. It wasn't normal." Besides, I was there in case mom needed help. Mom moaned just then very, very loudly. Terry pushed past me and picked up the phone and called Barbara and cancelled. It wasn't long before Terry quit receiving calls from her old friends, and she didn't develop new relationships. Her world became the small closed circle of Norma and Norma's needs.

A few minutes after Terry had cancelled her outing with Barbara the phone rang again, and Norma answered it in a very weak, sickly voice. It was dad. He could meet her for a cup of coffee at the Barbecue Inn, a restaurant they frequented. Mom's voice gained strength as she cheerfully accepted his invitation and threw back the covers, swinging her legs over the edge of the bed and reaching for her clothes on the back of the desk chair. Terry and I looked at one another, marveling at the miraculous recovery we were witnessing. Mom hung up the phone and ran to the makeup mirror where she began to apply her bright red lipstick.

"You sure seem to be feeling better," I accused her.

"Yes, I think all I needed to do was lie down and rest a few minutes."

"So, I guess Terry can go to the movies now." Mom thought just a second and agreed.

Terry called her friend but was disappointed to discover that the teenagers had already left for the movies. She asked mom if she could go with her to the Barbecue Inn since she was hungry and there was no food in the house. Mom was brushing her long red hair now with the expensive boar bristle hairbrush that only she was allowed to use. She said without pause, "No, I want to be alone with your father." She was out the door within a minute and a half of dad's call.

Terry began to cry. I pointed out to Terry that Lauren and I had left home early for good reason. Mom was not normal and she had better get signed up for college classes and get out of there. Twelve years later she was still at home.

When Terry showed up in court along with Norma to take the witness stand and testify that I was a terrible mother instead of telling the truth that I was a wonderful mother, I was not at all surprised. I had taken care of Terry until I left home at age sixteen, and she was indeed abandoned by me to a situation of neglect.

After the situation at home, taking care of only myself was such a tremendous relief. I remember my first meal in freedom, a peanut butter sandwich on white bread with a glass of milk. It tasted so good. I didn't have to care for a baby, an insane grandmother, a delusional great aunt, a hateful little eleven year old sister who thought meals just fell prepared from the sky, and a needy, whining mother. I made one sandwich, only one, and it was delicious.

Anyway, I was worried about the human pet family pattern repeating with Elizabeth when one day I got a desperate call from my cousin Carrie telling me she was eating alone at a restaurant off I-10 called Ciro's and wanted me to join her. She was pleased that I wasn't doing anything and could drive straight over.

When I arrived she was agitated. She said she was soooo happy I could join her because she had been sitting there all alone for twenty-five minutes. She felt like everyone was staring at her, and she didn't know what to do with herself while she waited for me to drive to the restaurant. Thank God she was friends with the owner and manager and could talk to them some while she waited.

I told her I was surprised she would feel so uncomfortable since her mother, my Aunt Mabel, had owned Teddy's Steakhouse, and she grew up in the restaurant business. I remember sitting on the bar at Teddy's Steakhouse with Carrie holding a funnel while she poured liquor into the liquor bottles mixing name brand and off brand liquors for the second shelf liquor that would be served to customers after they had had so many drinks that they couldn't tell the difference anyway. Now, I know from my Greek boyfriend, Ulysses that this is highly illegal. Carrie and I were childhood criminals, and we didn't even know it.

My aunt also used to take the bread leftover from the bread baskets cleared from customers' tables and place it into the bottom of baskets for the next customers seated just placing three fresh, untouched rolls on top. Four rolls were repeatedly used again and again. At the end of the night all the unused bread was then turned into croutons. Teddy's had the best croutons in town.

My aunt is going to be upset when she reads this, but she also knows she's getting off lightly. She'd better not complain too much because I've enjoyed writing this book and there will certainly be a book two, in which I might be far more forthcoming.

My aunt and uncle are very colorful characters. My uncle once shot one of his customers in the parking lot. I was too young to be privy to the details, but the consensus was that it was the right thing to do.

That was in the days before you had to have a grand jury if someone died. The police sort of showed up and asked people what happened and if the story was good all around they just dragged off the body and called it a day. You could kill nearly anyone with the right set of witnesses.

My aunt and uncle also had to once rouse a pack of fifteen or so gypsies out of a rent house. They loved to buy little houses in the poorer section of the city, fix them up and rent them out. At one point they owned two whole blocks of houses and had them fixed up like little dollhouses. They hardly made any money at all from the rentals because they got such a kick from fixing them up and put far too much money into the homes to ever really make much of a profit. It was a fun hobby for my uncle, who loved to build things. The homes were his joy.

He got a call one day from one of the renters that one of the houses seemed to have a lot of people living there, more than a dozen. They were loud and coming and going at all times of the day and night. My uncle had rented the home to a married man and wife with no children.

Uncle Gerald went over to investigate and was greeted at the door by a stranger who told him to take a flying leap. He wasn't moving no matter what the lease said. My uncle could just take them to court.

What this gypsy didn't know but was about to find out was some people in this world don't play nicey nice and take others to court. My uncle had seen inside the home. His baby, his pride and joy had been stripped of all its beautiful light fixtures and they had put up red flocked wallpaper in the entryway – RED FLOCKED WALLPAPER!

My uncle knocked on the door and the nasty man opened it again and laughed at him saying, "Oh, YOU. You are still here. I thought I told you to bug off!"

My uncle told him he had one minute to clear everyone out of the house, or he wouldn't be held responsible for what might happen to them. They were there on his property illegally and were trespassing.

The man said, "Yeah, yeah right. I'll see you in court, asshole."

My uncle has this sawed off shot gun that he took off of a would be thief who once entered the restaurant and tried to hold up my cousin Carrie at the cash register. As the man held the shot gun level at my ten year old cousin's head, my uncle came out of his office and in one punch knocked the guy out. The holdup man went flying up off the ground and landed in the little fish pond by the front door. My uncle ordered Cleo the cook to drag the man by his feet out the back door and put him in the trash dumpster.

My uncle loved that sawed off shot gun. I could write a whole book just about my uncle's adventures with his sawed off. The gun itself is illegal. Let me remind the reader at this point that this book is entirely fiction. Anyway, my uncle just walked back to his car and got his sawed off, I can't remember what he had named the gun, but it had a woman's name like Lucy or something. I'll have to ask my cousin next time I see her.

He got his sawed off and stood in the front lawn and started firing blasts through the front of that little wooden house. He'd chamber and fire and take a step to the right, chamber and fire and take another step to the right until the entire house was cut into two pieces by the blasts. More than a dozen people came flying out of that house like crazy. Then, my uncle burned the rent house down.

"Sometimes that is the only way to get rid of vermin," he explained later.

Needless to say, from then on all the other renters up and down those two blocks paid rent on time.

Anyway, when I arrived at the restaurant my cousin said she was relieved that I was there. She didn't see how I could eat often in restaurants alone. She had never eaten a meal in her life alone, not a meal at home and not a meal in a restaurant.

I couldn't believe it. That was simply incredible to me. "Carrie, how old are you?" I asked. "You mean you are middle aged, your daughter is going off to college next year and you've never eaten alone?"

After meeting Carrie for lunch that day, I gave Greg money to get their daughter a safe car and gave Elizabeth a lecture about becoming independent.

My dad's brother, Uncle Gary, lived his entire life taking care of his mother. He had almost married at a normal age, but his mother had disapproved and had stopped the marriage and Gary never had another girlfriend, spending all of his free time running errands for his mother and driving her to church. He had no life.

When his mother died he asked my good sister, Lauren, what he was supposed to do with his time after he settled all of her affairs and closed the house. He had never lived his own life. She had dictated every moment of it to him. He was in his late sixties before he ever had his peanut butter sandwich point of epiphany.

Greg, Carrie's husband, came over tonight to talk to me about his finances. I had to tell him I wasn't willing to loan him any money. Mr. Guillory stopped by and said he thought I had handled everything very well.

He said Greg had 'left happier than a faggot in the army' despite the fact that I had turned him down. I had even told Greg that I was having a party Tuesday, and that he and Carrie were not invited even though their friends Mike and Tina were coming. I was going to try to seduce a new man and I would feel uncomfortable with them watching because I was going to throw myself at this guy, and I would feel embarrassed with them witnessing my slutty behavior.

I told Greg that my neighbor who was a financial advisor could give him advice. Greg would then have a plan, a way out of the situation and that in itself would relieve some of the stress. Derek did this for a living and would consider it an interesting puzzle and then

Greg and Carrie would have privacy and not have to be embarrassed to have their problems laid bare for me to see.

I told Greg that Derek once had two hundred financial experts working under him. He worked for the White House and had advised three different Presidents.

He had helped with his own parents' situation when his father found himself laid off unexpectedly and unable to find work during an economic downturn because the owner of a privately held midsized company decided to retire and close the company. Derek's father was without adequate retirement savings and was too old for most companies to consider hiring. So, Derek put together a plan for the employees to buy out the company and keep it running. Derek's dad became president and major stockholder and things ended very well.

I had already told Derek about my unrepaid loan to Greg and Carrie, and he agreed that he would have done the same thing under the circumstances. They were hit hard by Greg's illness that nearly killed him the year before and found out the hard way that Carrie couldn't bring in any sales at all. Greg and Carrie had always thought that if Greg ever died that Carrie would just keep the shop running. Now, they knew that they needed a different long-term plan for the future for Carrie and Elizabeth, which was better than not knowing even though the facts were unpleasant.

I explained to Greg that I had loaned money to people that I loved and trusted for various reasons, good ones. None of the people could pay me back. I told him that the biggest loan was to a friend who had suffered from brain cancer, and that I had called him and left a message that I couldn't remember if he was supposed to repay me this January or the next which was a lie. I knew that the man was supposed to pay me back this January but by saying it that way it gave the man an extra year extension and allowed him to save face.

He was a good man and could be trusted to repay me if he had the ability and the fact that he didn't return my calls meant that he must be going through some major crisis in his life. He and his wife didn't need to be pestered for repayment of loans. I just hoped that things got better for him. I explained to Greg that my money manager had told me to live my life as if I would never be repaid and simply not loan any more money. Greg didn't get a loan from me but didn't seem upset.

After Greg left empty handed, I asked Mr. Guillory to sit on the couch and let me read aloud to him from my book. I read the chapter about meeting Ray Calhoun. I said that I had discussed Ray with my friend Taylor and Taylor had begged me, "Please, Penelope, no more stray kittens. Find someone happy who has his life together."

I told Mr. Guillory that Ray had so much need that I thought I could give him all of my energy until I expired and it would still not be enough.

I said, "Remember how Ulysses used to be in the beginning? He just had to be near me to feel better. I don't know if I have enough to give to heal this man. ALL I have may not be enough."

I had once become angry with Ulysses, telling him I wanted to be someone's girlfriend, not their drug. Now, I was considering walking into a similar situation with open eyes, knowing just what sort of a challenge I faced. I told Mr. Guillory I just couldn't stand seeing such a beautiful person in so much emotional pain. I thought it over and decided to throw a party and invite Calhoun.

"What if he comes with a girlfriend?" I worried.

Mr. Guillory laughed and said, "I doubt it."

I told Mr. G. that if Calhoun did not come with a girlfriend, I was going to put my arm around him at the front door and ask him to be my date for the evening and give him loads and loads of touch all evening to make him feel better.

Mr. Guillory is always on the alert for any man on the horizon who might topple Ulysses from his position as the man in my life. Kit warned me that Mr. Guillory might have Ulysses' interest in mind and try to sabotage me if he saw Calhoun as any kind of a threat. Kit recommended that I not invite Mr. Guillory for that reason. I explained to her that Mr. Guillory was responsible for the entire party, the guest list and the band. He told me tonight to expect fifty people. He hired a five piece band. He couldn't get the band I usually get, Lou Holtz's three piece band.

"Five piece, that gets more expensive," I explained to Mr. G.

He said, "Okay, I'll tell them only three pieces."

I said, "No, don't do that, tell them all to come. It is just more expensive that is all."

I have no idea who is coming to my party or how many to expect. Mr. Guillory's fifty can sometimes become two hundred.

I'm going to tell Calhoun, "Thank God you are here, now I know someone at my own party," and lead him into the kitchen and ask for his help with the red beans and rice.

Of course, my fantasies are all shot to hell if he shows up with a date. He has had weeks to think about me, if he has given me any thought at all. If he has been thinking of me, I'll know it when I see him. I told his best friend I had a crush on him for goodness sakes.

In addition to that, I called Robert Newhouse and told him that Calhoun made my heart race and my knees weak and even if the feelings were not reciprocated at least now I knew that it was possible for me to feel that way. I had thought previously that that part of me had died a long time ago, I explained to Robert. My voice was shaking on the phone when I told him. I hadn't expected to get all shaken up like that when I talked about Calhoun. Robert's voice was very serious, and he said he wasn't one of Calhoun's main core friends. He was pretty close to Ray Malloy and would pass the message on to Ray and let Ray tell Calhoun.

I told Robert that Ray had asked me out, and I had turned him down. So, I wasn't so sure if the message would get passed. He said he thought it would. Ray had been with Sharon about five weeks now, if he had ever felt slighted he was sure enough time had passed that there would be no ill will.

Ted called Ray Malloy and extended the party invitation and Ray had said both Rays were coming. I had invitations printed without my phone number, so I handwrote my cell number on two invitations and gave them to Ted to give to the two Rays. Now, Calhoun had my phone number.

This reminds me of the expression, you can bring a horse to water, but you can't make it drink. What if he just wrote me off as too young and some other woman had been with him for weeks, and I didn't even know about it? I am going to go absolutely cuckoo by tomorrow night.

Tomorrow, I have a Greek lesson at 9:30 a.m., and then I have to go to the liquor store. After that, I have to make red beans and rice. Tony Mandenelli's is catering. I've never used them before, but I am a regular at their restaurant. The bartender, Lisa, is my massage therapist.

Jesus, the other regular bartender, almost punched out my neighbor one time when we were seated at the bar. I turned down my neighbor's marriage proposal, and in retaliation he made a nasty comment about my weight. Jesus stood on the other side of the bar with his fist doubled up raising his chin quickly, twice with raised eyebrows, indicating to me that all I had to do was signal, and he'd pop him one.

Later, when Jesus and I were laughing about it, I told him, "You just can't go around hitting customers; you will get fired."

He said, "No, I'd just pop him one real fast and tell the manager he was drunk and fell off his barstool. I wouldn't get into any trouble."

Jesus is friends and gambling buddies with Ulysses' uncle. I had gone into the bar at Tony Mandenelli's and gotten rip roaring drunk after I started the affair with the neighbor. Ulysses had called the next day to say he was wrong for speaking to me that way, and that he took it all back. He wanted me to wait for him. I shouldn't be with another man if I wanted to wait for him.

OOPS! Jesus was my bartender the evening of my regretful confessing. Jesus got me loaded and told me I shouldn't tell Ulysses what I had done, and just keep it secret. He wouldn't tell and neither should I.

Vanessa was with me, and she got loaded too. We both kissed a waiter. Evidently we grabbed him by his necktie and both really laid one on him. Big kisses, holding nothing back. With tongue! Augh!

A week later Vanessa, her boyfriend and I all returned to the restaurant and the hostess remarked she was going to seat us at our favorite waiter's table. She seated us at a table with a waiter I had never seen before in my life. I even told him so.

He said, "If that is the story, I will stick to it."

Vanessa and I both commented that the behavior of the waiter and the hostess seemed a bit odd. We asked the hostess why she thought this waiter was our favorite and she related the kissing incident.

"Oh, they are playing a joke on us," I told Vanessa. "I would never kiss a waiter." Vanessa said she wouldn't either. How ridiculous. We looked over the menus, and the waiter arrived to take our orders. I told him that they couldn't fool us with their joke, so they could just stop it. Neither of us would ever kiss a waiter.

The waiter blushed. Deep red splotches appeared on his cheeks, his neck and his ears. Vanessa and I both looked at each other wide eyed and open mouthed.

"Oh, my god! Penelope, we really did kiss him! Look at how he is blushing! No one could fake a blush like that."

"Was it a really bad kiss?" I asked, apologizing. He said he had not been kissed like that in four and a half years. He was a married man. We had grabbed him by the necktie, and he couldn't get away.

When I related the story to my florist friend, Bob Walker, he said he once had had a similar experience drinking that same drink, the lemon drop martini. He was working in Beverly Hills, and it was back in the days when he hobnobbed with the 'in crowd' of fashion designers, organizing fashion shows and dressing movie stars.

He had started drinking lemon drop martinis at lunch. That day he drove a Rolls Royce and was wearing a Bill Blass tuxedo. He could not remember ever leaving the restaurant, but the rolls was found crashed into a palm tree on a major boulevard and Bob had had a fist fight with a police officer and ended up in jail. When he woke up, he was leaning against the corner of the cell of the drunk tank, and his tuxedo looked like someone had taken a box cutting tool and shredded it into two inch wide strips. For all he knew that was exactly what had happened. He had no recollection of any of the events of the day. That was the last time Bob took a drink. No, he didn't think he was an alcoholic, but the incident was a wake up call and he never drank again.

The staff from Tony Mandenelli's should be pretty good. I invited Lisa to stop by after work and bring her boyfriend if she wants. She said she wants to see my house. I told her the party would be super casual, and she could come directly from work. I ran into the president of the blues association, Eduina Greenleaf, and told her she could come. I met a couple at the Argentine Grill who were listening to Mr. Guillory sing, and I invited them.

The party was supposed to be for Jean Paul the pianist who allows Mr. Guillory to sing on Thursday nights when he plays at the Argentine Grill. Jean Paul has played piano in Houston for twenty-five years. I told him that was something to celebrate. I'd invite twenty people and he could invite twenty people, and we would have a party next Tuesday.

A couple of days later, Jean Paul called me and told me he had suffered a tragedy of horrendous proportions and was not up to a party and would not be attending or inviting his twenty guests. I told him, if he did not mind, the party would go on. If he felt like stepping out on Tuesday, he should come on over and enjoy the party. Maybe we would be able to cheer him up.

Today at the Memorial Park track, Mike ran past, and I stopped him to invite him and his wife Tina to the party. I dropped five invitations off with Roland Dvorsak, the man who sold me my baby grand piano. I had taken him and his wife to the Stones concert the week after his aunt died. He was very close to his aunt and she had raised him, so it was like having his mother die. I had only recently met him, and it made me feel really good to be able to help him through the week to give him something to look forward to.

Parker is coming and bringing four friends. Kit is coming. Taylor might come after group therapy is over, but that will be later in the evening. I told him I hoped he was getting his money's worth out of the group therapy or at least some good sales contacts to sell art. He said he didn't feel that he was until the other night he had had a real break through, a real blubberfest crying and crying over something that he thought he had resolved a long time ago but evidently he was still hanging onto it. Therapy - how exhausting. I would rather dance.

The party is tomorrow. I've told everyone that I hope my big crush Ray Calhoun doesn't show up with a date, or I will be devastated.

Mr. Guillory laughed at me when I told him. "Devastated? Heh, heh. You won't be devastated. Not you. You will just go on and be the life of the party and show him what a mistake he made. I know you. Devastated? Heh. Heh."

I am adding this now after the party. The party was a great success. Jesus bartended and at the very end, as people were leaving, he poured me a tanqueray and tonic that you wouldn't believe. The valet guy told me the next day, when he came by to say that a guest had complained to the valet company that a gun had been stolen out of his car after he had turned it over to the valet, that the guests were all talking about how terrific the party was as they were leaving. One guest had said he had not expected to have such a good time or to stay so late because he had not known anyone at the party, but that I really knew how to show everyone a great time.

I told the valet that I didn't know most of the people at the party and that he shouldn't sweat about the missing gun. I was not angry or accusing him of anything. I leave money in my car all of the time when those same valet guys park my car at the restaurant and I know that they are honest from personal experience. The person at the party was probably not remembering that they had taken the gun out of the car earlier in the day and would later find it at home. Or they were some liar trying to make an insurance company claim. Either way, worrying about it was not going to solve anything.

"Wait until life gives you something real to worry about," I told him. "Don't torture yourself with anticipated things that you might have to worry about in the future that may or may not even come to pass. Look at the perfect sunny beautiful spring day with all of the azaleas in Houston in full bloom. That is reality. You are a very young man, and you are ruining this perfect spring day for yourself by your thinking. I need to let you know that this kind of thinking can wreck your life. Are you or are you not standing here in the wonderful springtime, a young man in perfect health?"

"Yes," he answered.

"Then, why the hell are you creating problems for yourself for what? For nothing! Someone might accuse you of something. So? You did not do it. You know this. So what? Enjoy the sunshine. Believe me, in your long life there will be plenty of real problems to tackle that God will give you to learn from and this is not one of them. Are you sitting in a long hallway in a straight-backed chair holding your wife's hand as you wait for hours for your child's chemotherapy report?"

His face was stricken. "No," he responded.

"Then YOU DO NOT HAVE PROBLEMS. Don't insult God by ruining this perfect day he gave you. Quit being silly."

He left my doorstep with a different outlook for about five minutes. These defective thinking patterns can be overcome if the person wants to adopt a different world view. Often, these people gravitate towards one another and surround themselves with others who have the same outlook. The most important thing I look for in people I spend my time with is their speech patterns and thinking patterns. There are no 'problems.' In fact this word doesn't even exist for my friends, only 'situations,' and 'situations' are simply addressed.

I met someone new recently and was very excited until he said he had several little 'problems' that I needed to be aware of before I entered any kind of relationship with him. He said I should not worry because the problems existed only because of the relationship with his ex-wife.

Hmmm, I was more concerned about his speech patterns reflecting his immature thought processes that I have noted lead to impoverished thinking because he still existed in a world of 'problems.' I was further horrified that his explanation may be to try to lay the responsibility for his situation at another person's feet. I will find out later when he 'explains the several little problems.' At least he has learned the fundamentals of honesty.

Anyway, I needed to add to this chapter to tell you how the situation with Carrie and Greg unfolded over the course of the week.

After calling me on the phone once each hour for two days, Greg came to my door the night of the party just before the guests were due to arrive. Once again, he asked for twenty-eight thousand five hundred dollars.

Fortunately, Mr. Guillory was at my house helping set-up for the party, so I did not have to have the conversation with Greg alone. Greg explained to me that for the previous two years he had not paid the January and February car payments on his two luxury vehicles, and his relationship with the small local Houston bank allowed him this leniency. They understood the seasonal nature of this business.

"There is no income in those two months," he told me.

I was incredulous. This did not jive with his November 1999 promise to pay me back seven thousand dollars after his Christmas sales which he claimed were largely responsible for a third of his overall annual sales. He seemed to not remember previous descriptions of his seasonal business when he borrowed money. According to his promises in 1999, he should still be flush enough in January to make two car payments.

Anyway, he said that in the past that had been okay with the bank. He banked at a small bank that knew him and recognized that his business was seasonal. This year he did the same thing not realizing that with the small bank being bought out by a larger bank the small bank now had adopted all of the larger bank's lending policies.

He received a letter warning him about repossession of the vehicles on March first, which probably explains my cousin's phone call to me about that time. I had been sitting in Tony Mandenelli's restaurant eating a bowl of gumbo and looking over a catering menu to plan my party, when I received my cousin's call. A little old lady was seated at the next table and we were the only customers in the place, so she could overhear every word of my conversation.

"Hello Carrie? How are you? Yes, I haven't heard from you in a long time, not since the beginning of January. Why are you calling? Yes, I'm fine. Thank you for checking on me since you are my only family in town. I have broken up with my boyfriend. It probably would be a good idea for you to check on me more often. You know my friends Josie and Miguel call me twice each week for that very reason. I am like their adopted sister. Mr. Guillory does the same. But I haven't heard from you in ages. I thought you were embarrassed because you were supposed to pay me back that seven thousand dollars you owed me back in December and you never did. You know you do have to pay me back, Carrie. You borrowed the money for a few weeks and it has been a year and a half. It is time for Greg to start paying me something, anything each month."

The lady seated next to me smiled with a twinkle in her eye. Her facial expression said she had been there before with her relations, and she thought I was handling it well.

"Oh, you are NOT embarrassed? I would think that you would be, at least just a little."

I had been witness to their many expensive dinners out over the year in which they would order one or two bottles of wine. Once, when they were my guests, they had ordered a second bottle of ninety dollar wine after I had already announced that I would not be drinking anymore. I never order a bottle that costs more than forty-five dollars because Hank's has an excellent selection in that price range, and there is simply no reason to spend that much money on dinner out. They each had one glass out of the bottle and then Greg gave it to the waiter to wrap up and take home. I always had left the remainder of the bottle for the waiter to take home to his wife in addition to a generous tip. The waiter brought the bottle back corked and beautifully wrapped in foil that had been twisted with artistic flair. I assumed that since I was paying for dinner that the bottle was for me to take home. No, I simply got the check. Greg lifted the bottle off the table without even consulting with me to see if I was interested in taking it home.

He knew, of course, that I was not much of a drinker. So, he probably felt he knew, and accurately, how I would respond. No, I was not interested in a bottle of wine to go. I don't even bring home doggie bags. I think it looks tacky.

I knew in that moment how Greg felt about me footing the bill and that I would probably never see a penny of my seven thousand dollars. I talked about it with my neighbor and told him that it was a cheap price to pay to put me in the position of saying 'no' to them the next time they came to me for money.

I could point to that one loan and say, "Sorry, you never paid me back last time."

That is precisely what I said but not in so many words Sunday evening. I listened to Greg and as I began to hear about the repossessions of his vehicles I stopped him and told him that maybe I shouldn't be hearing so much about his personal finances. That was private. He said, no, he didn't mind me knowing.

I offered immediately that if he had come to ask permission to sell the vehicle that I had given to his daughter that summer not to worry. Elizabeth would have to understand she was a member of the family, and they were going through a rough patch and needed emergency money and would have to sell my gift. They could buy her another car after the spring golf season. I wouldn't tell anyone, I promised, about the repos.

Mr. Guillory said I should have seen the look of shock on his face when I suggested they sell something of their own to come up with the money. I told him I did see the look of shock. Call it shock, bewilderment, dismay. It obviously had never once occurred to him as a possible way out of his situation.

Greg said, "Oh, no. We could never do that to Elizabeth."

"So what are you asking me then?" I asked knowing full well. "I thought you didn't want to hurt my feelings by selling my gift to your daughter."

Mr. Guillory told me later that he thought it was real smooth the way I slipped that in there about having already given them something that year, something worth quite a bit of money. I also reminded him of the seven thousand dollars.

"Greg, if you are needing more time to pay back the seven thousand dollars don't worry about it. I know you are going to eventually pay me back. You said you would pay me in December, but you had a slow Christmas. I know after the spring season you will pay me.

He said he had thought of a way that I could help him out, and he could pay me back the seven thousand dollars immediately. He had it all written out on a paper for me. He had looked up the blue book values of the cars and calculated the equity he already had in the vehicles, forty thousand dollars combined. He would lose that equity forever, he explained, once the cars were sold at auction on Wednesday. This was Sunday evening. The bank president told him he could not intervene on his behalf now that the bank was essentially under new ownership and new rules. Rules that could no longer be bent for Greg.

Greg explained that his credit worthiness would be ruined with two repos on his record. The bank president said if Greg had come to him before the cars were actually repoed, when Greg first received the letter, the value of the cars was such that the bank could have extended him a short term second loan using the cars as collateral.

But, Greg never talked to the bank president when he got the letters thinking things would operate as they had in the two past years when he slow paid in exactly the same way. Here was the problem. Greg had come to expect special treatment and wanted it without having to ask for it, without putting on a suit and making an appointment and explaining respectfully to the bank president that he had a situation again for the third year in a row.

Mr. Guillory agreed with me it showed a lack of respect and an attitude of entitlement that was ugly. Greg said that now that the repossessions had taken place that option was closed to him. Two repos made him not credit worthy.

'Good,' I thought. 'Now maybe they could get their lives back on track and quit living high on the hog when they should have been economizing last year and, by the way, paying ME back.'

This was not a bad thing. They would be forced to live within their means. This was positive, although I am sure I could never convince Greg of that.

Somewhere in my memory bank was the fact that Greg and Carrie or just Greg had a home foreclosure in their past, but I could not be sure. I did not know. Greg had alluded to the effort in rebuilding his credit worthiness and this made me think that he was referring to a previous foreclosure.

I told him that I was not going to loan him the money. He said he was not asking me for a loan. He was going to put the car titles in my name, and I would just therefore be buying him a few days time to sell one or both of the cars. With the proceeds of the sale he would pay me back the seven thousand immediately.

Coming to me on a Sunday evening before he needed the money Monday morning to prevent the cars from going on the auction block was putting undue pressure on me to make a decision. It was Sunday evening and I did not know if Pearle, my attorney and close friend, would be in court the next morning. I knew he had several balls in the air right now with more than one client ready to go to trial. He may not be able to drop everything to meet with me in the morning, advise me and draw up a written agreement which for something as complicated as Greg was describing and for so much money, twenty-eight thousand five hundred dollars, would require a written agreement.

"By coming to me in the eleventh hour, Greg," I explained, "You are essentially denying me legal counsel in this decision, so I must decide no just to be on the safe side. No.

Also, my money manager is out of town with his family in Destin, Florida and before he left we had a meeting because I had asked him to put me on a budget. Last year, I loaned out money to three people including you. No one paid me back, Greg, and everyone had very sound reasons for not repaying me. The most money was loaned to a man, a small business owner like yourself who suffered from brain cancer. I called him three times to ask him for the money and all three times my calls went unreturned. I am just glad I am on my side of the situation, that is all.

So, the last thing my money manager explained to me, Greg, before he left town was that I could live decently on my budget until I was ninety-five and have money to buy each child a new car at age sixteen and send them to college, but my budget definitely did not include loaning any more money to people."

I also explained the reason I had asked for the budget was that the

previous company my money manager had been with had a simulation computer program that had erroneously advised that I could
spend more money then I should have been budgeted.

"Fortunately, we figured out this was incorrect. Important vari-
ables had not been included in the simulation. I had spent a ton more
than I should have right out of the gate. Now, I need to be close with
my money for three years to get back on track, the first three years,
not three years a decade from now."

Greg said, "Well, you needed to blow it out that first year,
Penelope, after all that you had been through with Richard. My God,
you deserved it."

"Yes, Greg, I don't regret anything that I spent. But after awhile it
got sort of sickening. You only need so much jewelry and stuff, then
it starts to get gross."

"But one thing I notice about you, Penelope, is that you really
enjoy everything that you have. You wear your jewelry, you use your
dishes, you enjoy your art and your home and for a woman with
twenty-eight fur coats in Houston," he laughed at this point, "I must
say that you wear them all! And you got such good deals on everything. No one ripped you off."

"Greg, I am sorry, but I have to say no in order to be financially
responsible myself. I don't have Pearle or Ted here to advise me, and
I will not make decisions like this without them."

Greg said he understood, and he would have come to me earlier
except he just was trying to find any possible way out without having
to come to me. 'Anyway out that doesn't include selling their other
car, the Mercedes that I gave to Elizabeth,' I thought. 'If he had come
to me I would have pushed for that one.'

Mr. Guillory worked for a used car lot and sent his earnings to
help out Ulysses. He offered to talk to his boss, the owner of the
car lot, to see if he would be interested in doing the same deal that
Greg was offering me. Greg didn't leave completely empty handed.
Maybe the car dealer could float him a short term loan.

Hell, what were they doing with luxury cars and living in a big custom home if their business didn't make enough money to be viable?

If you want to be in a business for the joy of it and not for income then change your lifestyle. Live in a duplex and rent out the bottom half to cover the mortgage and drive used paid for cars for heaven's sakes! Then you can build golf clubs to your heart's delight and not be too concerned about how much money the shop earns.

The next day Greg called me five times just during the hour that I was working out with my personal trainer. I took two of the calls. In the first, I explained I was working out. In the last, I explained that I was still working out. I reminded him that I had not changed my mind. My answer was still no. He called me every hour and then every half hour throughout the day. I stopped answering his calls.

I went to Spec's liquor where I announced at the entrance I was there to buy thirty-five hundred dollars worth of liquor for a party and needed assistance and spent the next hour stocking my bar. I knew from previous parties what to get including seventy five Romeo and Juliets and four cartons of cigarettes. I put them out on the back patio table with a big crystal ashtray and tons of matchbooks in a way that says, enjoy!

I have an air filtration system in my home exactly like they have in nightclubs that removes all the smoke from the air. It cost five thousand dollars and is worth every penny. Everyone can smoke like demons, and you can't smell it the next day. Because there is a Picasso behind the piano and three Chagalls downstairs, it is better to encourage the smokers to linger outside. The pile of tobacco in this central area does that. My close friends know they can smoke inside though.

I was at Specs when Carrie and Greg both came by my house and Yesenia told them I was out. Fortunately, the security guard, Dan Dealba, had come by to discuss the recent hate mail that I had received and to offer to help with the party.

"They were surprised to see Dan," Yesenia said.

Dan told Yesenia to lock the door and not let them inside under any circumstances.

"They should not come to the house to borrow money and bother Mrs. Bernard on the day of the party. She has already told them no and it is disrespectful."

I had told Mr. Guillory that they never would have asked me for the money if I was married. It is because I am alone that they think, erroneously, that I am easy prey. Yesenia agreed with this. She said my cousin Carrie acted like she owned the house and did not show respect to me on Thanksgiving telling me what was going to be served for dinner. Yesenia remembered how Carrie was surprised when I cooked my own favorite version of the traditional turkey dinner with dishes that I preferred, not letting her order me about in my own home. We had two complete turkey meals - hers and mine.

Carrie had really crossed the line the morning after Thanksgiving as we cleaned the kitchen together, Carrie told me that she and Greg had discussed it, and they really would prefer seeing me with someone of my own social caliber and not with the French-Algerian guy.

I told her that I had not asked her opinion of my choice of boyfriends, and I thought she was being horribly rude to say anything at all to me about it especially as a guest in my own home. She did not apologize although I demanded an apology including a demand that she never tread on that territory again. I reminded her that I no longer associated with Tessa because of her lack of boundaries in that area and the very same fate would be hers as well if she did not regain control of herself.

She forged on, bringing Greg's name into the conversation as if that made it okay. We, we, we she began all of her sentences. I felt like saying when her opinion alone could carry enough weight maybe I would feel like listening to it.

I stopped her again. I reminded her that I was not only older than her, but I had more life experiences and I knew more than anyone else what brought me happiness. I, for example, would never have chosen Greg for a mate, but in all the years I had known Greg and Carrie I had respected her choice and had simply been happy to see her find happiness after such a disastrous first marriage. I expected the same respect from her. Especially in my own home, I emphasized. She said she thought I could do better and that was all.

I was enraged. Her place at my dining table that Thanksgiving came not from being earned by friendship but simply from the fact that she was lucky enough to have the same blood running in her veins. I wanted to have some contact with real family after losing my children, my husband, my mother, my father and my sister in one courtroom battle. If it were not for this need that I felt this holiday and her good fortune at being my relation, she would not have earned an invitation on her own.

I had never stepped foot inside Carrie and Greg's home in all the years that they had lived there, although presumably they live quite near my former home in The Woodlands, which my mother now lives in after she testified against me in court.

I told Carrie that I knew myself pretty well, and I liked the French-Algerian guy. "Well, he is good looking," Carrie said, "and young."

"That is not why I like him, Carrie. I respect him."

She laughed an ugly guttural 'you've got to be kidding' noise, "Respect?"

"Yes. He has good values. He is working hard to achieve the American Dream. He has a masters degree in engineering."

"Oh, I didn't know that," said Carrie. "I thought he just worked for Continental at the French desk and delivered pizzas."

I refrained from rubbing Carrie's face in the fact that she had never gone to college. Who was a peg up in her very own scale of social caliber on that one? She would not have qualified to have his job, and he was polite enough not to point this out to her even though she had asked for his recommendation to help her get a job where he worked. So was his job not good enough? She wanted to work there!

He spoke five languages, was well traveled and accepted people of all different backgrounds and cultures. His world view was broadened by exposure to all sorts of people and experiences. Carrie didn't even speak Spanish, and I knew her family threw the word 'n****r' around like backwater bigots.

I told her I respected the fact that he had not given up and returned to Algeria when his wife left him unexpectedly debt ridden. He had borrowed from neighbors, co-workers and friends and worked all the overtime Continental allowed and delivered pizzas on the weekends for his friend's restaurant to repay everyone as quickly as possible.

She had made fun of him for being a pizza boy, but he had not allowed his home to go into foreclosure. As he put it, it was not the bank's responsibility that he had chosen a bad wife who would run off on him after secretly placing money aside in her own account that he thought had gone to pay the bills. She timed her departure to coincide with all of the utilities being shut off and the foreclosure notice from the bank's arrival. He came home one day to discover that she had rented a Uhaul and taken almost everything. His son had been his joy and now Amir was living in the heart of the KKK in Georgia.

Once, when he was delivering pizzas in a predominantly black area of town, a man had pulled a gun on him and held it to his head. The crazed man bragged to his gangster looking girlfriend that he was going to 'pop this guy.' He pounded on the roof of my boyfriend's Honda and yelled profanity for several minutes, waving the gun around recklessly and then pressing it to my boyfriend's forehead and then ranting some more.

I had asked later, "Weren't you afraid?"

He said, "No, not really. You see I had really wanted to die. I was so miserable. I had wanted to blow my own brains out but hadn't been able to bring myself to do it. I would think of my son, Amir, and I would stop. So, I was just waiting for this guy to do me the favor and hoped that he would do it right. It was a nine millimeter, so I was pretty sure that I would die and not just become a vegetable. He was putting it right at the center of my forehead. After awhile the guy just started to wind down, and I began to wonder if maybe the gun wasn't even loaded. That would be just my luck for that time in my life, the gun wouldn't have any bullets. He just looked at me sort of curious after a long time of yelling at me because he was saying all kinds of horrible things to me, horrible, horrible things. Saying everything that had ever gone wrong in his life was because of me.

I wanted to say, 'Hey dude I just met you,' but I didn't want to interrupt him. Nothing he said bothered me because I knew it wasn't true. This was just an angry crazy man showing off for his girl.

Then, he called me 'white,' and I bailed out of the car and grabbed him by the shirt and he almost fell down because he wasn't expecting it.

I yelled at him, 'Don't you ever call me white, you mother!'

He said, 'You are white.'

I said, 'I am more African than you. I was born in Algeria! Do you know where the hell that is? Algeria! That is in Africa! I just got here a couple of years ago. You can say anything you want to me, but don't call me white!'"

Carrie thought she was socially superior to this young, hardworking man. When she crossed the line again we were out to lunch, a lunch she couldn't afford if she had any plan of ever repaying me. I lashed out at her that it wasn't the borrowed Gucci leather stretched across her ass that gave a person class. It was how one conducted their life and treated others. I demanded an apology then and there in front of her daughter.

I refrained, of course, from letting Elizabeth know about the unpaid debt. It is how I conduct myself.

Sonya Bernhardt

10

Lorenzo's Petition To God

Lorenzo never understood before why he had suffered so many ups and downs in his life. Why had he made so many mistakes that he created a hell in which he had to live for a time and suffer until he found his way back to joy? But God is always at work in our lives even when we cannot see it.

Dear God,

I am focused on my work and my children only now. My years of chasing women are behind me. I want only to be healthy, prosperous and happy, and I want this for my children also.

But it would be nice to have a woman at my side, someone to talk to, someone supportive of me. I still have not yet grieved the passing of my brother, and now my father has died. I feel more alone now than ever before in my life. Sometimes it overwhelms me when I least expect it. I am happy and fulfilled by my work, and then I am hit by grief with such force I cannot breathe. I turn to share some good news with

Sonya Bernhardt

someone and no one is there. When I had too much work, seven jobs going at the same time there was no time to notice their absence. Now, things are slower and the hours are not so overfilled.

I promise you God, if you send someone into my life I will be good to her. I will pamper her. I will not make the mistakes I have made in the past. Why can I not have the fifty-three year marriage that my mother and father enjoyed?

Please send a woman into my life and I will cherish her. Please God, send a good woman who will treat me kindly, a sensual woman, an honest woman, a woman with passion for life who understands that it is not about struggle but joy. If she is beautiful and good with children and can cook this would be nice too. I need comfort in my life, the kind that only a woman can provide. I promise I will have my eyes open to recognize her, and I am ready to be good to her.

A couple of weeks ago, I began inviting people to my party. I had been in the piano bar at the Argentine Grill eating steak prepared in a manner that makes the steak particularly tender and tasty and a salad with a special South American dressing. I enjoyed a nice Chilean red wine.

The pianist Jean-Paul had previously allowed Mr. Guillory and his fellow aspiring night club singers to accompany him at a restaurant on interstate ten called the Redwood Grill. Now, Jean-Paul had moved to the Argentine Grill, and the singers followed him. They looked over their notes and music for a good half hour or more mustering the confidence to sing, making the decision of what to sing that evening, a new song that needed to be tested before an audience or one that they had mastered.

I enjoyed the company of these people. They were from all walks of life but had in common a desire to perform in front of an audience. Most took their singing lessons from the same teacher and had grown to know each other well over the years.

A customer fired up a Romeo and Juliet and sat next to his wife in the deep leather chairs in the bar area. I leaned over and thanked him, saying it was my favorite cigar.

"Do you smoke?"

"No, I love to invite people to smoke cigars, so I can enjoy them."

He joined me causing his wife to become angry, but she stayed in her chair. I went over to sit near her, leading her husband back to where he should have remained in the first place. Men have no sense at all sometimes.

I introduced myself to her as Mr. Guillory's friend and told them both about the arrangement between Jean-Paul and the singers.

"We are here every Thursday night," I explained.

They said they were regular customers and had never been in on a Thursday before. The man asked if he could sing next. I said, "Sure, just ask Jean-Paul." The wife was now friendly towards me and told me that her husband had the hobby of singing with a band. He was a very successful man and in fact they lived near me. He enjoyed singing, so he and a group of friends had a band.

He sang about five songs very, very well. When he was seated again, I invited them both to my party. For several days before the party, I invited everyone I ran across that seemed like they'd add to the fun.

When I drove out to visit my friend Kit and her family at their beach house in Surfside, I invited her to the party also.

"Don't expect much. The house is basically a wooden shack," warned Kit when she spoke to me on the cell phone giving me directions to their beach rental.

My children were with their father for Spring break. I had been working on my book and needed a little break from writing, or I was going to throw my back out again. I packed my little laptop, towels, shampoos, a bikini, sweats and a turtleneck and in five minutes I was on the road in my little 'rocket' Mercedes with the top down.

My friends all have joked with me when they see me having a

good time, "Richard WON?" Everyone, including the children them-selves are happy to see me happy, but it is a much different life than I thought I would have at this point.

The morning Richard was so terrible to me I could no longer live with him I stood under the shower with my face upturned sobbing and praying to God. "Please, God. I know you did not mean for me to have misery in my life. I have been nothing but good my whole life, and I know you want me to be happy. Certainly you do not want me to suffer. I must be doing something wrong."

I could no longer stand. I wailed and sobbed and curled into the fetal position. I promised God I would open my eyes. If only he would show me how to have a happy life, I was willing to accept the changes that he could work in my life. I would not question His wis-dom. I would accept those changes knowing He was moving swiftly and efficiently to bring me to a happy place as quickly as possible.

Then strange as it may seem, I had a vision. It would make you laugh, reader, but as the water that was running over my back turned cold, I watched it flow down the drain grate opening and I quite liter-ally saw a sign. I saw a real estate sign from the home directly across the street from my friend Andrienne. Her neighbor had renovated a home and had it up for sale. The phone number was there in front of my eyes.

I stood up thinking that if I laid there any longer I could suffer hypothermia. I pulled a towel around me and walked to the phone. I called Marta Warner Realty and asked to speak directly to Marta, no one else. I was told that Marta was in a meeting. I told the reception-ist that I was an abused woman and was leaving my husband that day and had been told to speak to Marta.

"One moment please, I will interrupt the meeting."

I introduced myself to Marta and told her I needed to purchase a home in River Oaks that day. I would be paying cash. I had three boys so safety from highly trafficked roadways and a big back yard were important. If she knew of a home with small children living on the same street, I would take it and pay for it that same day. "I only have about two and a half hours to look so in essence you will be picking my home, Marta, but you know the area and I trust you can do this for me."

She asked if Pearle Wiley was my attorney and I said, "Yes, why do you ask?" She said she had helped Pearle's clients with emergency housing in the past.

I told her Pearle had not told me to call, so she owed him no commission. I told her to not think it silly, but I had prayed that day and God had told me to call her.

"I am not a nut," I promised. "I just am terrified. I must be moved out of here before my husband comes home today, or he will kill me. I know if I am here when he returns I will not live until tomorrow. I want to move the children into a home, not a temporary residence or hotel and then move again. I only want to move the children once."

I said I knew that wealthy families from Mexico often sell a home with all of its contents. That would be perfect for me. Marta called Pearle and he verified that I was 'for real' and, in fact, the wealthiest client of his entire career. That was, of course, before the stock plummeted and our total worth fell from one hundred and ten million to twenty-six million after tax penalties.

I called Tessa and her mother, and they met me at the rent house and walked through it with me. It was a furnished rental and had a warm homey feel. I said I would take it and read the rental contract finding a couple of things I did not care to have in the agreement. For example, I would not tolerate the leasor to have access to my home any time she wished to inspect for damages or do repairs. I required twenty-four hours written notice. I might have been horribly frightened that day, but I could still think.

I went to Pearle's office and negotiated my contract with him. He told me later that he had never before in his dealings with clients had a client read the 'standard' contract much less change it and many of his clients had been leading attorneys. He said most people are in such a state of mind when they come to him to seek his help that when he casually pushes the contract towards them to sign they automatically do so.

Instead, I took the paper from the desk, stood and walked to the door of his office and asked his secretary, "Kim, could you fax this for me now?"

Pearle looked baffled when I returned to my chair and sipped my diet coke. He asked me if I minded explaining what I had just done with his contract. I told him I had a friend who was a family law attorney and another friend who was a family law judge both waiting in their offices to look over and amend the contract.

Pearle wanted to talk about the facts of the case, the ages of the children, et cetera. I told him if he didn't mind I would just wait for the faxes to come back and discuss how we were going to amend his contract. I was exhausted from the trauma of the morning and just wanted to sit quietly. If he agreed to change the contract as my friends recommended then we could talk about the divorce.

Pearle then knew he didn't have just any old housewife on his hands. We amended the contract, signed it and I was on my way. In three hours I hired a lawyer, rented a house and bought five hundred thousand dollars worth of art at Vermillion Art Gallery. I purchased the art in twenty-five minutes on a day the gallery was closed, so I dealt directly with the owner and had him discount the overall cost of the art by the amount he normally would have paid in commissions and delivered a cashier's check to the gallery in that amount. Then, I had lunch at La Griglia where I called the Mercedes dealership to tell them that a friend of mine would be coming by later to pick out two cars for me. I also called the hospital and the doctor to inform them of my new rent house address, so I could keep my health problems secret from the children's father. After lunch, I drove down the street to a store to pick out china, crystal and silver for my new home. I was home in time to greet the children as they walked from the bus stop.

Pardon me, reader, my mind has drifted from the party. Anyway, in the two weeks preceding the party I invited all sorts of interesting and fun people as I met them, including the owner of a beautiful home that I had been admiring.

I often find myself at my own party looking around wondering 'who the hell are all of these people?' I do not fool myself that they are my friends, just a bunch of beating hearts all tipsy and looking to get laid having a grand ole time in my home. My chief security guard once joked I should run for mayor. I know enough people. The thing is that with my memory problems I don't remember any of them a couple of weeks later.

The purpose of this party was to lure Ray Calhoun to my home and give him loads of attention, not bed him, but give him affection that he desperately needed. Taylor, my friend, begged me to have no more stray kittens, but I am sorry that is what I like to do. I like to come into someone's life and heal them.

"Do what it is that you do in a Christ like way," my bible study teacher preaches. I heal others, with touch, with listening, with being near. I was so psyched to hear that Ray Malloy, the Ray who had the guts to ask me out and his friend Ray, the one who made me weak in the knees were both coming to the party. I would show Calhoun that I was not too young for him. Hell, I don't think I have a friend UNDER fifty for goodness sakes.

I was going to greet him at the door and put my arm around his waist and ask him to be my date for the evening and then ask him to help me in the kitchen. I would keep my arm around him for the entire party and never leave his side. The party was just a reason to see Calhoun again. I sat near the door with my friend Parker and his new girlfriend, Joanne.

I had embarrassed Parker to death and pleased her to no end when they arrived, when I told Joanne that Parker had cried because she was unavailable to go out with him the previous Saturday. Parker was horrified.

I told her I was glad that he had finally gotten up the guts to tell her that he thought about her all of the time and wanted to call her but was afraid that she would not want him to bother her so much. She had told him that because he had not been calling she assumed that he wasn't really that interested and had been disappointed. I got the two love birds on the right track with my advice.

Meanwhile, following Parker's 'do not call him or he will think you are psycho' advice I had lost my little museum love god. Of course, I was correct to say, call when you have your life in order.

It could have taken months for him to get away from that leachy woman if he managed to do so at all.

I jumped up when I saw Ray Calhoun's friend Ray Malloy and his girlfriend Sharon enter the front hallway. They were the only people at my party that I greeted at the door, and the only ones to receive a tour of my home. I told them that I knew next to no one at my own party and was happy to see them. I probably appeared manic to them, talking too fast, rushing them from room to room of my home.

I told Ray, "You showed me your home, and I am delighted to show you mine."

I pointed out the hand carved furniture from Nicaragua and explained that I had donated money to start the woodcarving school there. I showed them the closet space and how I had organized everything.

I wanted to jump up and down and shout, "Where the hell is Ray!" but I resisted until we were walking downstairs again. After we had made the turn on the stair landing that has the grandfather clock I stopped, essentially blocking their decent. I directed my comment to Ray, "I was hoping you would have your friend, Ray, with you. You know I have a huge crush on him. I was looking forward to seeing him tonight."

Of course, inwardly I was screaming, "Where is he, where is he, where is he?" The whole damn party was for him. I was ready to just leave.

Ray smiled and so did his girlfriend. She really did not like me I was certain from our first contact at Ray Malloy's house where I told her she would not make the short list of lawyers who would take my case. If she had any knowledge at all that my gushing affections for Calhoun were not reciprocated then she would not be smiling but smirking with the ugly knowledge that I was going to be let down. They both smiled at my childish openness.

So what? I was nuts about someone. I am a very open person. Ray said that his friend had really wanted to be there, but it was his visitation with his children and he was with them in Dallas. He had really wanted to come he told me.

He was beaming as he said this, not looking uncomfortable. I supposed one or the other of them would have looked uncomfortable if I was throwing myself so openly at a man who was uninterested or had found another girlfriend in the time since I had seen him last. Not so. Their eyes were flashing, and they looked very happy when I made my inquiry.

I led them back to the main entry hall and asked that they sign the guest book to make certain that they would be invited to future parties. Ray signed in. He said Calhoun had to be extra careful since he had filed for divorce that week, and he was afraid to come to the party since my attorney's firm Tiro and Wiley was representing his wife.

My jaw dropped open. I had thought of every possible scenario for the evening including the dreaded 'what if Calhoun showed up with his new girlfriend on his arm and I had to simply leave my own party and fly to Canada to visit friends' scenario. I could definitely never stomach THAT. But 'could not attend due to possible wife's spies at party and had filed for divorce' had not even occurred to me as a possibility.

I was thrilled. I told Ray that I guess that it had been completely unnecessary then to ask my bible study mom about the moral dilemma caused by my affections for his friend when his friend had not yet filed for divorce. Ray smiled a huge smile, nodding his head up and down affirmatively as he signed in the guest book.

His friend had already had a girlfriend a year ago, one that had not survived to the stage of actual filing for divorce. I was NOT going down that road. He could get himself together, and then I would be interested. The party was just to remind him that I was still in existence.

I told Ray that I had talked to my bible study mom and had invited his friend with the plan of throwing myself at him. I said this with his girlfriend standing at his side. She was grinning like a Cheshire cat. I told her that my heart raced when I was around Calhoun. The first time it happened I thought I had just gotten ahold of some coffee instead of decaf by accident and after three days of my heart racing

I had gone to the cardiologist for a stress test. Sharon laughed. I told her then my heart raced once more the next time I saw Calhoun. It was awful. It was like I was seventeen years old again. It made me afraid to feel this way I told her. I didn't even know if my affections were returned, but I told Ray it was good to know that it was possible to feel this way.

I told Sharon that I didn't mean to be too forward, but I wanted her to feel my heart racing just talking about him. I took her hand, with her permission of course, and placed it on my chest. My heart was indeed pounding. I couldn't help the way that I felt, and it was nice but scary too.

I pointed to the two bars that were set up and invited them to have a good time. From time to time I would catch a glimpse of Ray out on the patio with Sharon sipping on his drink and looking into the house from the open French doors watching me screaming and jumping up and down, dancing, applauding, sitting in the laps of male friends and hugging people.

At one point a party guest came rushing up to me saying that someone outside was about to get caught on fire and would not listen to her to get away from the chimenea. I ran outside, congratulating myself once again for not drinking at my own parties for just such emergencies. Indeed, someone had put mesquite chunks from the garage supply of cooking wood into the chimenea instead of the chimenea artificial wood logs made for the outdoor fireplace. The fire blazed out of the top of the clay fireplace two feet into the air and every twenty seconds or so a fireball rolled out of the chimenea's belly bursting forth a full four feet, much further than any guest would expect the flame to reach. A crowd had gathered near the chimenea at what they had presumed to be a safe distance, never guessing that they were in danger a couple of times each minute of the flames licking their asses.

I ran up and pinched the man who was the most in danger on his rear end, hard. "Watch out!" I yelled. "The fire is going to get you."

He turned around laughing saying I was just looking for an excuse to pinch his rear when another ball of fire rolled out and nearly ignited his frontside.

"Whoa!" The entire group exclaimed.

"Now, do you believe me?" I asked.

I turned to see that Sharon and Ray were watching. As I passed them they told me it was a great party. Ray said his friend would have loved the party. He was a real hell raiser too, he explained.

Too? Good then. His friend had observed me and deemed me a common hell raiser. Maybe they would put this annoying 'he's too old for you' garbage aside and just accept me as one of the rare people on earth who just loved living. Isn't that worth something? Isn't that what his friend needed in his life the most? Carpe Diem you bastards. I told them I was glad they were having a great time and went back inside. The party was now in full swing.

I had intended to spend the day at Avalon Nail Salon getting a manicure and pedicure. I had also planned on buying a hundred small bowls for serving gumbo and red beans and rice. I also wanted to take a nap that day after I picked up cake for sixty people at the bakery.

However, midafternoon a handsome Latin man named Lorenzo that I thought had been introduced to me by Ben as Ben's 'wife' or male life partner, stopped by to tell me Ben would not be able to attend the party. He had come over to apologize on Ben's behalf. He further explained that he would also not be able to attend since he had a hotel in Louisiana that was undergoing renovations, and he needed to make the four and a half hour drive to make payroll. He was just stopping by on his way to make the long drive and wanted to thank me for inviting them to the party.

I invited him in to have a quick tour of my home. He loved every detail. At some point during the tour it became apparent to me that I had misinterpreted his relationship with Ben.

Inside the loop with so many gay couples it can be confusing sometimes, the straightest looking people will correct your wrong assumptions about their sexuality and introduce you to their same sex life partners. This is what I thought Ben had been doing when he introduced me to Lorenzo, his remodeling contractor, as the genius behind Ben's home renovations. "Lorenzo did it all," Ben said. "He made all the decisions."

"We've been invited to attend a party," Ben explained to Lorenzo immediately after I had told Ben he and his wife were invited.

'I had been politely corrected,' I thought. I hoped they would not be insulted by the wording of party invitation 'musicians and freaks only.'

As I was showing Lorenzo through the house, I could feel his eyes on the curves of my body, and I began to feel self conscious and, yes, aroused by the nearness of him. I had thought of nothing but Calhoun, and my heart was racing at the thought that in a few short hours I would be showing Ray through my home just like this.

Lorenzo noticed every detail and said I should do home design for a living. I said I had enjoyed remodeling homes in my youth working alongside a boyfriend who bought duplexes and fourplexes in the area. My aunt and uncle also remodeled homes their entire lives. It was in my blood. I had considered buying some small homes, fixing them up and selling them completely furnished and decorated just to do something fun, but my real passion was for shoe design.

He said he had built a home for a well known shoe maker and told me the story of his first shoe design. He had made them for nine dollars a pair in Brazil. His first order from a single store had been for fifty thousand pairs. I told him when the children were older I planned to go to shoe design school in London. He said I should meet the man who built the shoe empire. Maybe I could work for him or learn the ropes to have my own shoe company as he had done.

I showed him my favorite shoes and talked about proper balance and toe bed and why my favorite shoes were superior to others. He told me that he knew what he was going to do. He was going to buy me a pair of shoes. He asked my size. He stood in the doorway of my shoe closet and asked if my friends called me Amelda Marcos. I told him yes they sometimes did, and that I did not consider it an insult at all. I said it was not crazy to have that many pairs of shoes if that is what you loved. People collect all kinds of things.

He said Amelda had many of her shoes because her country had factories that manufactured shoes, and the manufacturers would send shoes to her as gifts so that they could say the wife of the leader of the country wore their product. She was simply an ambassador of the country and that was a major manufacturing force there.

I sent Yesenia to pick up the cakes at the bakery. I called the caterer and told him to bring the bowls. I seasoned the red beans, added the sausage and made four cups of rice while Lorenzo told me stories about unusual homes he had built for wealthy people.

I invited him to have some beans, and he sat at the dining room table. He loved the food and said my home was so comfortable it was difficult to move from the chair, but he was obviously detaining me from my preparations and he would have to go so I could get ready. He asked if he could take me to dinner when he returned from Louisiana. "Sure," I said. He was handsome and easy to be with, in that I would love to throw you under the table and have my way with you right here kind of sex appeal way.

He joked that he felt like we had already had our first date since I had made dinner for him. I told him I looked forward to our second date as we said goodbye on the front step. He kissed me on the cheek sweetly. He had only come by for a couple of minutes to apologize and had left his cell phone back at Ben's house, so there was no way for his workers to contact him. He went back to Ben's to make sure that everything was under control and then drove to Louisiana.

Interesting. Well. That was unexpected. I guess if Ray shows up with a date I don't have to be so disappointed now I thought. I had a dinner date with Lorenzo to look forward to.

What was happening to me? I was becoming sex crazed after two years of waiting for Ulysses. The first day of Spring 2003 was approaching, the day I had promised myself that I would 'get on with my life,' and I was definitely ready to move on.

Maybe Taylor was right about my misguided attraction to Ray and how appealing his loneliness and heartache was to me. He told me I needed a real partner, someone who 'had his act together' and was happy and fulfilled; someone who would make me their focus instead of me focusing on helping them with their problems.

When I told this to Lorenzo on our second date, he said it reminded him of the scene in the Jack Nicholson movie *As Good As It Gets* when the actress is bemoaning the fact that what she wants is a NORMAL boyfriend, one who doesn't have any problems. Her mother says that she was sorry to inform her, but that doesn't exist.

Lorenzo said very sweetly as we entered the restaurant that he had wanted to kiss me so badly at my house, but he 'had not wanted to mess up.'

He had called me from Louisiana as he began his drive back to Houston to invite me for a late lunch or early dinner. How sweet. He wasn't going to wait to see me that evening at dinner. He wanted to see me as soon as possible.

Ray Calhoun get a clue. This is how a girl needs to be pursued, not this turtle hiding in his shell for months, never calling once after she broadcasts to the entire known universe that you make her go to the cardiologist for stress tests she is so attracted to you. At least call and say, 'sorry not interested' for Christ's sakes. How insulting. Who needs that?

Taylor is right. No more stray kittens. I want someone ready to be in a relationship and treat me very well. I want a boyfriend, not a project.

God, Lorenzo is easy company. He had also written a book, already published and gave me a copy. He was going to inscribe it 'to the woman whose lips I cannot kiss' because I told him I regretted to inform him that the previous time he saw me would have been the best time to kiss me since my lip was now bleeding. My acne medicine had dried out my skin and lips so much, and I had been to the dentist that day and even though the dental assistant kept moisturizing them with Vaseline, my lips were cracking and hurting. It would be impossible for me to kiss anyone that night, sorry.

I invited him over and told him I wanted him to read a couple of chapters. "I love to watch people read and laugh out loud," I explained.

I was happy that the book had even held the attention of three teenagers when I had visited my friend Kit at her beach house. Kit and I went out on the front deck and drank Bacardi and diet coke and enjoyed watching the surf and left the teenagers alone in the house with my book on the kitchen table. Kit could see them hovered over it at the kitchen table reading a page and then passing it around. She said, "You won't believe it Penelope, but they are all in there reading. You can't make a teenager do anything they don't want to do, and they are all in there reading your book."

I couldn't believe it. I had been thinking more of an adult audience for my memoirs, housewives who might learn from how much I had enjoyed my freedom from oppression and find some humor and escape from their daily routine in the descriptions of my parties and travels.

"I must include my travels," I told Kit, "At least the time I was charged with white slavery in Spain."

I had accidentally taken my children to a two week orgy known as the Running of the Bulls event. Every marijuana smoking, backpacking college student from all over Europe was there having sex in the doorways and boulevards for all the world to see. My two youngest never noticed a thing, but my oldest would hold his hand next to his face to cover his eyes and point in the direction of the exhibitionists and chuckle. We didn't see examples of every page of the Kamasutra, but let's just say it wasn't the educational family trip I had envisioned.

Anyway, I invited Lorenzo back to my house and printed out a couple of chapters and asked him to join me in the family cuddle chair. I felt fairly safe because I had already told him he wasn't going to get a kiss out of me. I wanted very much to be held. He laughed out loud as he read, and I kept asking him to point out what he had found so humorous.

Then, he wanted to kiss me. Sorry, no. My lips were at the point of bleeding they were so cracked. The acne medicine had worked so well I had stupidly used it more often than prescribed. He kissed all over my face very gently and on my lips, very, very gently.

This gets me nowhere. I don't know where guys get the idea that this is anything other than annoying or boring. He said he wanted to kiss me all over my body gently from my head to my toes. Okay, time to go home. Women want to feel a man's hands on their bodies, and not meek hands asking permission in their timidity. Not rape, but not indecision either.

Suddenly he caught on, and was on his knees at the base of the reading chair sliding his hand up my thigh and exploring like a man who does not need a map. "Lets go upstairs," I said. "We are in full view of the entire neighborhood in this chair with the front window blinds open."

"Really?"

"Well, sure. Do you want to put on a show? Kids live on this street. Don't get any funny ideas though. I just want you to hold me, I just don't want you to do it in full view of the street."

I was enjoying this yes, no, yes, no concept that my friend Parker had introduced me to so recently when I told him about the guy from the museum. I folded back the covers and climbed into the bed fully clothed.

"Come hold me." He took off his clothes down to his underwear and slid into bed beside me. I told him, "I want to rest my head on your chest." He had a beautiful chest. How young was he? He said he had been happy to hear that I was nearly forty-two when we were talking at dinner.

He said he was so attracted to me but almost didn't ask me out because he thought I was in my twenties and too young. Then, he decided to not let it matter. He concluded that I was thirty-two after I told him I had a twelve year old son. He calculated I had probably been twenty when I had my first child. Lorenzo explained that, if it hadn't been for the hint that I had a twelve year old he would have guessed younger and not asked me out. But forty-two made him feel much more comfortable, not like he was robbing the cradle. What is it with these guys? I thought it was supposed to be good to look young, but young must be pretty scary.

We played a pretty wild game of yes, no, yes, no. If we were keeping score we'd have to say Lorenzo won but only on style points. Four hours into yes/no I leapt from the bed, ordering him out of the house, and he promised that he would behave. Moments later I was begging him not to behave but he never wavered from the line I had drawn. He said he was going to get a vasectomy on Monday, and he meant it. He was not joking around. We moved to another bed, having destroyed the first one and napped. He had to go to work at seven but he ended up being an hour late due to an extra tie breaker round that ended tied again.

He promised me he would give me no disease and would not make me pregnant. I had made him completely crazy and happy at the same time.

I had my head resting on his chest and asked him sweetly, "Do you want me to be your girlfriend, Lorenzo?" I think he was as shocked to hear me ask as I had been to hear the words come out of my own mouth. I could hear his heart race, panicked.

"Do you want to be my boyfriend, and I will be very sweet to you all the time and you will be very, very happy, I promise?"

"Yes." He said. "I would love to have you be my girlfriend."

"Lorenzo and Penelope sitting in a tree K-I-S-S-I-N-G," I sang. Thank God I am a mature woman of nearly forty-two. Can you imagine the hell men go through with younger girls? But I was interested in him and a very direct woman. If there were any other honies around I wanted them cleared out immediately and yes, a vasectomy on Monday was an excellent idea.

He called me four hours later when he left his crew and arrived at his office asking if he had awakened his sleeping beauty. He said it was time for me to get up soon and go get the children at school. He has called me a few more times since then while visiting with his daughter from his divorce, and I have my children for the weekend. Sunday evening I will go to Josie's house to celebrate her birthday with her, and Lorenzo's kids sleep over on Sundays unlike mine who return to their dad's house.

I told Lorenzo that I had looked forward to seeing a man that evening at my party, a man I had been chasing, but he had disappointed me and remained in Dallas and not called personally. Timing is everything, and it is very possible that he was never interested. I will never know. A girl likes to be chased, not do the chasing.

Lorenzo said he had not planned on being so aggressive with me; he just lost control because my skin was so very soft to touch. He had never felt any skin so soft in his entire life. I asked him if I could title my next chapter 'The Man Who Dropped in for Five Minutes and Stayed for Ten Years.' He laughed and said that sounded like a good chapter title to him.

Who would have guessed? I didn't even know this man two weeks ago, although I had admired the home he was building and wanted to own it. I am reading his book now, and he has a beautiful island home and a positive outlook on life. He spent ten years writing the book and confesses to his imperfections and the mistakes he made during his marriage that led to divorce. He describes his philosophy of life. What a nice way to get to know someone.

The first day of Spring arrived yesterday, and I called Mr. Guillory to tell him I am no longer waiting for Ulysses. I have moved on and have hopes that this new man I have met will turn out to be wonderful. I will soon know.

"Have you told Ulysses?" asked Mr. Guillory.

"No. No need to tell him. He knows. We are so connected that way. He knows."